Show Me A Family For Christmas

Cowboy Crossing
~ Book 6 ~

By

ALEXA VERDE

Since his wife died, all Conner Strauss wants is a big family, other children to put a smile back on his little girl's face. His wish might come true when his mother finally tells him who his biological father was. To get close to his new siblings and their children without giving himself away, he starts courting the family nanny.

Once jilted, Gwendolyn Meyers concentrated on her career as a bodyguard, eager to prove she's just as good as her late father was. Now, as a simple favor to a friend, she's working undercover as a nanny to protect the Clark family's children since strange things started happening on Mending Hearts Ranch. But when a stranger in town sparks her interest and his lonely daughter rouses her compassion, she might be given the chance at happiness where she least expected it.

When she starts seeing shadows of her past, she's determined to find the truth behind her father's death. However, someone close to her is even more determined to keep secrets hidden forever.…
Can love and a big noisy family heal two broken hearts this Christmas?

From Alexa: I had an idea to write this book before Jenna's story, so there is an overlapping timeline. This book starts a few weeks before Christmas, before Connor, Gwendolyn and Daisy appear in Jenna's story. I hope I won't cause any confusion, and I hope you'll enjoy their story.

Dedication

This book is dedicated to Renate, a wonderful reader and a friend. I love your wisdom, your encouragement, and your knowledge and am grateful forever for all support you've given me.

CHAPTER ONE

THIS QUIET SMALL TOWN decorated with garlands around lampposts and gigantic snowflakes in shop windows could be charming for some people.

Conner Strauss wasn't one of those people.

His gut tightening, he recalled the opulent mansion belonging to the wealthiest family in town—the family who owned all the land the eye could see here.

The mansion he should've grown up in.

The land that should've belonged to his daughter, too.

If his biological father hadn't abandoned their family. If it hadn't taken Conner's mother nearly forty years to tell him who his father was. She probably never would've broken her silence if she hadn't suffered that genetic disease scare.

The tightness in his gut squeezed further as he made a turn and Christmas lights on every storefront mocked him with their festive mood.

It was only a few weeks before Christmas. All his life he'd known he'd been a mistake on his mother's part. Even more in the eyes of the man who didn't want to acknowledge that mistake in front of his *real* family. But how could he refuse when Conner's family had been in dire need, not once but three times? That cruelty had cost lives.

The frosty fresh air did nothing to calm his raw nerves.

Pain sliced him as he slowed for an upcoming bump. His daughter could be easily startled. Once upon a time, he'd wanted justice, then revenge. Now he needed hope and information.

Not for him, but for his little girl. One genetic disease scare in the family was more than enough.

Foisting off a smile, he glanced back. "Are you okay there, Sweetie Pie?"

"Yes, Daddy. I wanna apple turnover for breakfast. Can we?" The impish smile on his favorite face in the world warmed Conner.

"We sure can."

Fine, it was far from a healthy breakfast, but so were most of those sugary cereals other children ate. At least breakfast was usually healthy in their house. Fruits, yogurt, oatmeal, scrambled eggs. He did try his best.

He returned his attention to the road and put the pastry store's address in the GPS.

Then his fingers squeezed the steering wheel, pressing in deep. He didn't need the wealth of a family who'd never been interested in him. He'd done well for himself, first as a foreman, then as a gallery manager.

But he didn't want Daisy to grow up lonely like he had, spending more time with horses than with people. Besides, who'd take care of his precious girl if something happened to him? And, after his mother's genetic illness, he needed to know whether his girl had anything else in her medical history to watch out for, to prevent from getting serious.

It was bad enough that he didn't prevent…

No, better not to think about it.

First, however, he had to make sure the Clarks weren't as cruel as his father was. Conner's eyes narrowed. Having Daisy's mother die and her family shut off his little girl was devastating. No way would Conner subject his daughter to further abandonment, further knowing she was unwanted.

His heart ached every time he thought about it.

He parked his rental truck near the pastry store and lifted his daughter from the harnessed booster seat in the back. Then he tugged down her cute multicolored knit hat with a pompom nearly as large as the hat and pulled the hood outlined in faux fur on her head for good measure. Mid-December was cold, even in Houston, Texas, where they lived, much more in Missouri. The gray sky hung low and heavy as if in solidarity with his mood.

"Ready, Sweetie Pie?"

"Yes, Daddy." She smiled shyly up at him.

Unlike Annika, who'd had an outgoing personality, Daisy had always been shy. She had difficulty engaging with other children. Visits to the child psychologist didn't help much, but the woman had suggested that having Daisy spend time with cousins or other family members would help.

The issue was that Daisy and her cousins didn't know about each other's existence, and neither did their parents. That was about to change—after he'd researched whether the Clarks could be trusted, of course. He'd been deceived and disappointed too many times not to know better now than to trust strangers, even if they were blood related.

"Let's go then." He pressed playfully on her upturned nose and made sure her scarf was tied tight but not too tight.

Her tiny hand in his, they approached the store. Warm air rushed out to greet them, drawing them in and wrapping them in a homey hug scented with just-brewed coffee, pumpkin spice latte, and freshly baked desserts.

His stomach grumbled. The aromas mixed with the scent of pine needles emanating from fragrant branches forming centerpieces on the round tables. Tablecloths with holly patterns draped those tables, and a myriad of snowflakes danced close to the ceiling above the snowmen cutouts decorating the walls.

Annika would've loved it here. She'd loved all things Christmas, had gone all out every year with decorations and baking German Christmas desserts. The pain of missing her was always sharper during the holidays.

His gaze stopped on the Black Forest cake, a fruit bread with nuts, spices, and candied fruit called stollen, and the German chocolate cake on the display. He wanted to close his eyes.

But if he did, he'd only see her face.

Then again, he saw her face every day in their daughter, Annika's spitting image, the large brown eyes, the slightly upturned nose. His throat constricted as his fingers tightened around Daisy's little palm while they approached the counter.

Two elderly ladies, the only others in line, looked at him and his girl. They'd clearly pegged him as a newcomer.

An outsider.

Story of his life, first as a maid's son among well-off ranchers' children and now as an art gallery manager where he didn't belong.

He felt… stuck.

Stuck within four walls while he loved open spaces. Stuck in suffocating crisp shirts and tailored suits when he preferred Wrangler shirts and jeans. Stuck with a forced smile, chatting up potential clients or praising famous artists when he wanted quiet. Okay, he'd relegated that duty to his assistant, more often than not retreating into his grouchy self.

Yes, he was an outsider. And an outsider was something he'd never wanted his child to be.

He resisted the urge to clench his teeth and lifted his daughter so she could better see all the choices behind the counter. "Would you like anything else?"

She shook her head.

Okay then. He placed her on the tile floor. "Two apple

turnovers, please."

Daisy's eyes widened. "Daddy, but what are you going to eat?"

Conner chuckled. "Make it three apple turnovers, please. What would you like to drink, Sweetie Pie?"

She scrunched her nose in a manner he found endearing. "Apple juice."

He ordered that and a latte for himself. As he paid for the pastries and drinks, the bell over the door jingled, and a woman with three children came in. Since he'd researched online, he knew who she was.

Gwendolyn Meyers, the Clark family's nanny. His heartbeat increased. She might be his ticket in.

No one knew people's secrets better than someone who worked for them. He'd overheard his mother, who'd worked as a maid most of her life, telling her friends things that made them gasp. Rich people seemed to consider maids invisible, part of the wall, and didn't realize "part of the wall" had great hearing and even better eyesight.

Nannies could be the same. And if the Clark family were as snobbish and disrespectful as their late patriarch, Gwendolyn could be a disgruntled employee.

A valuable source.

A twinge made him wince. He'd never used people for his purposes. But the reason for his intentions was looking at him right now with big, trusting eyes as he placed their food on the table and helped her up on the chair.

Once he removed Daisy's warm coat, he stole a glance at Gwendolyn. Her expression was slightly pained as the three children shouted their orders. It probably didn't help that each one was tugging at her sleeve and the little girl with pigtails of nearly the same hue as his daughter's hair was changing her mind for the fifth time.

Gwendolyn was pleasantly plump, and her clothes were a mixture of grayish colors as if she tried to blend into the background—like part of the wall indeed. Dark reddish-brown hair framed her round face in messy waves. Dangling mismatched earrings—one several silver teardrops and one glittery golden hearts—danced in her ears as her head moved swiftly, turning from one child to another. Her makeup, if she wore any, was subtle.

She looked about forty, but the freckles speckling her nose and cheeks—like sprinkles covered the Christmas cookies on display— gave her a more youthful look. Remnants of a snowball melted into the back of her blazer, probably from the children getting into a snowball fight earlier.

Then she smiled at the two boys and the girl, suggested they point to the things they wanted, and initiated the game, "Whoever says the first word will lose"—which insured immediate silence.

He took a sip of his pumpkin spice latte and moved the pastry plate toward his daughter. Daisy was a slow eater, which had created issues in daycare where she was always the last one to finish her meal. He'd hired a babysitter after a daycare teacher had yelled at Daisy to hurry up, and he'd barely suppressed his anger after finding it out.

He found his daughter watching the girl with the pigtails. He recalled his research again. Danica Clark. Danica and Daisy. If the two girls ended up spending time together, things could get confusing.

Dressed in a canary-yellow coat and matching boots, Danica resembled a spot of sunshine that didn't want to stay still. He imagined if Gwendolyn blinked, she'd be searching for Danica through the entire town. Probably neighboring towns, too.

But most likely, the cat ears on Danica's knit hat attracted Daisy's attention. She'd been asking for a "kitty" for a while. He'd give up his life for her, but when he thought about a cat, the image of the one running across the road always appeared in front of him.

The screech of tires. The scream. The pain. The scent of burning rubber before he passed out.

He took a deep breath of air scented with pine needles and pastries to bring himself to reality.

As Gwendolyn struggled with dessert boxes and paper cups, he gave his daughter a reassuring smile. "I'll be right back, okay?"

"Okay, Daddy." Daisy took a tiny bite of apple turnover.

He hurried to the counter. "Let me help."

A sigh escaped Gwendolyn's pink lips as she herded the children to a table. "Thank you."

"I'll carry it!" Danica reached for the orange juice cup.

He placed the dessert boxes on a table near his, then strode back to the counter to pick up Gwendolyn's caramel macchiato.

"Noooo!" Danica shrieked behind his back.

As he pivoted back toward the table, he slipped on the tile, and the drink that once had been his favorite flew into the air. From his horse riding lessons, he'd learned how to fall without hurting himself, but that didn't stop him from landing on the floor.

"Daddy!" Daisy screamed.

"I'm okay. I'm okay, Sweetie Pie." He'd constantly had to reassure her that he was fine and wasn't going anywhere. After all, she only had one parent to rely on.

"Sorry if I scared you." Danica gave him an apologetic smile. "I spilled the orange juice."

"I'll clean it." The woman behind the counter came over with napkins.

"It's no biggie. The only place that's hurt is my dignity." He pushed himself to his feet just as Gwendolyn leaned down and offered him her hand.

Up close, her large eyes were a warm shade of honey with crystalline dots in them, and his heart made a strange movement.

Those eyes widened as if… as if she felt something. Then she looked away. He glanced at the floor, expecting to see the macchiato there and ready to buy her a new one. But it wasn't there.

It was… on the table.

Huh.

So she'd caught it. She must have quick reactions, but then that might be a necessary skill while working with children.

"Well, I guess we got the embarrassing part of the introduction out." He pulled out chairs for everyone, then sat in his chair again, but faced it toward the group.

He curved his lips up with an effort, wishing he'd shaved today. The beard made him look like the grouch he was. At least he didn't look like a Sasquatch—yet—but he was moving in that direction.

Well, apparently, he didn't scare off the children who eyed him and his daughter with curiosity.

"My daughter and I are new in town. Is there a place here that's fun for kids?" The sweet liquid soured in his stomach. This woman seemed kind and naïve, and he didn't want to deceive her. A pang of conscience made him wince.

Then, as his daughter seemed to recoil into herself at the sight of other children, he reminded himself that, if Daisy ever had to go into foster care, she wouldn't survive.

She'd need a family to take care of her, and there was a chance the Clark family could turn out to be a good one. Not all rich people were snobs like his biological father or Annika's parents. Despite inheriting an art gallery from her grandmother, Annika was one of the kindest people he'd ever met.

"Sure." Gwendolyn smiled at him, and for some reason, his heart skipped a beat. "The park is great in better weather. Christmas lights are fun to look at."

Daisy took another bite of her apple turnover and chewed slowly. Then she whispered, "Daddy, can we go to the park? I wanna build a snowman."

His rib cage constricted at the memory of him and Annika building a snowman, Annika laughing, deliriously happy.

Next to Gwendolyn, Danica perked up. "Yeah! We're gonna go to the park today, too. Right, Miss Gwendolyn?"

Gwendolyn blinked as if realizing her mistake. "We are?"

The woman at the counter waved at them. "That's a great idea. I'm sure this nice man over here and his little girl could use some company. We're a friendly town, after all."

Gwendolyn's mouth slid into a perfect *O*. "But—"

Danica slipped from her chair and marched to them, holding out a cookie on a napkin, her pigtails bouncing with the skip in her walk. "I'm Danica, and over there are my boyfriend, Nehemiah, and my cousin, Landon. Come with us to the park today."

Daisy just blinked at her.

Danica didn't seem to need an answer. She left the cookie on the table and hurried back with a grin as if after a job well done.

Wow.

This was much easier than he'd thought.

People in small towns were too trusting. Or was this what small-town matchmaking looked like?

He braced a hand on Daisy's chair as she reached out for the cookie. "What do you think, Sweetie Pie?"

"I like it."

He wasn't sure whether she meant the dessert or the idea of joining Danica and her friends, but he gave Gwendolyn his best smile. Let's hope she liked men with beards. "We don't want to inconvenience you, but we could use some company. While I pride myself on being my daughter's best friend, she might like to spend time with kids her age."

Something he couldn't read flashed in the woman's eyes, and her smile frayed at its edges. "Well, if you don't mind the company of a dog, as well…"

Daisy's eyes widened, and she clapped. "A dog?"

Well, then it was decided. Just like him, his shy daughter had found it easier to relate to animals than to people, though she preferred cats.

He hurried to say, "Thank you so much. Oh, let me introduce my daughter and myself. I'm Conner, and this"—he rested his hand on his daughter's shoulder—"is Daisy."

"I'm Gwendolyn. Great to meet you." A smile illuminated her face, making it pretty in a girl-next-door way. Sweet and warm, just like the hue of her eyes or her freckles.

A spark of attraction caused an irritating surprise. After Annika's death, he wasn't in the market for romance. Losing someone he'd loved had hurt too much.

Besides, what would this soft-spoken woman think when she found out he used her to get information about the Clark family?

CHAPTER TWO

THE BELL OVER THE DOOR rang again, and running to the woman who entered, the children cried out, "Auntie J!"

She hugged them in turn, smiling, and waved at Gwendolyn.

So this must be Jenna Clark.

As she flicked long dark bangs from her eyes—*electric-blue eyes*—her gaze rested on him and sliced open his insides. Anger bubbled from those opened wounds like hot lava. It wasn't just because of all the siblings she resembled their father the most.

She didn't resemble the relative he hated as much as the relative he loved, and that made looking at her more painful.

The tall height, the challenge in her electric-blue eyes, the enviable confidence in her stride as she sauntered to the counter—even what he now recalled of her history of academic achievements before she'd skipped town—reminded him of Tara, his stepsister. Of the way he'd failed to help her and she'd run away.

He suppressed a shudder and turned away so Jenna wouldn't catch his expression and get suspicious. She was an investigator, after all.

Even after Jenna left with her latte, her fresh, expensive scent and his sense of regret lingered.

He'd begged his mother to ask for help from his biological father. After all, the man owed them for years of child support his mother refused to press for. Conner had needed to put Tara somewhere she'd be safe. When she'd disappeared, he was desperate to find her. But once again, his mother said the man refused to help them.

Just like he'd refused to help when Conner's little brother was sick and needed expensive surgery. Fine, those weren't his father's children. But Conner was. Didn't his dad have the humanity to help desperate kids in a matter of life and death?

Conner's mother's marriage in his teen years was a disaster. He could still feel the metallic taste of blood from the hit to his jaw when he'd tried to stand up for Tara, could still hear the wail of his tiny brother's cries at night. A shiver ran through him as if he were in the apartment that was often cold because they'd always owed for electricity.

Just imagining his daughter ever being treated like he and Tara were treated twisted his gut worse than those pretzels displayed on the counter.

Guilt assailed him again. Guilt for being unable to protect his stepsister. Guilt for not saving his wife. Guilt for failing his little brother. Guilt for being born. He'd overheard his mother saying her life would've been so much easier if she hadn't gotten pregnant with Conner.

Then he squared his shoulders and plastered on a smile again for his daughter. "Are you doing okay, Sweetie Pie?"

Okay, he smiled for Gwendolyn's sake, too. No one would want to go on a date with someone filled fuller with regret than the clerk filled his cup with latte, ready to spill if he wasn't careful, and burn the person close by.

Man, guilt stung.

He doubted that, after everything was said and done,

Gwendolyn would still think it was great to meet him.

Gwendolyn was so not meant to be a nanny.

She'd had to guard pets before—though many of those pets would disagree who'd guarded whom—and had worked protecting teenagers, seniors, and many ages in between. But taking care of children was a different matter.

As she drove to the park with three children belting out the Christmas song on the radio at the top of their lungs—despite those lungs being relatively small—she wondered again why she'd taken on this job. The scent of french fries clung to the leather seats, though she'd searched high and low for any remnants of food.

At least, the Newfoundland mix was in the truck bed, or she'd join in this attempt to make Gwendolyn's ears bleed.

She made a turn and suppressed a sigh. Okay, she knew the reason for taking this assignment all too well. Her friend Vera — and she'd had too few genuine friends—had asked her to help out and work as the children's bodyguard undercover.

That was what Gwendolyn was, really. She became a bodyguard like her father, skilled in weapons, martial arts, and foreign languages. Not a nanny! She'd never babysat siblings since her estranged sister was a year older than she was. Had never worked as a babysitter in school.

A longing stirred her. She was so close to becoming part of the elite security company her father had once worked for. There could be a vacancy anytime. She could nearly taste her goal like she'd tasted the cookie in the pastry store. Instead, she was in a small Missouri town playing the uncomfortable role of a nanny.

Her gaze moved to the rearview mirror.

Then she tensed.

Hadn't the same older navy-blue sedan been two cars behind

her when she'd stopped to get the children pastries? Her gaze zoomed in on the license plate. Snow covered it, and she didn't like it one bit.

A cold shiver traveled over her spine despite the warm air the heater spread comfortably through the truck cab. The sedan looked achingly familiar, not just the color, the make, the model, and those tinted windows.

The decorations, too. Her father had often decorated his car—exactly like this one—with a red bow for Christmas. Another thing gave her shivers. A pennant for her father's favorite football team hung on the antenna.

She returned her attention to the road just in time to spot the traffic light.

Red!

She pressed on the brakes too fast. When the truck stopped, she jerked forward. Based on the yelp in the back seats, so did the children.

Dara, the family Newfoundland, let out a howl.

Ugh. She should've known better than to let ghosts from the past distract her. It could've been worse. Had she slammed on the brakes, the Newfoundland could've flown forward and landed on the rear windshield. She and the children loved that goofy dog too much to let that happen.

"Sorry!" She glanced back. "Everyone okay?"

Dara gave out a cheerful bark. Phew.

"Yeah!" Three heads bobbed up and down. "Are we there yet?"

"Almost." She'd lost count of how many times she'd heard that question even on a five-minute drive.

She moved forward on the green light and went slow. The car crept behind her without passing.

The yelling—um, singing—resumed.

She drew in a shaky breath and concentrated on the road as

she slid her purse with her gun closer. The identical twin of a car was a coincidence. It had to be.

Her guilty conscience couldn't have conjured up the image. She'd had nightmares before, yes, but never hallucinations.

Continuing her father's legacy couldn't make up for never finding the person who'd shot him. Being a heartsick teenager at the time didn't excuse her. Her shoulders hunched against the guilt's familiar pressure.

If she hadn't chosen dinner with a cute boy over hanging out with her father that evening, her dad might've still been alive.

Overhead, the clouds seemed as leaden as the weight in her stomach. And okay, maybe she was on edge because it was so close to Christmas. Her father had been shot on the night before Christmas Eve, and no matter how many years had passed, she had difficulty getting in the spirit for the season.

Forgive me, Lord.

Another slow turn.

Several cars passed her, one of the drivers asking her whether she was okay. A tractor could've passed her now. But the navy-blue sedan decided to crawl at a turtle's speed, too. What in the world?

The children interrupted yelling the next song long enough to ask, "Are we there yet?"

"Soon." She hoped.

Finally, the dark-blue sedan moved by her, and relief whooshed out of her lungs. It signaled changing lanes as if winking at her like her father often had.

Then her breath caught in her throat again. The bumper sticker…

It showed allegiance to the same military branch her father had been in before he'd been honorably discharged and joined the security business.

Hmm, and wasn't it strange that the license plate in the back was plastered in snow, like the front one? It was as if someone had deliberately used it as a target for snowball practice, and the owner never cared to clean it.

Another logical explanation could be that they didn't want their car tracked down. She pursed her lips. Or maybe she'd been in the security business so long she'd become accustomed to being suspicious of everything.

She suppressed a grimace as she sped up on the outskirts of town. She hadn't wanted to go to the park because they'd be a much easier target in the open. Though her friend, Vera, had assured her things should be fine now, Gwendolyn wasn't so sure. Yes, during a whirlwind romance with Maverick Clark, Vera had uncovered who'd been after him and caused his accident. Yes, she found the woman responsible for sabotaging the tractors and other vehicles. But other unanswered incidents still left Gwendolyn uneasy, so that car wasn't helping her nerves.

The next Christmas song ended, and she used the temporary quiet as she turned on the road leading to the park. "We're almost there."

"Yay!" the children squealed, and Danica high-fived her boyfriend, then her cousin as if they'd never visited the park before.

Gwendolyn smiled at their enthusiasm, her heart warming up. She loved kids. She did. She just wasn't great with them.

However, when Vera had contacted her and asked for help protecting the Clark family children, she couldn't say no.

Vera's recent wedding had been lovely. Gwendolyn sighed, long and deep, releasing the pressure in her chest. She wasn't jealous. Really, she wasn't. After all, after the kind of childhood she'd had and a ruined engagement, she wasn't the marrying type. Her dream job as an elite bodyguard traveling the world on assignments wouldn't be great for a family, either.

All the things she'd told herself almost enough times to start believing them.

Almost.

She was happy for Vera. But having her best friend married now changed things. Seeing her so deeply in love changed things, too. Made Gwendolyn ache for something she'd chosen to live without.

Then the image of the newcomer at the pastry store appeared in her mind as she parked near the playground entrance and surveyed the territory for anything suspicious.

Would he be at the park with his daughter? Did she want him to be?

Of course, she couldn't let a stranger close to the children without the Clarks' permission. So she'd done a little research, finding out he was a former ranch foreman who worked as an art gallery manager now, and Vera had also looked into him and said it should be okay.

Sadly, Gwendolyn didn't have time to investigate his family history. Maybe because those smoldering brown eyes in his photo set something inside her ablaze.

The pleasant wave washing over her surprised her.

Was it attraction?

Yes, the man was handsome. A strong nose and jaw. Chiseled features. Mesmerizing brown eyes. Even the beard gave him a ruggedly handsome look.

But she didn't plan on staying in town much longer since the need for guarding the children seemed to be gone now. Just a few weeks to make sure. No point in starting a romance and risking her heart being broken a second time.

She studied her surroundings as she turned off the engine. Everyone knew the routine by now and stayed in their seats. Okay, all seemed clear.

"Let's go." She opened their truck door, and the children scrambled onto the ground fast. "Don't run too far. I need to be able to see all of you all the time. Promise?"

Three nods followed, but she wasn't convinced.

She untied the dog, making sure to hold onto the leash firmly. The large pet loved to roll in the snow and was surprisingly fast for her size. Gwendolyn had found out the hard way that being dragged by the leash in the snow wasn't fun at all, except for the children who'd watched the spectacle.

As the children started building a fortress, she joined them while remaining on high alert. Though she kept her attention on her surroundings, her thoughts kept returning to the mysterious sedan. What were the odds it looked exactly like her father's and even had the same decorations and sticker?

Longing swept through her whole being, covering her like the snow covered the ground. Twenty-five years after his death, she missed him as if it were yesterday.

Lord, is that car a sign I need to investigate his death?

He deserved justice.

Dara barked and tugged on the leash, so Gwendolyn reluctantly let the dog go. The dog needed exercise, or Gwendolyn would be chasing the Newfoundland around the mansion later, catching furniture and vases on the way.

Minutes later, she realized her mistake.

"Dara! Stop! Please stop!" She rushed after the gigantic dog as Dara dashed to an unsuspecting passerby.

No, no, no..

Chapter Three

GWENDOLYN CRINGED as she caught up to the pet.

The Newfoundland mix lifted herself on her hind legs and unleashed a nice flood of saliva on Conner.

To his credit, he remained standing, which she could imagine was no easy feat. She was no weakling herself due to years of training, and still, Dara had nearly knocked her down when they'd met. What a day that had been! Considering Danica had put glue on Gwendolyn's chair and extra pepper into Gwendolyn's food, it hadn't been the best first day on the job in history.

"I'm so sorry." Gwendolyn made it to him fast and pulled the dog back.

"It's okay." Despite his words, his tone was clipped.

Huh. There was no reason for her heart to flutter as she looked into his smoldering eyes.

No reason at all.

Her heart didn't usually act like that in men's presence. Working with guys for years, she had to prove to be their equal, to make them look at her as a reliable, trustworthy partner and not a possible date.

She reminded herself of her duties as she kept the children in her peripheral vision. By now, they'd abandoned building the fortress and joined them.

"Are you okay, Sweetie Pie?" His voice turned soft and tender.

Did he… Did he just call her sweetie pie? No one had used that term of endearment on her before. Why would it make warmth spread through her? And why would he ask whether she was okay?

He leaned down.

Belatedly, she realized he was talking to the little angel hiding behind his legs. If ever the term *sweetie pie* suited someone, it suited this girl. She looked sweet and shy. Unusually shy. She seemed a fragile flower, just like her name suggested. But then again, Gwendolyn was far from a child psychologist.

He was worried Dara could've scared his daughter. Probably that was the reason for his clipped tone.

Gwendolyn crouched before the little girl. "I'm sorry if Dara scared you. She only wanted to greet you."

The dog gave a cheerful bark as if to confirm Gwendolyn's words. The girl hid her face in Conner's jeans.

Guilt slapped Gwendolyn as she straightened out. "I didn't mean for that to happen. Dara is very friendly. Well, sometimes *too* friendly."

She should've had a much faster reaction. Was she kidding herself that one day she could become as good as her father had been?

"Hi! Glad you made it. Wanna play with us?" Danica tapped Daisy's shoulder. "Remember Nehemiah, my boyfriend? And Landon, my cousin?" Contrary to Daisy, Danica didn't have a shy bone in her small body.

"Yeah! We gonna make a snowman." Nehemiah joined his girlfriend of several months and grinned. Adorable dimples made their appearance in his cheeks.

Yup, girls these days started having boyfriends at five while

Gwendolyn had gotten her first boyfriend at twenty-three and couldn't keep him long. Gwendolyn suppressed a sigh. Was she so pathetic that, if she ever became interested in romance, she needed to take lessons from her five-year-old charge?

Daisy peeked from behind the safety of her father's legs.

Maybe Gwendolyn needed to pique the girl's curiosity to get her out of her shell. Gwendolyn smiled. "You know what, Daisy? We'll build a snow*woman*."

"Would you like that, Sweetie Pie?" Conner straightened out the cute multicolored knit hat on the girl's head.

The large pompom lifted up and down as Daisy studied her little cowboy boots with pink embroidery. No fair for a child to have such amazing eyelashes. Gwendolyn would never have the skill to apply mascara and eyeliner like God had naturally blessed this little girl with.

Hmm. Gwendolyn had never cared about makeup. Why now?

A moment stretched out, but she had loads of patience. One needed oodles of it to spend nights on stakeouts and double heaping oodles to work with children.

Finally, Daisy stepped forward. Those lashes winged up, and big curious eyes blinked at Gwendolyn, touching something inside her. "A snow… woman?" Barely audible, her words formed a puff of humid air as soft and nearly silent as falling snow.

"Yeah. Why should men have all the fun?" Gwendolyn high-fived Danica, then turned to Daisy, offering a high five but from a distance.

Conner visibly tensed.

His tension ricocheted inside Gwendolyn. Was she overstepping some kind of boundary?

Then Daisy lifted her hand. The weak gesture didn't exactly reach Gwendolyn's palm.

"I promise to keep Dara away." Gwendolyn glanced at the dog, whose tongue hung out and tail thumped on the snow as if to signal *she* made no such promises.

A tentative smile further softened the girl's angelic face. "Daddy, can I?"

His expression relaxed, and gratitude flashed in his brown eyes. "Of course. I'll join you."

The smile widened into a grin. "Yeah, Daddy."

Relief flushed over Gwendolyn as if she'd completed a difficult assignment. "Great. Let's do it, then."

She'd just met this girl, but she felt an immediate connection. Maybe because she'd been painfully shy as a child. Or because she'd grown up without a mother, who'd taken Gwendolyn's sister and left after the divorce when Gwendolyn was five, the parents dividing children as if they were property.

Tugging her gloves from her pocket and making sure the children had theirs on as well, she switched her thoughts to the fun present from the painful past.

Thankfully, she'd had the foresight to bring a few carrots and a pack of jelly beans to make the snowman's—ahem, the snowwoman's—eyes and mouth and even buttons on the, well, dress. She scanned the park and the playground and listened intently. So far, so good.

"Where do you live?" Danica asked Daisy as they rolled a snowball.

"Houston." Daisy's voice was quiet again.

"Cool," Nehemiah said as he petted Dara and by some miracle managed to keep her in one place. *Thank You, Lord!* "I used to live in Chicago."

"We got his dad married to my auntie Liberty, so Nehemiah could stay here and be my boyfriend." Danica shrugged like it was no big deal. "My auntie is awesome. Wait till you meet her."

The boy nodded with an air of self-importance, those dimples making another appearance. "Gotta help those adults."

Conner raised a brow at Gwendolyn, a question in his eyes as they started making a big snowball for the base. "Are they for real?" he whispered.

She hid a smile. "You'd better believe it."

Danica glanced back as she and Daisy were rolling a different snowball, a twinkle in her eyes, and Gwendolyn stilled, feeling caught in the girl's crosshairs.

Uh-oh.

The little matchmakers might be at it again. Did... did Gwendolyn want them to be? Her heart skipped a beat.

She didn't come to this small town to start a romance. After her disastrous history, she wasn't looking for romance, period. Then why did her treacherous heart shift?

Danica said something, and Daisy grinned.

"Thank you." Conner moved closer. His breathing came out in foggy puffs in the frosty air.

A little closer, and she'd be able to feel his breath on her skin. No thinking like that!

She couldn't afford distractions, especially such handsome ones. She checked her surroundings again.

Then the meaning of his words filtered through a mental fog she shouldn't be having. "You're thanking me for... what exactly?"

"My daughter doesn't smile often. No matter how much I try to cheer her up." His voice cracked and deepened, then perked up. "She's been smiling much more today."

It tugged at Gwendolyn's heart as they moved the base forward. It should be big enough to stop, but neither of them did.

What had happened to the girl's mother? The question was on the tip of her tongue, but she held it in. It was none of her business.

As it was none of her business whether the lack of the ring on his ring finger meant he was single indeed. She wasn't going to ask about his marital status, even though she ached to know.

She sent him a warm smile of her own. "I'm glad if we made

your daughter smile. I take it your wife…" She stumbled, heat rising to her cheeks.

So much for not asking.

"Annika…" His voice dipped. "She died when Daisy was twenty-three months old." No inflection, no emotion accompanied the words, which probably took a lot of effort.

Something raw tore through Gwendolyn's heart, and she almost moved her gloved hand to cover his. Instead, she whispered, "I'm sorry. That must be difficult."

"Tell me about your occupation. It must be… interesting to work for the richest family in town." He obviously tried to change the topic.

She opened her mouth, then closed it, reminding herself about her duties. "I can't tell you much about *the richest family in town.* There's such a thing as client confidentiality."

Disappointment flashed in his eyes. "How about the things the entire town already knows anyway?"

O–okay. "The Clarks are people who care about each other, even if they don't always show it. They are not perfect, but they are God-honoring and help others in need. They have great children who I'm sure would welcome Daisy anytime she wants to come for a playdate."

His eyebrows rose as if it wasn't something he expected to hear, and her instincts woke up. Why did he react this way?

"We're waiting for you!" Danica interrupted, her hands on her hips in a trademark gesture Gwendolyn grew to associate with the girl who was as stubborn and outspoken as her auntie Liberty.

"Uh-oh. We overdid it." Conner chuckled as he patted the oversized ball he and Gwendolyn had created. Then he placed the much smaller ball the boys made on top of it and added the other smaller ball the girls had rolled for the snow woman's head.

Danica rolled her eyes. That girl often acted way too grown-up for her age. "It's gonna be a humongous snowwoman."

Daisy giggled.

"I guess she's going to be plus-size." Gwendolyn spread her hands. "Like me or your aunt."

"Okay." Danica nodded with authority. "My aunt says she is beautiful. The more of her, the more beauty."

Daisy nodded again, and another giggle escaped her lips.

Conner's eyes widened. "I can't believe this."

Alarm rang inside Gwendolyn. "What happened?"

He was reluctant to answer, so she glanced around for any possible threats, then stepped to him. "Um, would you mind helping me bringing carrots and jelly beans from the truck? And I have a scarf we could use as the snowwoman's skirt. I parked close, so we'll see the children from there."

He hesitated as if reluctant to leave his daughter even for a minute, then followed her.

"What happened?" she asked again as she handed him the supplies from the truck, keeping the children in the corner of her eye.

"Daisy giggled." Shaking his head, he rubbed a hand over his face, and his eyes glistened. "I can't believe this."

He loved his daughter very much.

Admiration unraveled inside her, and she wanted to linger and ask more questions. But he obviously didn't want the children to stay alone, and neither did she. So they headed back.

Gwendolyn leaned to the children. "Daisy is our guest today. How about we let her do the honor of decorating our snowwoman?"

Everyone nodded. "Yeah!"

With her lashes sweeping upward, Daisy's eyes brightened. "Can I?"

Gwendolyn grinned at the girl. "Of course!"

More gratitude filling his eyes, Conner lifted his daughter.

Gwendolyn helped place the carrot, then the jelly beans just right. "Ooooh, she now has beautiful brown eyes. Just like you. Great job!"

Daisy peeked shyly at her with those long-lashed eyes, and a slow grin widened her pink mouth before she ducked her head against her dad's shoulder.

Conner hugged her tighter. "Great job indeed, Sweetie Pie."

The rest of the children clapped, causing Daisy to lift her head from its hiding place, her cheeks pink.

"You're amazing. You know that?" Conner whispered in Gwendolyn's direction when he put his daughter down.

This time, heat warmed her insides, so her cheeks probably pinked as much as Daisy's. "Oh please." She waved off his praise.

Yet it touched her deeply. Weird how it gave her nearly the same sense of accomplishment as when she'd saved her client's life.

The little girl also stirred her compassion. Being raised by a single dad had made it difficult for Gwendolyn to relate to girls her age. It might be the same for Daisy.

Besides, Gwendolyn knew firsthand how hard it was to be an introvert in a world that seemed to favor extroverts, how painful to form friendships and approach new people. In her teens, she'd been envious of the popular, confident girls who'd seemed to have it easy with their bright smiles and outgoing personalities.

"Now, let's have a snowball fight," Danica announced, interrupting Gwendolyn's musings.

"What?" Daisy's lower lip trembled.

Gwendolyn's heart squeezed, and she gave the girl her best reassuring smile. "You don't have to do it. But I'd love to have you on my team. It's going to be just us girls."

Conner gave his daughter a quick hug. "We can go home if you like."

Why did the idea of him leaving any moment make her heart dip? She pulled her shoulders back. She had a job to do. Besides, based on the way he'd talked about his late wife, he was still grieving. So he probably wasn't looking for romance, either.

No reason for that to stab her with disappointment.

Head tipped to one side, that pompom bouncing by her ear, Daisy thought a moment and shook her head. "I wanna play."

"Great!" Danica grinned and high-fived Daisy. "I like you. Wanna be my friend?"

A soft whisper of air slipped from Daisy's mouth as her eyes went big again. "For real?"

"For real." Danica nodded. "Now, let's play. I'll show you how to make a good snowball."

Daisy's lips turned up a little. "Okay."

While the girls made the snowballs, Gwendolyn patted Daisy on her shoulder. "You're doing great. Both of you."

Danica beamed. "I know." No humble bone in that small body, either.

Conner chuckled, and so did Gwendolyn. Huh. Who'd think that even while they were on the opposite teams a bond could form?

"If Nehemiah and Danica stay boyfriend and girlfriend through their teens, he has his work cut out for him," Conner whispered to her, his breath caressing her ear.

Gwendolyn laughed while her insides warmed. The sky looked much brighter now, the clouds gone, and the sunlight created a myriad of tiny sparkles on the snow. Some of those sparkles reflected in Daisy's eyes as Danica told her she was doing "real good."

Although Gwendolyn's aim was great, she had to divide her attention between the game and the outer perimeter.

While Dara ran in circles around the snow fortress as if to make sure no one stepped inside that circle, she wasn't the best watchdog. A few times, squirrels got her attention, and she spent a long time under the tree, hoping for them to return, barking with surprise that the squirrels didn't want to meet her.

Even if the Clarks thought the danger had passed, this was still Gwendolyn's job. So she needed to pay attention to every distant motor or every crunch of snow under someone's feet at the park's other end.

Due to her doing this double duty, the girls nearly lost. But in the end, the guys seemed to let them win, as true gentlemen. Her cold-kissed cheeks and eyes aglow, Daisy beamed when Nehemiah and Landon congratulated her and Danica on their win.

Then Gwendolyn's foot slipped on the snow, and overly distracted by looking at Conner, she didn't regroup herself to avoid the fall. Her arms flailed, and she had to hold onto something.

That something turned out to be Conner's scarf. The earth moved in front of her as she landed on the snow, dragging him with her.

What...

What just happened?

She cringed. She was supposed to have much better reactions than this.

Unforgivable.

But, as she looked up into his brown eyes, heat pooled in the pit of her stomach. Having him so close, looking into those depths, feeling his lips near enough that if she moved a little she could kiss him made her breath lodge in her throat. The scent of his spicy cologne, mixed with frosty air, wreaked havoc on her senses.

"Are you... are you all right?" His breath warmed her skin.

She couldn't find her tongue. She couldn't find her limbs, for that matter.

"Daaaaaddy, are you okay?" Daisy's worried voice made him hop to his feet, then pull Gwendolyn up, too.

"Yes, Sweetie Pie." He dusted the snow off Gwendolyn's coat while she felt like a fool.

Some bodyguard she was!

She cringed as embarrassment spread through her. If any of her colleagues had seen her, she'd be a laughingstock. Worse, she could expose her client to danger if she behaved like that. Not only had she fallen, but she'd also taken a guy with her. Then she'd been so distraught she'd forgotten her charges.

Just great.

All because of a sudden attraction to a guy she'd met today. Okay, she wasn't falling for the man—not yet, anyway. She was falling *with* him, and that wasn't much better.

She needed to walk away from this man, never see him again, and concentrate on what she needed to concentrate on. She'd let a handsome face distract her once, and her father had paid for her mistake with his life. Something hard slammed her heart. She should've learned her lesson then.

"Children, we're going home."

A collective groan met her words.

"How about hot cocoa and cookies when we get there?" Yes, she was offering a bribe, but she needed to collect her bearings.

Hot cocoa and cookies met a more enthusiastic response.

Danica waved at her new friend. "Come visit us sometime. Miss Gwendolyn makes yummy cookies. And cocoa."

Those eyelashes feathered over her cheeks as the girl focused on her cowboy boots, but another shy smile was curving up her lips. "Daddy, can we?"

Conner stepped to Gwendolyn, giving her a whiff of his intoxicating cologne again. Her insides went liquid like the cocoa they discussed. Oh for crying out loud!

Danica elbowed Daisy. "Say pretty please. That gonna work."

Her head jerking up, Daisy blinked and whispered, "Pretty please?"

"Nah. Like this." Danica fluttered her eyelashes, lifted pleading eyes at Conner, and singsonged in a high voice. "Pretty pretty please?"

Daisy repeated the words in a more hushed voice.

Conner spread his hands out. "How can one say no to those eyes?"

Nearly getting lost in *his* brown depths, Gwendolyn had to agree.

"Good. It's decided then." Danica high-fived Daisy.

What? Oh boy.

Gwendolyn had to watch out with that little matchmaker who was getting more and more skilled in what she was doing.

Danica placed her hands on her hips. "Miss Gwendolyn, Daisy will need your phone number."

Daisy blinked. "I will?"

"Both of us would like to have your phone number, please." His lips widened. Wow.

He was handsome even when he frowned, but when he smiled, she nearly swooned. What was wrong with her?

She scanned her surroundings again. Giving her cell phone number wasn't a good idea. Yet she rattled it off.

"We... I... We've got to go." Her mind seemed as foggy as her breath. *Concentrate!*

"I look forward to seeing you again." He looked at her, his protective hands resting on Daisy's shoulders.

"I..." Gwendolyn stared at him.

Danica sighed as if asking, "Do I have to do everything myself here?" "Miss Gwendolyn says she looks forward to seeing you, too."

Gwendolyn didn't know whether to laugh or cringe. She chose to do neither and herded the children and their gigantic dog to the truck.

As she was about to take off, her phone rang, and she fished it out of her purse. Her eyes narrowed at the unknown number on the screen. A telemarketer?

"Hello," she answered as she studied her surroundings,

prepared to say she didn't need an extended warranty or wasn't going on a cruise in the near future.

"Hiya, Gwennie," a deep male voice said. Then the line went dead.

Unable to move, afraid to breathe, she stared at the phone. That was the way her father used to greet her.

Chapter Four

LATE IN THE EVENING, Gwendolyn stretched out in her guest room bed at the mansion.

The room was almost as big as her apartment and boasted emerald-green Missouri summer landscapes, a large antique oak desk with a matching chair, a bronze lantern night-light lamp, and a mustang herd galloping over the rug. Strangely, this room suited her more than her own place with its minimalist furnishings.

This one had character and legacy, and her place was like a blank slate still waiting for her to decide who she was. As if, when she'd lost her father, she'd lost part of her identity, and even a quarter of a century later, she hadn't recovered it.

That call earlier still spooked her. She'd wondered if God was nudging her to investigate what happened to Dad. Now, it seemed maybe someone else was, too. Tracing the caller's number got her nowhere. Probably, a burner phone. No joy tracing the caller's location, either. She didn't have the contacts here to dig deeper, but Vera did. God willing, her friend could help.

So instead of thinking about the blue sedan and the call, things she didn't want to think about, she found herself remembering the guy she'd met today, and humming. She probably had a goofy smile as she thought about Conner and his little girl.

What about the man drew her to him so strongly?

Was it his obvious love for his daughter? Gwendolyn and Conner's bond over their painful pasts, with him losing his wife and her losing her father? His charisma? His Texan twang, great build toned by years of working outdoors, or handsome features?

Probably all of the above.

Though probably not so much the great build. Muscular men surrounded her in her line of work. Most of her colleagues were buffed as if it were a job requirement. After all, people preferred to hide behind broad shoulders. Those muscles had never affected her before.

Lord, I have horrible judgment about men. I've made my share of mistakes. Is Conner going to be one of those mistakes? Or is he the man You created for me?

Wow. She was going too far with the last statement.

Her phone rang and her pulse accelerated. Reaching out for her phone on the oak nightstand, she picked it up, and her heart skipped a beat at Conner's name. "Hello," she whispered into the phone.

"Hi, Gwendolyn. Um, Daisy and I are going to look at Christmas lights tomorrow. You mentioned how beautiful they are."

Did she? Oh yes, she did.

Conner cleared his throat. "Would you... would you like to join us?" There was a voice in the background. He chuckled. "Daisy told me to say pretty please."

Despite her best intentions, she smiled. "I... I don't know." She closed her eyes. She'd avoided looking at Christmas lights for over two decades. Worked through the holidays. Didn't put up a Christmas tree.

Besides, it wouldn't be a good idea to see him again.

"Oh. My daughter told me I was saying it the wrong way. I

need to do it like Danica did." He pitched his voice higher. "Pretty pretty please?"

Laughter bubbled in her chest, and she heard herself saying okay.

"Great."

"Yay!" An excited scream came from the background.

What had she done? "I mean—"

"See you tomorrow." He disconnected.

Her phone beeped, signaling an incoming text. Then the smile slid from her face as she stared at her phone screen.

The text was from Vera, and her stomach clenched as she opened the message.

I'm working on it.

A low groan slid loose, and Gwendolyn banged her head back on the sturdy oak headboard. What was wrong with her? *She* should be participating in the investigation. *She'd* been the one in Springfield when her dad had been murdered. *She* was the one who'd let him down. *She* was the one seeing and hearing things that reminded her of him.

Instead, she'd pawned it off on her friend. What kind of daughter did that?

A guilty daughter. A daughter who didn't want to remember her mistakes.

Her throat clogged up as she forced herself to think about what had happened a quarter of a century ago, the memories she'd done her best to push away but couldn't ignore any longer.

At first, she'd been hurt when her father had accepted an assignment two weeks before Christmas. It had taken her a long time to realize he'd accepted that job, not because of the generous pay but because he could relate to the case.

Brea Cohen, the daughter of a famous sculptor, was back from drug rehab, and her father wanted to make sure she didn't relapse. He also didn't want certain friends anywhere near her. Brea was fifteen, and the sculptor had been raising her on his own.

Gwendolyn closed her eyes, willing the image to come to her mind. Though her father had never mixed business and personal life before, the small Cohen family was friendly, and with the holidays approaching, he'd taken Gwendolyn to his client's place filled with beautiful sculptures several times. He and Mr. Cohen became somewhat close to friends.

With long, straight, beach-blonde hair, an hourglass figure, and outfits rich in price and poor in fabric amount, Brea looked nothing like Gwendolyn.

Teenage Gwendolyn had dressed in khaki pants and gray hoodies, doing her best to blend into the background. Gwendolyn's hair was boy-short—a compromise with her father as he'd preferred military cut. She'd already been chubby despite her exercise routine.

While Gwendolyn's father had been strict with her, toughening her up for her future life, Brea had been obviously spoiled. It was as if Mr. Cohen had tried to overcompensate for being unable to give Brea a mother figure by giving her everything else she'd wanted.

But while their appearances and characters were different, the situation itself must've raised Gwendolyn's father's protective instincts.

He'd called Gwendolyn regularly while she'd stayed with her grandpa. He'd told her with a chuckle he didn't understand what he was paid for. Brea stayed inside the house, glued to her phone. She hadn't tried to sneak out at night—one of the female house employees watched the girl's room at night due to sensitivity issues. He'd insisted that was part of the contract so he couldn't later be accused of any lewd behavior.

Even then, Gwendolyn had been surprised that a teen who'd had issues in the past would stick to the house regimen. Gwendolyn should've brought it up, and again, guilt jabbed her.

Guilt had been her loyal companion since the day he'd died. The day before Christmas Eve, he'd called her, saying he'd asked for the holidays off and wanted to spend three days with her.

She was excited, but she was supposed to have a date with a cute guy she'd met at the grocery store of all places. Her father agreed to her going on the date, though she could tell he was disappointed. But she'd always done what he'd wanted, so wasn't it time to do something for herself, too?

What happened on the night of December 23 still sliced her insides sharper than any knife could. Her father was found shot in the parking lot of an abandoned warehouse many miles from the posh neighborhood he'd been surveilling.

Why had he gone there? To meet with someone who didn't want to be seen?

Even then, why didn't he tell anyone?

Gwendolyn stared at the ceiling as if she could find answers there. She rubbed her throbbing temples, a migraine brewing as it did every time she'd thought about the horrible day.

According to the police, Brea had said she had no clue what had happened, and Mr. Cohen had said the same thing. He'd confirmed his daughter had spent all the time in the house, and so had the female employee who'd been watching her.

Could he… could he have lied for his daughter and paid his employee to do the same? Gwendolyn threw her shoulders back. She needed to talk to Brea, something she should've done twenty-five years ago.

Migraine getting stronger, Gwendolyn slid out of bed and picked up her laptop from the desk. After powering it up, she searched for internet updates on her father's last client and his family.

Her heart sank.

Oh no. Brea had overdosed eight years after Gwendolyn's father's death. Since then, Mr. Cohen hadn't done a single exhibition despite many requests. He'd stayed away from any kind of media, becoming a hermit. To this day, he didn't have any social accounts, unless he'd done it under a fake name. He'd never remarried, either.

Compassion stirred her, but then doubt wriggled in, elbowing the more sensitive emotion aside. Was the man plagued by grief—or guilt? Had something her father overheard or witnessed in their house created a need for his elimination?

She needed more plausible theories, of course.

Despite a million hammers knocking in her brain now, Gwendolyn searched her memory for her father's cases, for any people who could've wished him dead. She started making a list for her friend and for herself, grading the people by probability.

Amazingly, remembering details of the things that happened twenty-five years ago was easier than remembering something from a few days ago. Gwendolyn massaged her aching temples again. She did her best to dredge up anything the police officer investigating the case had cared to share with her, which wasn't much. But then, all she'd done during their conversations was cry.

Her phone rang again, and she reached for it.

Uncle John, her father's best friend and colleague.

She called him an uncle since she was a child, though she wasn't related to him. Uncle John had a paunch, a receding hairline, a goofy smile pushing up round cheeks, and an affection for sweatshirts with fun quotes. He smelled like the cookies his wife baked and he'd often brought Gwendolyn.

He didn't look—or smell—like bodyguards Gwendolyn later had worked with. But, before he retired at sixty, Uncle John had more saved lives under his large belt than any man Gwendolyn knew. He'd told her he'd used the surprise element to his advantage and had taught her to do the same. Though the man could look like an elephant, he moved with the agility of a leopard.

Thanks to Uncle John, Gwendolyn had stopped lamenting the

fact that she didn't look like a bodyguard and saw what could be her shortcoming as her strength. She'd made many clients see her point, too. And a few times when she'd worked with a partner bodyguard, Gwendolyn had been the one who'd saved the day. While her partner had been a target, Gwendolyn had stayed in the shadows and, just like Uncle John, used the element of surprise in her favor.

Uncle John's wife died two years ago, sadly, but his grown-up children and grandchildren often kept him company.

Realizing she'd lingered too long, she swiped the screen to answer, nostalgia stirring inside her. "Hello, Uncle John."

"Hello, Gwendolyn." His deep, tired voice somehow reduced the pounding in her temples. "How… How are you holding up?"

First, he'd visited, then called her before Christmas every year. Not to wish her happy holidays like other people.

To make sure she was okay.

Those first two years, it had put her grandpa on guard. But she'd never sensed any romantic interest on Uncle John's behalf, and there was none on hers. While he hadn't turned into a father figure, he'd checked on her throughout the years, had helped her get training and her first bodyguard assignment, becoming her mentor.

He was understanding, too. With him, she didn't have to smile through the holidays and pretend all was merry and bright. "I'm hanging in there. You?"

"You're welcome to spend Christmas with me and my children and grands." As always, the invitation came.

As always, she declined. "Thank you, but no. I appreciate it, though." She paused, then told him about the navy-blue sedan.

He whistled. "I don't think it's a coincidence. Seriously, you should stay with us for the time being."

She shook her head as if he could see her. "I can't go into hiding. What kind of a bodyguard would that make me?" She wanted her father to be proud of her, not ashamed of her. Her fingers wrapped tighter around the phone's edge.

"An alive one? Okay, never mind."

"Could you please email me anything you know about… well, when my father was shot."

"Will do. Remember, the invitation is still standing. Any time."

A beep signaled an incoming text. "Thank you. It means a lot to me."

"Take care of yourself. Please." He disconnected.

She opened the text from her friend.

Cohen is going to have an exhibition. The first one since his daughter's death. I'm going to email you a flyer and the info.

Gwendolyn typed the reply quickly.

Thank you. I have a list of suspects I made. I'm going to drop it off at your room in a few minutes if that's okay.

The phone beeped immediately.

Sounds good.

Eyes narrowed, Gwendolyn logged into her email on the laptop and opened the flyer. The sadness and pain in the small bronze figures pictured was palpable.

She covered her face with her palms. What did this mean?

Had Cohen healed after nearly two decades? At least enough to show his pain to the world?

Or was there another reason?

Early the next morning, Gwendolyn checked her phone for updates. Vera might be busy with the baby—or her husband—so Gwendolyn didn't go knocking on her door. Not that Vera's husband was a big baby.

Gwendolyn's heart started beating fast. Vera had sent an email with an encrypted attachment. A password to open the attachment waited in a text, so Gwendolyn hurried to look through it. She had little time before the children woke up.

The first suspect, Ron Amspoker, an abusive ex-husband of her father's client, was in prison at the time of her father's murder but could have an accomplice. Vera had checked whether any people Ron was in prison with had been released at the time of her father's murder. The answer was no.

Grimacing, Gwendolyn slumped further against her wooden headboard as she studied Vera's next file. She'd gone through the list of people who'd visited Ron in prison. Two of Amspoker's relatives had been overseas at the time of her father's murder.

O–okay.

Several women who weren't blood related to him had been among his other visitors.

She zeroed in on the names and photos.

Romantic interests?

She cringed. Yes, from what she'd learned about him from his life history, he might be a charmer who could spin a great tale. She studied the photo of an attractive clean-shaven man with shoulder-length brown hair, sly eyes of an unusual green, and a square jaw. So he was handsome. But how could those women disregard that he was a known abuser?

Could he twist the truth that skillfully?

She sighed.

Wasn't she gullible when her ex-fiancé had lied to her? That meant she shouldn't be trusting the handsome newcomer in town, either. Her treacherous heart skipped a beat. Despite her thoughts, she couldn't wait until the evening to go see the Christmas lights with him and his daughter. And she didn't even want to see the lights.

Concentrate.

She forced herself to study the women's files. He'd had three female visitors, and two of them stuck around for a while.

Interesting. She nearly held her breath, her curiosity piqued.

One, a weary-eyed thirtysomething woman named Odetta had not only stopped visiting him but had also moved to a different state shortly after said visits.

Hmm. She was a waitress who lived in government-subsided housing. The apartment she'd moved to was much more expensive, and it had taken her two months to find a new job. How did she afford the move?

Vera had done a lot of work in a short time. Had she stayed up all night? Argh.

Let's think.

The throbbing in Gwendolyn's head resumed full-force, and she grimaced.

Odetta had already been in several abusive relationships and had grown up in a household where domestic violence calls had been made on a regular basis. Gwendolyn resisted the urge to grind her teeth. It appeared abuse was all Odetta knew, and she kept coming to such men instead of avoiding them. Codependency issues?

As pressure built in Gwendolyn's chest, she said a prayer for the woman.

Then doubt shivered through her. What if her father had a protector's complex? He might've gone to that abandoned warehouse if he thought he needed to help a woman in distress.

Odetta could've played that role if Ron asked her to, couldn't she? Gwendolyn looked at Odetta's photo at the time. Long dirty strands fell on the woman's slumped shoulders, and despair dulled her gray eyes as though she'd lost heart after years of abuse. A thin charcoal scarf wrapped around her neck, tied too tightly as if it were a noose ready to be pulled.

The pressure heavier, Gwendolyn said another prayer for Odetta.

Done with the file Vera had sent her, Gwendolyn started researching first on social media, then on the internet overall. It was disturbing how easily someone's address could be found online.

Gwendolyn let out a low whistle when she found the national house sale and rental site displaying photos of the mansion where Odetta was living now. The amount it sold for was more than impressive.

Odetta had become a suburban wife with two teens and a dog. Not to mention a dentist husband whose teeth—based on the photo—were as white and straight as their picket fence and probably the best advertisement for good dental work.

Gwendolyn found his dental clinic. Huh. Odetta was his office assistant. Gwendolyn studied the photo on the clinic's site. Wow. Over two decades later, she seemed to look better instead of worse.

Her much shorter hair, now professionally styled, had a rich chocolate hue to it. Gone were the dark circles around her eyes and their haunted expression as if she needed to jump back in case she'd get hit again. Her bright smile spoke highly of either her husband's character or his professional skills.

Maybe both.

A cheerful turquoise silk scarf hung loosely around her neck. Peering into those no-longer haunted eyes, Gwendolyn hesitated. Odetta had put her past behind her and didn't need anyone to drag it out and wave it around. Or pull it around her neck like a noose, for that matter.

Then Gwendolyn's desire for closure won over compassion. She glanced at her watch, then at the business hours on the site. The dental clinic should be just opening up. She punched the dentistry office number into her cell phone. Her pulse quickened for more reasons than one as she waited. She needed to hurry up and get ready, too.

A melodic female voice named the dentistry, then said, "How

may I help you?"

"May I speak to Odetta?" Gwendolyn said the woman's married name.

"Speaking."

In that split-second, Gwendolyn decided to go for a direct approach. "My name is Gwendolyn Meyers. My father was murdered twenty-five years ago. I have reasons to suspect Ron Amspoker had a grudge against him. I need to know whether twenty-five years ago Ron asked you to call my father and arrange a meeting with you."

A sharp gasp answered her.

Chapter Five

GWENDOLYN CLOSED HER EYES, then reopened them. "I see. He did. Then, once you shot my father, that guy paid you to move out of state and have a better life."

Was it so simple and so tragic?

"No!" Then, in a much quieter voice, Odetta said, "No. Listen, can I please call you on my cell phone?"

Gwendolyn went cold. She'd made a mistake. She had no proof whatsoever. "Um, okay." She disconnected.

Seconds stretched like her taut nerves as she stared at her phone screen. Odetta didn't have to call, didn't have to talk to her. So stupid to blurt out her suspicions! She resolved to let Vera do most of the investigating from now on, if not all. Otherwise, Gwendolyn might mess things up instead of finding her closure.

Finally, the screen lit up with an unknown number.

This could be a telemarketer, but she hurried to answer. "This is Gwendolyn."

"Listen, Ron did ask me to do what you… what you just said." Odetta's hushed words tumbled out fast. "But that made me realize what kind of man he was. It was like my eyes… opened. I'd been saving to hire him a better attorney, so I used those funds to move.

It's going to sound stupid, but I was afraid I'd go back to him if… if I stayed."

"Why should I believe you?" Tiredness seeped into Gwendolyn's bones despite it being the beginning of the day.

"Because it's the truth. Besides, I was at the diner, working late the day he died. Lots of people can confirm it."

"You could still place the call getting him to the location where someone else could shoot him. Besides, why didn't you tell this to the police?"

"I… I was afraid of Ron." Odetta's voice shook. "I wanted to start my life over with no ties to my past—that meant not getting involved with police reports and testimonies."

"Would you be willing to report this to the police now?" Not that it would do much good at this point, but still…

There was a pause. "My husband… I…"

A lump formed in Gwendolyn's throat. "Do you realize that, if you reported this twenty-five years ago, my father could still be alive? Did you consider that Ron might've asked someone else after you refused to help?"

"I… I'm very sorry." Something soft entered the woman's voice. "I really am. I was a different person then than I am now. I'll report it to the police. Honestly. I've got to go now. I need to get back to the office."

"Just one more thing. Your husband… does he treat you well?" Appearances could be deceitful, and pain could hide behind flashy white smiles, too. Gwendolyn knew it all too well.

"Yes, he does. He loves me and our children. I learned that love and pain don't have to go together." She sighed. "I'm very sorry about your father."

"Thank you." Once the line went dead, Gwendolyn placed the phone onto the nightstand, her mind and muscles weary.

She called Vera and relayed the conversation.

"Thanks," Vera said. "I'll check Odetta's alibi. I'll look at the other two women who visited Ron Amspoker, as well. If he asked her for help, he could do so with others. I'll let you know what I find out."

"Thank you." Gwendolyn disconnected the call.

Then she rushed to the bathroom to brush her teeth. Her thoughts whirled like water disappearing into the sink as the mint flavor filled her mouth. She considered calling Uncle John, but then her brush froze in the air.

All the assignments her father had been receiving had gone to Uncle John after her father's death. Uncle John had a motive.

She groaned as she resumed furious brushing. She didn't know where to turn or who to trust.

Or maybe she did know. She could trust Vera, and she needed that more than ever. She brushed her hair fast, not bothering with makeup, like always. She needed to talk to her friend as soon as Gwendolyn could feed the children and get them to play a game.

If she ever wanted to have a future with someone—for some reason, the image of Conner came to mind—she needed to know about her past.

And why the navy-blue sedan looked so much like her father's.

In the evening, Gwendolyn stared out the window as Conner drove past the Christmas lights along the quaint small-town streets she'd started to like more than she'd wanted to. She was used to moving from one place to another, trained herself not to get attached. It had been easier that way.

Then why did Cowboy Crossing feel different?

Lord, is this the time for me to put down roots?

Her relationship with the Lord wasn't ideal. But her father and grandpa had taught her Christian values, and her fragile faith had survived while many other things hadn't.

Wouldn't it be amazing to have a home for Christmas… and for many Christmases to come?

This seemed like a good place with a caring community. She stole a glance at Conner's handsome profile, illuminated in the car's dimness by all the streetlights. Pink and yellow hues made everything look mysterious and fun.

Her treacherous heart jumped into her throat as he smiled at her. "Beautiful, aren't they?"

"Oh yes," she whispered.

Then she reminded herself that, just like her, Conner and his precious daughter were passersby here, probably leaving for Houston soon after Christmas. The thought left bitterness in her mouth, and she turned to the lights again, doing her best to soak up holiday cheer.

She glanced back at Daisy to make sure she was okay. The girl sat there, obviously mesmerized by the lights, her hand pressed to the window as if she were trying to hold onto them.

Gwendolyn hoped the girl would be more successful than Gwendolyn had been.

"Look, there's a herd of deer!" Daisy squealed as she pointed to the left.

"There sure is, Sweetie Pie." Then Conner winked at Gwendolyn. "Does this remind you of your childhood?"

Her stomach clenched. "It's going to sound horrible, but after my parents divorced, we didn't celebrate Christmas much. Dad and I moved around a lot. I never knew what town we were going to spend the holidays in."

"That's… sad."

Her lips pursed. She wasn't complaining. Honestly, she wasn't. She notched her chin up a bit. "It wasn't bad, really. Most of the time, he did take me to see the town tree in whatever town we were staying in, and he bought me a present every year. A practical one, like a sweater or shoes."

He'd sent her sister expensive gifts for Christmas as if he'd needed to buy Vanessa's affection while he'd already had Gwendolyn's by that time. She preferred to ignore a twinge of disappointment. She probably would've done the same thing.

"He did his best," she continued. "It's not easy to raise a child on your own."

Especially after…

No, better not to remember.

Conner gave a slow nod. He probably knew it too well.

Then she brightened as he turned the corner and a Christmas tree with garlands and lights towered into view. "One of my favorite presents was an unusual one for him, a Christmas ornament with our names on it. It was bright and cheerful and… promising, I guess."

"I can see that." His voice softened as if he understood the lonely little girl she used to be better than she did.

"And then…. He was shot the day before Christmas Eve," she kept her voice as low as possible so Daisy wouldn't overhear them.

"I'm so sorry." His voice became a whisper, too. "My condolences."

Her lungs constricted. "Thank you. The year after he died, I tried to decorate a tree and dropped that ornament. It shattered into sharp shards." Kind of like her heart. If anyone had tried to win her heart after that, he'd only get cut on sharp edges. "I haven't put up a Christmas tree ever since."

His left hand stayed on the steering wheel, but his right one reached out to her. He took her hand and held it while he slowed near a yard where snowmen shivered in a circle. "I am sorry to hear that. Would you… would you like it to be different one year?"

Delightful tingles traveled over her skin from his touch despite the pain. Somehow, breathing became easier. "I… I don't know."

Holiday cheer didn't seem to exist for her, not when it could too easily turn into tears.

"I realize the real reason for Christmas, of course. But believing God loved me, especially when I couldn't understand why He'd taken my father, was difficult." She tried to keep the bitterness out of her voice. She failed. She'd had little in the sense of family and even less in the sense of friends. Her faith became as fragile as that ornament, and she was desperate not to drop it.

Longing unraveled her defenses again as a family with three boisterous children spilled into a front yard, laughing, on the way to a car decorated with fir tree branches and red bows. For a long time, she'd told herself her job was enough.

It wasn't any longer. She'd love to have a close-knit family like the Clarks, a cozy inviting home like theirs, and…

And a certain man with a little girl appeared in her imagination. They were sitting on a carpet near a fireplace where three stuffed stockings hung. Beside them, a large tree glowed, its twinkling lights reflecting off the bows of many presents underneath, and Gwendolyn was reading the girl a children's book with a happy ending.

He moved his hand away, and she missed its warmth. That was why she'd learned not to get attached—it hurt too much to walk away when the time came. She'd carried her loneliness with her like a turtle carried her shell, a mini mobile home where she could hide anytime needed.

But right now, it wasn't about her. She turned to Daisy and said loudly, "How about we go through a drive-through and get hot cocoa with lots of marshmallows? If your father approves, of course."

The girl's face lit up. "Yay!"

Gwendolyn's heart shifted. She remembered the last conversation with her father, filled with the promise of the same joy. He'd taken time off for the holidays. She'd looked forward to going to the children's Christmas play and to the Christmas parade the town held on the twenty-fourth.

He'd said things were going to be different from now on. They were going to stay in the same place for a while.

Her fingers tightened around the seat belt as if it was the reason she had sudden difficulty breathing. If only she'd spent the evening with him that day instead of going on a date where the guy had never even showed up. A fresh onslaught of emotion—regret, shame, guilt—blinded her like a ruthless blizzard.

Conner cleared his throat, pulling her out of her trip down memory lane. "I... I heard that the town needs volunteers for the Christmas drive to distribute gifts to the children from underprivileged families."

She tensed. She'd heard it, too. She stared at his profile, waiting.

He glanced at her, his gaze uncertain. "Daisy surprised me. She said she wanted to be an elf. So you know who volunteered for the role of Santa Claus. Would you... would you like to join us?"

"Pretty please!" Daisy chimed from the back seat.

Gwendolyn froze like the reindeer herd in the next front yard. As it was, it was hard to escape the reminders of the day she'd lost her father. Add to that her discomfort around people she didn't know, and she'd squirm in her seat if the seat belt allowed it. "I... Well, I'm not really a Christmas person."

"I understand. But... Maybe this Christmas can be different. If you let it be."

With his voice so quiet, she had to strain to hear it against the motor's low rumble. Yet his words echoed inside her, then—just like the lights outside—illuminated the deep-seated longing. The longing to believe in God with *all* her heart, not just part of it.

The longing to believe in herself.

"Pretty pretty please!" Daisy singsonged again.

That sincere and naïve plea touched a soft spot. Did the girl long for a mother figure like Gwendolyn once had? Did she sense a kindred spirit in Gwendolyn who could understand her better than other people because they had so much in common?

A new kind of longing unraveled the tightness in her chest. The longing for a family and a daughter.

She plastered on a smile for the girl's sake as she turned back. "I'll think about it."

Daisy sighed. "Danica says when adults say 'I'll think about it' or 'We'll see' that means no."

The sadness in the girl's voice spurred Gwendolyn on. "You know what? I thought about it, and I'm going to join you on the Christmas gift drive."

"Yay!" The girl clapped.

"Thank you," Conner whispered and glanced at her before turning his attention to the road. "That means a lot to me." He coughed a little. "I mean, to both of us. Daisy and myself."

Her heart fluttered from his words. Daisy looked happier than when she'd met her. She wished she had a friend during her childhood as fun and confident as Danica.

"I'm glad Daisy and Danica became friends. Children in the Clark family take after the adults. They treat me like a friend instead of an employee, too," she said.

For some inexplicable reason, a muscle moved in his jaw. "Gwendolyn, I need to tell you somethi—"

"Daddy, Miss Gwendolyn, look!" Daisy yelled, pointing at a display of shimmery angels.

"Yes, Sweetie Pie. They are beautiful," Conner said.

Her rib cage constricted. Once Conner and Daisy returned to Houston, then—just like Gwendolyn had to do many times—Daisy would have to say goodbye to people she'd grown to care about. Gwendolyn had lost count of how many times she'd had to do that. She ached thinking of this little girl feeling what she'd felt.

Lord, please help Daisy. Please guide me on what I need to do to help her, too.

One couldn't rewrite the holidays.

Couldn't change their past.

She'd stopped believing in miracles after her father's death, and something inside her had shut down. Turned out, she still needed that closure, and she needed to figure out the mysterious signs about her father she'd had this Christmas season.

He'd been her world once. The only way to fill at least part of that gigantic void was to continue on his path. To do what he'd been doing. She'd worn out the clothes and shoes he'd given her and had broken the ornament. But, by becoming a bodyguard, she could keep a part of him with her forever, continue the legacy like the family she worked for now continued theirs.

One couldn't outgrow a profession.

Or… could one?

Chapter Six

GWENDOLYN'S GUT TWISTED. She'd thought she wasn't cut out to work with children. Yet she'd enjoyed spending time in Cowboy Crossing with the rambunctious family way more than she'd ever enjoyed any of her bodyguard gigs, even those that had come with stays in luxury hotels complete with spas and Jacuzzis.

Maybe it had something to do with a certain child whose shyness and need to be loved reminded Gwendolyn of herself at that age.

And with a man who'd affected her more than she'd wanted. A man who didn't know who she truly was because keeping that secret was part of her contract. She ached for him to know her and maybe even like her as much as she liked him.

Unexpected fatigue weighed on her muscles. She loved the Clark family, but she was tired of new contracts, new clients, new gigs. She was used to moving and moving on, but she didn't want to this time.

Nothing in her contract prohibited her from telling others about her past, though.

"I want to tell you something...." he started again as he made a turn.

She interrupted while she had courage. "Wait… I want to tell you something, too. I used to work for a security company, then in security for a few affluent people. Okay, for a lot of affluent people." She paused at his sharp breath intake. "I wanted to be like my father."

Liberty had told her she'd become a veterinarian like her mother not only to continue a legacy but also because it made her heart sing.

Being a bodyguard had never made Gwendolyn's heart sing. Had she chosen the wrong path all those years ago? If so, could she have a chance to choose a new one?

"Now, I wonder. Maybe I also did it because it's easier to follow a path that already exists than to make our own. But that's not the right way to find ourselves, is it?"

"No, it's not," he said slowly.

"My dad became my hero." She sighed. "I guess I also wanted to become someone's hero."

Conner smiled. "Well, based on the way my daughter looks at you, you're already her hero. And frankly, I think the most heroic thing people can do is to have the courage to do what they love and offer a few acts of kindness along the way."

"Don't be sad." Daisy's voice made her look up. "Wanna be my friend?"

It took Gwendolyn a moment to answer. "I'd love to." She turned to Conner. "I have very few friends."

Why did she say that? Unwanted memories appeared in front of her eyes.

Moving from school to school because of her father's jobs had come with risks and not only for him.

Just like the horse herds her grandpa had worked with, schools often had a hierarchy. And as a new, plump—some popular skinny girls considered her fat—not well-dressed girl with no makeup, Gwendolyn had often found herself at the lowest level of the pecking order.

She didn't fit in with any groups. She was okay at math but not brilliant and didn't have any singing or acting talent so no hope of being accepted by geeks or into some school production. Not athletic enough to be part of the jock crowd. And she certainly didn't have any necessary qualifications to become popular. She'd been a loner and learned to stay low, blend into the background the best she could. It worked sometimes—but not always.

When it didn't, the skills her father had taught her had come in handy. People often took kindness and shyness for weakness, but they respected brutal force.

Once her fighting skills were known, she was left alone. She hadn't come to challenge hierarchy but to survive until the next move to a new place. Who knew some schools could become such great preparation for bodyguard training? One always had to be on the lookout.

Things changed when she was twelve, and she shut her eyes at the memory. She'd managed to blend into the background well enough and watched her back at the new school.

Then a girl from her math class joined her at lunch. She had short thin hair, braces, and slumped-forward shoulders. "I'm Gillian. Do you want to be my friend?"

Joy filled Gwendolyn. Her sister was her best friend once, but since the separation, the only person Gwendolyn could rely on was herself. Finally having a friend felt amazing.

Three days and three lunches later, Gwendolyn realized the kind offer was extended partly because Gillian was bullied before. Gwendolyn was too thrilled to care if Gillian's friendship had underlying reasons.

The next time popular kids started using Gillian as a punching bag, Gwendolyn stood up for her.

There was no hesitation.

There couldn't be. That was what friends did.

The next day, Gillian invited Gwendolyn to her neighbor's backyard for a barbecue. It smelled of leaves and fresh hope that day, and Gwendolyn was excited about a new beginning.

Once Gwendolyn stepped inside, she guessed what was going to happen. There was no scent of barbecue.

Older and stronger kids waited for her there, and a few more stepped behind her to cut off her escape. Gwendolyn glanced at her friend. With a sinking heart, she realized this was Gillian's ticket into a popular crowd—or at least to be left alone for some time. As Gillian said when Gwendolyn's father and the school administration conducted an investigation later, Gwendolyn was going to move soon anyway, and Gillian was going to stay.

Gwendolyn learned there could be a limit to human cruelty, but there was none for betrayal.

Trembling, she moved with her back to the fence, her muscles tense, prepared to fend multiple hits. She was going to lose, but she'd give it her best. Her heart thundered in her ears louder than the mockery. She was prepared for bruises, for the taste of blood when someone's fist connected to her jaw while she'd blocked another person's punch to her solar plexus.

Gathering every ounce of her training, she prepared herself for the excruciating pain when her bone was crushed, barely minutes after her heart had been. Even with all that pain, she couldn't afford to pass out, and she did the special breathing her father had taught her.

But there was something Gwendolyn wasn't prepared for. The last thing she remembered before she'd fallen to the ground that day was that Gillian smiled.

It was the smile of someone with a job well done.

Though Conner had ulterior motives for coming to Cowboy

Crossing, he always wanted to give his daughter the most wonderful holiday celebration he could. Even if he couldn't incorporate Annika's German traditions yet. He just couldn't.

A strange thought appeared in his mind as he drove on the outskirts of Cowboy Crossing for the Christmas gift drive. Would Annika want him to remarry and give Daisy a new mother?

Especially if that person was nothing like Annika?

Unlike Gwendolyn, who was obviously shy, Annika had enjoyed being around people and could talk for hours to a person who dialed the wrong number. Annika loved festivities, and they had gone to many Fests in Germany, including the famous Oktoberfest. He'd joked she looked like a German milkmaid, with her habit to wrap her braid around her head and her affinity for dresses and aprons due to all the baking.

She'd laughed about it and bought them folk costumes, his complete with a hat and lederhosen, and they'd worn them to the Oktoberfest. He'd thought he'd looked ridiculous in leather knee-length breeches with suspenders, but he'd wanted to make her smile.

She'd looked so pretty in a dirndl, a traditional Bavarian dress with a tight bodice and a gathered skirt. To follow the custom, he'd paired his lederhosen with a white button-down shirt, and she'd paired her dirndl with a white blouse and an apron. Neither one of them drank alcohol, but her eyes had shone brightly as she'd enjoyed the festivities and the large costume and riflemen parade among about six million people in Munich.

He'd loved giving her the best holidays he could, too, and a fist wrapped around his heart and squeezed tightly.

Now he considered another person he'd love to give wonderful holidays to. The one sitting in the passenger seat right beside him. He'd tried to tell Gwendolyn who he was twice yesterday, but both times, he was interrupted. Was it a sign it was best to keep it a secret?

His allegiance should be to his daughter first. And so far, Gwendolyn hadn't provided much information about her employer, not that he'd insisted, really. He'd been too taken away with her kind hazel eyes and hurting soul.

Did that make him a bad father?

If only he could ask God for guidance! But he'd stopped praying when Annika died. Pain had filled his entire being then, not leaving space for faith.

He glanced back to check on Daisy. She was sleeping peacefully, obviously tired out by a day of running around and handing out presents to children. Her sweet smile tugged at him before he returned his attention to the road.

Making sure his daughter was happy and well taken care of was his priority, not falling for the lovely woman he'd never see again after Christmas. He'd tell Gwendolyn and the Clarks who he was soon.

Soon.

The secret already made him lie awake at night and gave him pangs of conscience now. But it seemed even more painful to say it.

"Daisy must be exhausted," Gwendolyn whispered. "Well, we only have one more house left."

"Yeah. Good." Okay, maybe not so good.

His heart shifted. He didn't want the evening to end. He'd met Gwendolyn recently. When did he become so used to her half-smile or her attentive way of listening to his every word?

"Tell me more about your work. I mean, do you love it?" Her voice conveyed his answer was important to her.

His fingers tightened around the steering wheel as he slowed around the curb. Then he lowered his voice to keep from waking his daughter. "I love... some aspects of being an art gallery manager. Like sponsoring an art studio for children that gives free lessons and then exhibiting their works."

"I imagine their parents might be more excited than the children." She chuckled. "It's nice of you."

Her praise touched him, but he didn't mean to be bragging. "I can't take the credit. Annika started it. I just needed to make sure the program continued. Taking care of the gallery was the right thing to do." Was he trying to persuade Gwendolyn—or himself? "The first few directors I hired messed up exhibitions, so I needed to take over myself."

"That was… noble of you. Does this job make your heart sing? I mean, if it's okay to ask." Based on the whiff of her delicate, fleeting perfume, she shifted toward him.

It was as if a fresh wind ruffled the pages of his story, turning it to a chapter he wasn't ready for.

Fine, he did feel confined within those four walls as if he were placed in one of the cubes in a cubism painting. "What choice did I have? Fulfilling my obligations should make me happy." His voice was too clipped, and he winced.

Gwendolyn had voiced the questions he'd been asking himself lately. Maybe being close to a ranch awakened memories of a place where he'd belonged.

The scent of her perfume moved away, and the voice grew quieter as if she withdrew more than physically, causing a void within him. "Sorry. I didn't mean to pry."

The urge to tell her who he was, to share his story, surged through him. Her eyes were kind and inviting enough that he could forget caution. He'd gathered some information through the grapevine about the Clarks, and she'd given the family a great recommendation.

Then his stepsister's scream the last day he'd seen her rang in his ears, and he felt it in his gut—the secret had to remain hidden for now.

So he told her the things he could.

About losing his little brother when surgery could've saved

him. About Annika's spontaneous personality, her love of everything art, her penchant for baking German treats as if the recipes were in her blood.

He could feel the sweet taste of stollen and Black Forest cake, hear Annika's warm laughter and soft humming of German songs, smell her favorite flowers—daisies, of course. She was raised in the US, but her ancestors were from Germany—and she'd never forgotten it.

She had an enviable confidence in herself and pride in her culture, including speaking German fluently. The most common native language in Europe, she'd said.

No words had sounded as beautiful to him as when she'd whispered "Ich liebe dich" for the first time.

I love you.

His fingers tightened around the steering wheel as if it were sparkling ornaments or painted porcelain village figurines they'd bought at the market. He and Annika went to Germany at the magical time of Christmas when they'd dreamed of having children and bringing them there one day to visit.

A lump formed in his throat. As much as he'd tried to keep Annika's legacy by working at the gallery, for some reason, he'd kept the ornaments and the figurines in the attic and had never tasted stollen, German chocolate cake, or Black Forest cake again.

He told Gwendolyn about those empty years without Annika when the pain wouldn't go away. About leaving ranching for the art gallery, even if he was still a cowboy at heart. About all the amazing horses he'd encountered while working at a ranch. While he'd made sure to establish the fact they could rely on him and he was the one responsible—the leader of the herd, if you wish—they'd been his friends. And often, his teachers.

He even told her about Snowflake, a beautiful Appaloosa who'd thrown the ranch owner when she bucked, landing him on the ground. Twice. Thankfully, the man had agreed with Conner that the horse was just scared of her new surroundings and he'd mounted her too soon. With a lot of patience, Conner had started making progress with Snowflake, a spirited horse who'd sadly been mistreated by her previous owners. Conner had found signs of the abuse on her body.

But then, the owner's young nephew came for a visit and, despite Conner's protests, took Snowflake for a ride. The guy wasn't experienced with horses but was arrogant and sure he'd needed to show the horse who was the boss. Snowflake's history of being difficult had added to his desire "to teach Snowflake a lesson."

Conner had begged him to give Snowflake some time, but to no avail. Sure enough, Snowflake came back alone. Apparently, she'd gotten spooked and fled, and the guy had lost control and fallen from the saddle, breaking his arm.

Snowflake was sold right after that, and Conner couldn't do anything about it. Later, he had learned Snowflake changed several owners until she'd broken her leg and been put down.

Gwendolyn didn't say a word. But she listened and seemed to understand. And somehow, that made the pain a fraction smaller.

Afar off, he spotted a house nestled by a red barn, and a fresh onslaught of pain sliced through him. The barn looked so much like the one on the ranch where he worked—eh, *used to work.*

He did miss being out in the open, riding horses, feeling the wind in his lungs, and the uplifting sense of freedom he couldn't find anywhere else, especially crammed in the gallery where he always feared he'd break something irreplaceable.

But then... hadn't he broken so many irreplaceable things before?

"It's just... if I couldn't have Annika any longer, this way I could have a part of her. Her legacy."

He glanced at Gwendolyn as he removed his foot from the accelerator pedal. Candy cane earrings danced in her delicate ears.

And more than compassion glowed in her eyes. Comprehension shone there as if she'd experienced herself what he was talking about.

Her fingertips brushed against his right hand, light as a touch of tinsel, but they still made his heart beat faster. "I understand. I understand it very well."

By previously working in security to keep part of her father in her life, she'd done the same thing he'd done. And like him, she must've been questioning it now if she'd started nannying. She got him, plain and simple.

An invisible bond strengthened between them. A bond that would have to be broken when he returned to Texas. It didn't make sense to fall for Gwendolyn, even if he could open his aching heart to her after Annika's death.

Then Gwendolyn glanced back at his sleeping child and said, "But don't you already have a better part of her?"

After about half an hour, Gwendolyn could guess why Conner had saved this family for last to give presents, and it wasn't about the geographical distance. They celebrated Christmas like they meant it.

At first, Gwendolyn worried about Daisy, but the girl seemed to get a second wind and enjoy herself.

All of them, including two parents and five children—all girls—sang carols, built a gingerbread house, enjoyed cocoa stirred with candy canes, and played a few games Gwendolyn had to learn fast.

She got so carried away that, despite being unable to carry a tune to save her life, she nearly joined in singing carols with Conner, Daisy, the family, and their two cats who, apparently, as the head of the family felt the need to explain, were both females.

Some families requested the child "earn" their gift, and this was one of them. So each cute blonde girl either recited a poem, sang a song, or in the case of the oldest, performed an acrobatic figure. Gwendolyn understood now why one of the gifts was a certificate for gymnastics lessons.

After sharing some contents of the basket with Christmas cookies Conner had brought into the house, she loved watching the girls' faces light up when they unwrapped the gift boxes with sweaters and coats, then the ones with toys, games, and books. But the highlight would be the bicycles in different sizes to suit each girl, every bicycle with a large red bow, that Conner secretly stowed behind the barn for the parents to give the girls on Christmas.

Tears shone in their parents' eyes when he slipped them a note explaining where and what the secret gifts were, and more thanks escaped their lips than Gwendolyn had heard in her life. As the woman hugged Gwendolyn oh so tightly and whispered yet another teary-eyed thank you, she warmed to her very core. She didn't expect any presents this year—just like the year before and the year before that—but this was already the best Christmas she'd had in decades.

By far.

"It was kind of you to participate in the Christmas gift drive," she told Conner when they were driving back, Daisy once again asleep in the back, so adorable in her green elf outfit.

He didn't even live in this town, and still, he'd done it for these children. So yes, it was more than chiseled features or generous muscles she was attracted to.

"I'm the one who benefits the most. And hopefully my daughter this time. I want to show her that the easiest way to feel better ourselves is to help someone else. Hopefully, it helped her shyness a little, too. I'm grateful to be able to buy her the gifts she requests. Well, besides a kitten. But not all parents can do the same. I wanted her to give gifts to children who are not in her situation."

It dawned on her. "It's not the first time you've done this, is it?" She should've guessed by how at ease he was while it took her a while to be more or less comfortable with people she didn't know.

"My late wife started this tradition. She said we should share our blessings." His voice dipped a little. "I... I haven't done it since she died."

Her heart clenched. The more she was getting to know this caring, honest, and yes, still grieving man, the more she liked him. But how could she compete with a woman who was no longer here and sounded perfect?

Of course, she didn't need to compete. She, Conner, and Daisy would go their separate ways soon enough, and she'd have the opportunity to retreat into her familiar cover of loneliness as if this amazing holiday had never happened.

Sadness pressed on her lungs.

Her breathing became shaky as she recalled the troubling calls, too. Four calls now. All saying the name her father used to call her. She'd gone to the police in the afternoon, but they couldn't help her. The calls had come from burner phones.

She'd been restless ever since she'd seen that old navy-blue sedan with tinted windows and snow-covered license plates.

Would she be able to put the puzzle pieces together with her friend's help? Or was twenty-five years later too late and were too many of those pieces missing? Or was she even putting the wrong pieces in the wrong places?

Could she put the pieces of her heart together like that puzzle and finally move on?

"Are you okay?" Conner asked as if sensing her change in mood while he made a turn.

She told him about the navy-blue sedan and strange calls.

He frowned as he slowed for an icy dip in the road. "I'm worried about you. You should talk to the police."

She sighed. "Done already. The calls came from burner phones."

"If you allow me, I'd like to hire you a bodyguard."

She chuckled without mirth. "I *am* a bodyguard."

The truck swerved slightly before he straightened it out. "What?"

Oops. She wasn't supposed to reveal it—her contract explicitly specified that. On the other hand, she didn't want to withhold the information from him like her mother had from her father.

Her fingers tightened around the truck door handle. "The Clark family hired me because they thought the children might be in danger. It looks like that's passed and I'm not needed any longer. That's why I'm leaving after Christmas."

"Oh, wow."

Cold seeped into her bones as if the blast from the past was freezing. So she took off her gloves and reached to the vent with hot air.

"Cold?" He turned up the heat.

She wanted him to reach for her hands and warm them up instead, but it wasn't like he could while driving—or would even want to.

Either way, it wouldn't help because her cold came from within.

Chapter Seven

GWENDOLYN'S SURPRISING STATEMENT about working as a bodyguard still bothered Conner the next day. He wasn't sexist, but that didn't fit this soft-spoken, bashful woman. Or was her act a role like the stranger in town he'd been playing?

No, he felt she was sincere with him. Unlike him, which gave his conscience a fresh pang.

Then he went cold. Her profession meant she could be killed. Even if they had a future together—which they didn't—he could easily lose her like he'd lost so many people in his life already.

Yet even after her confession, he couldn't stop thinking about her. His feelings were tangled up worse than the Christmas lights in his attic.

He stole a glance at Gwendolyn with Danica and Daisy at the table in the Clarks' mansion where Daisy was invited. One thing was clear: with the adoring way the girls looked at Gwendolyn and the way her face lit up, these children loved her, and she loved them.

First, they'd all made Christmas art today, which in this family meant more than drawings. Jenna Clark had given them a variety of unique buttons she'd brought from Europe.

While Conner played video games with the boys, Danica and Daisy had made a snow*woman* from pearl buttons glued to a sheet of poster board, then given her eyes from tiny sparkling buttons. They drew a Christmas tree nearby, and more buttons glued to the paper became ornaments. Gwendolyn praised and encouraged them, then brought yarn that turned into snow on the ground and clouds in the sky. And a cat, of course, with two green buttons for his eyes.

When Conner made a break to bring snacks from the kitchen, he checked on the girls' art. "Looks beautiful."

Daisy beamed. "Thanks, Daddy. It's a gift for you."

His heart swelled at the pride and joy in his daughter's eyes. And while Danica helped, he had Gwendolyn to thank for it. "I love it."

"And I love you, Daddy." Daisy hugged him, snugging her little face against his side, and he breathed in the sweet scent of her mango shampoo. "Always."

"I love you, too, Sweetie Pie." He'd cherish it forever, as well as that sweet smile. "Always."

Once Daisy eased out of his embrace, Danica high-fived her. "Okay, let's make snowflakes. Boys, you, too."

So they did, and a lot of silver and white snowflakes were soon taped to the walls. He worked with the children, helping them and making his own.

"You're a skillful snowflake maker." Gwendolyn winked.

He chuckled. "Well, that's something I've never been called before."

Then Gwendolyn made snowflake costumes for Danica and Daisy. Two of the boys were the stars, literally, and all the children were involved in a short play Gwendolyn had written for them. The children seemed to have a lot of fun as they learned their roles, though they jumbled most of the words.

Gwendolyn smiled and encouraged them, even when the

dance of the snowflakes left a lot to be desired. He found his lips widen in a smile, too, as something warm filled a place in his heart he'd considered shut down since Annika's death.

Gwendolyn was a natural with children. He could easily imagine her being a kindergarten teacher. Or a mother, for that matter.

His heart skipped a beat. Daisy already looked at Gwendolyn with such admiration that it tangled up his heartstrings. How could he explain to his daughter that this was only a temporary arrangement—especially when he didn't want to believe it himself?

Gwendolyn's words took root as his girl's eyes brightened at the praise. He *did* have a better part of his wife left than the gallery.

Daisy was the reason he got up every morning, the reason he breathed. But… was he smothering her with all his attention? Did he become one of those so-called helicopter parents?

His heart sank. He'd showered Daisy with love and gifts. But where was the line between love and hovering?

When she ran to him, he hugged her with all the tenderness swelling his heart. "You're the most beautiful snowflake ever!"

"Thank you, Daddy. Um, Danica invited us to look at ponies someday. Can we?"

Wow. Being in that familiar environment… He glanced at Gwendolyn as the sinking sensation in his heart lifted. "Would that be okay with the Clarks?"

She was grinning as she poured cocoa. "They told me to second Danica's invitation."

"Then sure." Pangs of conscience needled him again. Gwendolyn was sweeter than the drink she'd brought, and he was deceiving her. But he couldn't tell her about his connection to the Clarks in front of his daughter. Maybe when they all went to the stable?

Or was that reluctance inside him a sign he should wait? After all, when he'd tried to help Tara and revealed the family secret, it had ended tragically. Regret sliced him at the image of the necklace he'd given his stepsister.

That necklace was found on a dead Jane Doe two months after Tara ran away. His stepfather had identified the dead girl as his daughter....

"Thanks, Daddy." Daisy smiled, bringing him back from sad memories, and his heart went soft like marshmallows in his cup.

He had an idea as he looked into those luminous eyes. "What kind of exhibit would you like to have in the gallery?" Then he cringed. What was he doing? She was still too young.

Daisy didn't hesitate. "The cats."

He swallowed hard. "Cats?"

Of course, she didn't know. She was too young that tragic day, and thankfully, she was at home with his mother the evening he'd taken Annika out for their date night. The squeal of tires slashed his eardrums again as Annika swerved to avoid hitting a cat. She'd loved cats. They were going to get Daisy a kitten for her second birthday.

Another tragedy that could've been prevented if he'd acted differently and stayed at home with Annika that day.

Probably, another reason why he'd clung to Daisy so much. After all, too many people had abandoned him already.

God had abandoned him, too, or Annika, Tara, and his little brother would still be alive. There were things he couldn't understand about God.

There were things he couldn't understand about that horrible day of the accident, either.

Gwendolyn walked to them with a tray of cocoa with marshmallows and a stack of Daisy's favorite apple turnovers. "She probably means the history of cats, right, sweetie?"

Daisy nodded.

"There should be a lot of paintings and sculptures with cats. I can help with research," Gwendolyn said as she placed the tray on a side table.

"Me, too! I'll help, too!" Danica screamed, snatching a pastry.

Having hidden who he was from the family from the beginning pressed on his conscience now. But he couldn't be too cautious when things concerned his daughter. Yes, if he told it to himself enough times, he could believe it.

"I love cats." Daisy's quiet voice underplayed the louder girl as she eyed the goodies on the tray. Then she looked up. "But I love you more. And you, Miss Gwendolyn. And you, Danica."

"Love you, too, sweetie," Gwendolyn said.

For a moment, his heart stilled, and breath lodged in his throat. Whaaaat?

Gwendolyn loved him?

Oh. She meant his daughter.

She leaned to him and whispered. "I wanted to ask you. Is it okay if I bring some German treats? Incorporate German traditions? For… for Daisy's sake."

His insides tightened, and the moment stretched.

Then he drew her closer in a desperate need of human connection, of understanding, of support, even if he'd never admit it to anyone. His blood rushed in his veins at her proximity, the gentle scent of her perfume enveloping him. "That might be a good idea. I thought forgetting the past would make it less painful. It didn't."

"Okay," she whispered somewhere against his heart.

His heart made a strange movement in his chest, and he let her go. He kept a secret from her, so he didn't have the right to hug her. Didn't have the right to feel the way he was starting to feel.

As he placed the kiss atop Daisy's head, breathing in the sweet scent of her mango shampoo that mixed with the scent of cocoa, his chest swelled with an unfamiliar feeling.

Maybe this was what happiness felt and smelled like.

Only to disappear after Christmas.

He should tell Gwendolyn. Now.

He almost held his breath in preparation.

Then, as the image of his stepsister flashed in front of his eyes, he remembered why he was so reluctant to reveal who he was. It wasn't only because of his daughter.

Tara's words rang in his ears as if decades hadn't passed since the last time he'd seen her. After her father had beaten her up again—this time for a broken glass—Conner had made another desperate attempt to help her, asking his mother to talk to his biological father.

Conner didn't know what else to do. His stepdad had threatened that, if Conner went to the child protective services, he'd beat Tara to death and it would be all Conner's fault. His mother had said Conner's father had refused to help. Somehow, his stepdad had found out about the entire debacle.

This time, the man used the metal belt buckle to punish Tara for Conner's snitching and made him watch. When Conner had tried to interfere, he'd received hits on the arms.

He flinched and rubbed his hands over the sweater as if he felt the scars.

He'd never forget the salty taste of tears or the look in Tara's eyes as she'd whispered to him later when he'd tried to soothe her pain with ice packs.

You only made things worse. You're a snitch! Nobody is going to help us. Nobody wants us.

Those words echoed inside him louder than screams, sliced him worse than the metal buckle sliced his skin. Tara had disappeared that night. His stepfather hadn't tried too hard to find her. As he'd gleefully told Conner, it was all Conner's fault. Tears had burned Conner's eyes then, tears he couldn't allow to spill.

He'd packed a backpack and left for the streets to look for

Tara. He hadn't found her, but the police had found him and brought him back.

Minutes stretched into days and then months as he ran away more times to search for her. Then the horrible news came.

A Jane Doe who might be Tara was found dead. She'd worn the necklace he'd given her. His stepdad had identified her, saying that should be the end of the story.

And it was.

The event had woken up his mother from her lethargy, made her realize her son might end up like Tara. Especially when her husband had replaced the punching bag of a daughter with a stepson.

Conner and his mother had left together, first for the women's shelter, then for a small apartment as he had started receiving a bigger salary at the ranch. His stepsister's disappearance had saved him and his mother.

But it had forever imprinted in his memory—and into his skin—that secrets were often best left untold.

"It's a German tradition to have a wreath and light four candles in it." Gwendolyn hoped she was doing this right as she placed candles in the wreath days later. One couldn't always rely on information found on the internet.

As Conner lit them with a lighter, Daisy's eyes went big. "Wow." She clapped, her braids bouncing. "It's so pretty."

Conner's gaze was pensive, so Gwendolyn could only hope she wasn't pushing him too far. Then he looked up at her, his eyes misty. "Thank you for doing this."

Oh no.

Was he fighting tears?

Despite his words, her heart constricted. The next part should go better.

The mansion was unusually quiet. The Clark family was out riding horses, except for Vera, who'd traveled to the crime scene while investigating Gwendolyn's case—Gwendolyn had received the information from Uncle John and had passed it on to her friend. Heather, pregnant, was resting at home.

Gwendolyn had been told the kitchen was at her disposal when she'd asked for it, and everyone was okay with Conner and his daughter visiting for the evening. Liberty wasn't just okay, she'd cheered Gwendolyn on.

First things first.

Gwendolyn reached for the Advent calendar and handed it to Daisy as she crouched before the girl. "That's for you." She explained the calendar's meaning. "We should've started it earlier, but better late than never, right? It's got lots of chocolate, too."

An adorable grin pushed up the girl's cheeks. "Yay! Thank you, Miss Gwendolyn." She threw her little hands around Gwendolyn's neck.

It tugged on her heartstrings. Children's hugs, so trusting and sincere, could never get old.

"Hey, I feel left out!" Conner leaned in for a group hug.

The pressure around her heart intensified at his intoxicating scent. Hugging him would never get old, either, though in a different way.

She didn't know who pulled back first, but she did know she missed his warmth immediately.

Once the stollen was in the oven, she took off her apron and helped Daisy untie hers. "And now… how about we write a letter to Christkind?"

Conner raised an eyebrow. "Christ child?"

She fidgeted with her sweater hem. "Okay, I'm still rusty about German traditions. From what I understood, it's more like an angel. Christkind comes on the twenty-fourth of December. They even have a parade where a girl wears wings and represents an angel in Germany. And German Christmas market in Chicago has a Christkind every year."

Daisy blinked fast. "I wanna be an angel."

He brushed flyaway strands of hair back to her braids, and so much love shone in his eyes. "Sweetie Pie, you already are."

Once they settled down at the table, the girl scratched her forehead. "I'm not gonna write the letter."

O–okay. Gwendolyn gave Conner and Daisy an apologetic glance. "No?"

Daisy's head bobbed up and down, and so did her two braids. "Nope. I'm gonna *draw* it."

That was probably because she couldn't write well yet. Gwendolyn was about to offer her help but then nodded instead. "Let me bring art supplies then."

Once she did, Daisy chose colorful crayons. It didn't take her long to draw but much longer to write a single phrase in big letters.

Gwendolyn did her best to look away. But curiosity won, and she stole a glance.

Her heart nearly stopped beating. The drawing depicted a woman with reddish-brown hair, a man with a beard, a girl with two braids, and a white cat the same size as the girl. All of them gathered around a Christmas tree.

The large wobbly letters stole Gwendolyn's breath away.

I WANNA A MOMMY.

The girl stuffed the drawing into the envelope. "How am I gonna send it to Christkind?"

Conner brought glue and a few packets with glitter and sprinkles. "We're supposed to leave the letter on the windowsill. But first, let's decorate it with sprinkles and glitter to make it attractive."

"Sure, Daddy!" Daisy clapped, then did as he said.

When Gwendolyn caught his gaze, her sad wistfulness

reflected there. Could she trust herself to become the kind of mother she'd never had? She'd have no clue where to start. Would he open his heart to love—and risk of pain—enough to want her in his and his daughter's life after Christmas?

Then there was the mystery of her father's death and the suspicious calls she'd begun receiving. Not to mention the fact that she and Conner lived in different parts of the country.

He touched her hand. "I know what I'd write in the letter."

She steeled herself against the way he affected her. Did she take this too far? Did she make this small family a silent promise she wouldn't be able to fulfill, no matter how much she wanted to?

No matter how much she wanted to find a home in his broad chest with that snowman sweater, where she'd melt into his strong arms.

As if reading his mind, he opened his arms for her, and she walked into his embrace. Wow, her heart was never complete like this before.

"Group hug, Daddy!" Daisy screamed.

"Of course." He lifted his daughter up, eliciting a squeal, and hugged them both.

Gwendolyn was wrong a moment ago. Her heart was even more complete now. She imprinted the image into her memory, to cherish when… Best not to think about that.

As well as not to think about her mother. But the memories appeared uninvited.

The first years of her life she could remember, her memories were colored in bright hues. The house was breezy and large, with expensive chandeliers and polished hardwood floors she and her sister had enjoyed sliding on. They had fun playing with their many dolls, inventing stories as they went.

Her childhood home seemed like a fairytale castle, and she was a princess, a pink dress with the word *Princess* written in glitter to prove it. Her mother, of course, was the queen. She'd let the nanny bake cakes as often as the girls wanted, so the memory smelled and tasted like Gwendolyn's favorite white sheet cake with sprinkles. It was Gwendolyn's job to pour sprinkles, and she'd taken it seriously, so the entire counter was often decorated in them. Okay, part of the floor, too. Her mother had only laughed after telling the nanny to clean it up. Mommy had such a melodic laugh, like jingle bells.

Her long blonde hair—hair Gwendolyn sadly hadn't inherited—was often pinned up in an elegant updo, and she loved giving parties. She'd moved among her guests in a shimmering dress like true royalty, her flowery perfume following her with the admiring gazes.

Mommy looked so happy. But then the world looked much more… bubbly when one looked at it through the flute of champagne.

While the girls had spent most of the time with the nanny, their mother had often taken them for expensive trips because her daughters deserved it.

Wanna go to an amusement park? Let's go!

How about a zoo? It didn't matter if it was several states away. If the girls wanted to see a giraffe, their mother was booking the tickets.

They had gone to Disneyland like other families went to the movies.

Wanna a dollhouse? Let's go shopping!

A kitten? Sure!

Sometimes Gwendolyn thought they could've asked for a live giraffe and gotten it, too. Her sister, Vanessa, had certainly suggested it to her.

Their father had rarely been with them. Mommy said he cared about his job more than he cared about them. *Bad Daddy!* Gwendolyn screamed, and she and Vanessa had refused to kiss him in the rare times he came home from trips.

He was a grouch who didn't like parties. Worse, Gwendolyn had overheard him shouting at their wonderful, fun mother. Gwendolyn had stomped on the floor then, ran to him, and hit his legs with her tiny fists, demanding him to stop yelling at Mommy.

Bad Daddy, she'd repeated to herself when he'd awkwardly read her a bedtime story. She'd kept her eyes shut and hugged one of the many plush toys Mommy had lavished on her precious, precious, so precious girls.

Then something horrible happened. Her grouchy, cruel father took her away from the wonderful mother, friends, sister, and the cake-baking nanny. Away from the castle and their fluffy white cat.

"Not fair! Not fair!" she'd screamed until she was hoarse. She'd outgrown her pink princess dress, but she wanted everything else back.

They moved to a tiny apartment with gray walls that the dolls in her sparkling three-floor pink dollhouse would laugh at.

On the contrary, Gwendolyn wasn't laughing. She was crying. A lot.

Her grandpa moved in with them to take care of her while her father was on trips, making the apartment even smaller. Grandpa didn't smell of cake, but of leather and horses—she knew from the few times they'd gone riding. At first, he seemed as grouchy as her father.

It took her a long time to accept the new situation and warm up to her grandpa. Horses helped.

Grandpa worked part-time on a ranch and took his scared, hurting granddaughter to them. First to the ponies. She watched him groom horses, walk them, talk to them while he somehow managed to keep an eye on her. His kindness to horses finally allowed her to trust him.

That trust made her believe him when years later she learned the true story about her parents.

Amazing how her childhood memories changed over time. It was like one of her toys—a kaleidoscope, tiny pieces of colorful glass encased in a white tube. Every time she'd shaken up the tube, a different picture appeared through the glass peephole. The myriad of colorful miniature glasses remained the same. But they'd arranged themselves in a new way each time, the effect magnified by the reflections in many angled mirrors.

Wasn't it incredible how things—no, perceptions, but often perceptions was all that mattered—could change, once shaken up?

CHAPTER EIGHT

CONNER'S LIPS WIDENED as the children sang carols in front of one of Cowboy Crossing's homes. They were a little off-key, but what they might lack in musical talent, they made up for in enthusiasm—and volume.

The elderly couple in the doorframe smiled as they hugged each other. Their wrinkled faces were so peaceful, and their pale blue eyes were so shiny that wistfulness unraveled inside him.

Joining the tune, he stole a glance at Gwendolyn, who was mostly opening her mouth instead of singing. When he'd married the first time, he'd wanted to spend the rest of his life with Annika, loving her forever, growing old with her like this couple.

He'd wanted to tell her "Ich liebe dich" until the rest of his days.

Then he'd discovered nothing was forever.

Except maybe pain.

Gwendolyn's lovely face glowed while she placed her palms on the children's shoulders. His daughter sang the glory of God at the top of her lungs. As his heart soared with the rising tempo, he wanted to believe in that simple dream again, and something started changing inside him.

He'd spent so much time punishing himself, blaming himself for many things, from Tara running away to his mother's unhappiness to Annika's accident. Apparently, guilt and grief were best buddies who'd often hang out together, and he winced.

Enough.

As the song ended, the couple clapped and then rewarded the children with cookies.

As Conner, Gwendolyn, and the children walked to the next house, he said, "Gwendolyn, I love the costumes you made for the children. You have many talents."

Her cheeks pinked. "It's not a big deal. Jenna helped. As for many talents and skills, as you can see, singing isn't one of them."

He found her even prettier in the glow of lantern light and Christmas lights. "But humbleness is. Um, may I ask why you don't sing with us?"

Her blush deepened. "Because if I do, people will start asking who is torturing the cat."

Daisy looked up, her eyes big. "Someone would torture a cat?"

Such horror underplayed those words that he hurried to explain. "No, Sweetie Pie. Of course not."

Gwendolyn sighed. "But it would sound like it if I tried to sing."

Danica hiked her chin. "Sometimes you just gotta have fun. Right?" She turned to the other children.

"Yeah!" they said in unison, and Conner grinned. These children—his nieces and nephews—were quite the kids. And if the adults were like these children, maybe he'd made a mistake of not telling them who he was from the get-go.

His heart warmed as he readjusted his daughter's multicolored knit hat while they approached a redbrick house with inflated snowmen in front of it.

During their short time in Cowboy Crossing, the changes in

his child made his chest swell. With Gwendolyn's inclusion of her into the children's games, with everyone accepting her and outspoken Danica—so opposite in character from Daisy—taking his daughter under her wing, Daisy had smiled more than he'd seen her smile in years. She'd started to blossom under Gwendolyn's loving attention. And the children had accepted his daughter as one of them.

He flinched from a stab of guilt as he pressed the doorbell. He'd been afraid the Clark kids would be spoiled and maybe even arrogant, considering the family wealth. He'd transferred his prejudices from his biological father onto innocent children.

The longer he kept his identity a secret, the more difficult revealing it would be. To the family and to Gwendolyn.

As they waited, an older navy-blue sedan drove by, the license plate obscured with snow, and he felt rather than saw Gwendolyn tense. He recalled what she'd said about this car.

His stomach clenched at the alarm in her eyes, and he leaned to her. "Again the same car as the one your father drove?"

He remembered the feeling of being watched sometimes in the last five years, but he could never explain it. But in her case, it wasn't a feeling. It was real.

She visibly swallowed. "Yes. I mean, I know it's a popular make and model. It's fine. I'm fine."

As she looked away, she clearly wasn't. Although an older model, the car could be a coincidence, but not combined with the decorations and the sticker. He needed to look into this. His protective instincts woke up. He wouldn't want anything to happen to her.

After the doorbell chimed again, a gray-haired woman in her sixties opened the front door, holding a calico cat in her arms, the feline appearing especially large against her petite frame. The cat's claws were firmly in the woman's Christmas sweater as if he was afraid she'd let him go.

Daisy darted forward. "Oh, a kitty!" Then she moved back as if remembering their mission. As they sang, the woman's face brightened, and even the cat seemed to smile.

Then… then he heard Gwendolyn joining them, at first tentatively, then a little louder. She was willing to venture off her familiar path now.

Was he?

Gwendolyn on a background of Christmas lights tugged at him. It was unfair she had associated Christmas with a tragedy, and he was eager to change that.

Sadness lingered in her beautiful hazel eyes, and he ached to erase it, too. He needed to be truthful with her and the Clark family, but he didn't want to ruin the holidays. He was going to tell them at Christmas.

He gave her an encouraging nod as the song lifted to the sky together with his prayer for a Christmas miracle.

Christmas Day was always the hardest for Gwendolyn. Granted, thanks to Conner and his daughter, this holiday season was her best one yet. But she'd learned the hard way that one never felt as lonely as among the crowd.

When she'd been a child, during Christmas, she'd stop by her neighbors' windows and imagine her family was the one by the fireplace, with both parents smiling at their children and a large fluffy cat curling up at their feet. Then she'd miss her mother and sister a little less for a few blissful moments before returning to reality.

As for the cat, due to her father traveling a lot, he didn't think having one was a good idea. But sometimes, she'd suspected he vetoed the cat because her mother had taken theirs when she'd left, despite Cuddles's loud protests. She'd said, obviously, they couldn't divide the pet in two.

Cuddles had meowed even louder when he'd heard that.

Gwendolyn's gut twisted at the memory. It must've been difficult for her father to lose a wife, a daughter, and a pet in one swoop. It had been heartbreaking for Gwendolyn.

A sting of guilt made her grimace, but she hid it fast. The adults exchanged gifts with the boys' help as messengers, excited and loud. It was a great ending to a day filled with enjoying the church service, giving thanks to the Lord, and savoring a scrumptious dinner.

And yesterday with Conner and Gwendolyn, dinner was just as scrumptious. She'd found recipes online and cooked a duck with apples and onion stuffing, then red cabbage for the side. She'd made potato dumplings, too, hoping it was all in German Christmas traditions. She'd bought pfeffernuesse before for dessert. The shine in Conner's and Daisy's eyes was the best reward.

Today, children's laughter mixed with the adults' many thanks, and the scents of pine needles overlaid the aromas of turkey and pies.

The nativity scene wasn't just for show. This was a God-honoring family and a charitable one, as well. Many families in town benefited from their gifts and the charities they donated to, not only during Christmas.

She did her best to smile.

This was Christ's birthday, a time to rejoice and be grateful.

Forgive me, Lord. Please. Thank You for Your amazing gift.

The question formed in her mind, and she did the best to hold it back.

Why did some people have large, loving, close-knit families while others had to be alone?

Even if the Clark family treated her like one of their own from the start, she *wasn't* part of them, and that stabbed sharper among the happy chaos. Instead of looking into the window at Christmas, like she'd done as a child, she was inside the house now. But she wasn't part of this family, no matter how much she longed to be.

And she missed her father like never before.

He was different from the man Mommy had portrayed him to be. While he'd worked all the time to provide for them, Mommy had lived beyond their means. If he'd cut up her credit cards, she'd gotten new ones. She'd borrowed from their friends because she knew he'd grudgingly return debts when back. After a fight, he'd get loans to cover her purchases.

She'd drained him like doctors drained patients' blood in old times. Like those doctors, she'd somehow believed she was doing the right thing. She and her daughters deserved the best things in life. Dad loved her so much he forgave her every time.

Even when he'd come home to find both cars repossessed and the house on the verge of foreclosure.

Then Mommy had realized she'd drained him dry. He couldn't give her what she'd needed any longer. Or wanted—which in her eyes was the same. So she'd left him for a man with a new shining palace and a new shining carriage—ahem, luxury car. The hiccup in the plan was the man didn't want to raise two spoiled daughters who weren't his. He already had a spoiled daughter, so one more was a max.

Well, Dad was going to keep at least one daughter anyway and let Mom know, too. She hadn't flinched, just tilted her head coyly, and said, "Take Gwendolyn then. She's going to be less fun and more work. She takes after you, after all."

Her next husband wasn't as susceptible to her melodic laugh and carefree character and tried to curtail her spending. So she'd eventually moved on to another one, taking Vanessa with her.

Gwendolyn didn't warm up to her father overnight after that long and honest conversation with her grandpa. But then she'd remembered how her father read her stories even when she'd pretended to be asleep. She'd started noticing how he gave her the best food at meals, helped her with homework, and then found fun things to do that didn't cost much.

After some time, they'd become a team of three. She, Dad, and Grandpa. Until she became a team of one.

It had taken Dad years to pay off her mother's debts while living frugally. Gwendolyn learned there was a high price to pay for loving someone too much....

Back in the present, her gaze met Conner's across the room, and their gazes held for longer than they should have. Warmth pooled in the pit of her stomach, even as she shivered. She'd have to say goodbye to him and Daisy soon. Probably right after the New Year.

Someone touched her hand, and she winced and glanced in their direction.

"There's a gift for you." Vera pointed at Landon standing with a box in front of Gwendolyn. Vera's gaze was pensive as if she could guess Gwendolyn's thoughts. Concern etched in her friend's features.

Apparently, Gwendolyn had zoned out and hadn't heard her name called. Being so distracted wasn't an acceptable quality for a bodyguard and could get her or her client killed.

But she didn't expect many gifts, and the fact they had cared to do it touched her.

"Thank you." Gwendolyn accepted the box and smiled at Landon, then at Vera.

From the inscription, the gift was from Vera, and Gwendolyn gave her friend another warm smile. For the next few minutes, she paid more attention. The pile of gifts near her rose with surprising speed, and she smiled apologetically at a few people for whom she hadn't bought presents.

They hadn't done it just for her. Daisy had received a lot of gifts, too, and Gwendolyn loved the grin on the girl's face.

Could she have a ridiculous hope that Conner and Daisy would want to stay here?

More petals unfurled on that budding hope. She'd fallen in love with this small town as much as she'd fallen in love with this family, or maybe those things were related. Somewhere between watching Christmas lights in the quaint homes, participating in the gift drive, or caroling—her, singing, who'd think?—she realized she could see herself here.

Of course, if the Clark family didn't need her services any longer, she'd have to find a different job—a different career, actually. But hadn't Vera changed her life and become happy with the results?

Gwendolyn glanced at her.

Her friend leaned toward her and mouthed, "Are you okay?"

Gwendolyn wasn't, but she nodded nevertheless. "Thank you for everything," she mouthed back.

Liberty hand-delivered her present. "You're welcome to stay here indefinitely if you want to. The children love you. Actually, we all do."

A pleasant wave rose in Gwendolyn. "I appreciate it more than you know."

Lord, please guide me. Please help my heart find a home.

She needed to figure out who was behind her father's murder, so time off could come in handy. But it would be great to know she'd have a place to return to instead of leaving one assignment for another.

Conner got up as if he were going to say something, and she froze.

What was going on?

Then the youngest brother in the family and his wife, Heather, announced they were expecting twins. Conner sat down again. As much as she was happy for the growing family, longing for her own child to love unraveled in her heart.

Then longing sharpened as her gaze returned to Daisy, who grinned at her. Minutes later, Gwendolyn understood the meaning of that grin better when Nehemiah delivered Daisy's gift for her, a self-made necklace and a drawing. After Gwendolyn thanked the girl and placed the necklace over her Christmas sweater, tears she couldn't explain prickled her eyes.

Conner seemed to make a second attempt to speak, but a marriage proposal to Jenna interrupted him. Everyone joined in congratulations, including Gwendolyn and Conner.

Premonition twisted Gwendolyn's heart. What… what did he want to talk about?

"I'm so happy for you, Jenna." Liberty snatched her sister into her signature bear hug. "Well, look at us. All the Clark siblings finding love the same year."

Gwendolyn stared at Conner.

Could she find love like all the members of this family? Could he have feelings for her, too? Her feelings for him grew every day, but she forced her features to remain neutral. She'd worked as a human shield long enough to learn to conceal her emotions.

For the most part.

She didn't want anyone to know she was falling for Conner.

Including herself.

Chapter Nine

CONNER HAD NEVER had pangs of conscience this painful his entire life. He'd had the opportunity to reveal to the Clark family and Gwendolyn who he was—even with all the interruptions—and he hadn't used it.

Okay, okay, it wasn't too late. But a nagging feeling in his gut wouldn't go away.

"Daddy, can we stay here?" Hugging a plush toy cat she'd received yesterday among other gifts, Daisy lifted pleading eyes after he finished braiding her hair in their room in the B&B.

His heart about stopped. "Don't you… don't you miss our big house in Texas? Your room and toys?"

Gwendolyn hugged the toy tighter. "I like Danica. She's nice to me. And Miss Gwendolyn. And… everyone. And their house is nice. And they have ponies."

A lump formed in his throat. The idea sounded more appealing than he wanted to admit. But what about the art gallery? "I thought you liked cats."

"I do. I like ponies, too. I like Miss Gwendolyn and Danica even more."

Huh. He loved Texas, but this small town in the Show Me

state spoke to him, too. Or maybe it wasn't just the town but a certain hazel-eyed beauty who'd claim his heart if he didn't pay attention.

He sighed as he crouched before his daughter. "I've got obligations."

Daisy blinked. "Obla—What?"

"Things I have to do. Like take care of your grandma." Though his mother didn't do such a great job of raising him, he felt responsible for her. Besides, she'd changed a lot from the lethargic woman she'd once been. He should be grateful for the change.

Daisy's lower lip trembled. "Is Grandma sick again?"

He gave his daughter a reassuring smile. "No." He'd talked to his mother daily and kept in touch with her doctors, and she'd sounded more upbeat and energetic than ever. "But we have to stay close, in case we need to help her."

A sigh too big for such little lungs escaped Daisy's lips. "Ah. Then your job, right, Daddy?"

His kind daughter was understanding, but it didn't remove the stone pressing on his chest. "Yes, Sweetie Pie." Leaving the gallery would feel like betraying Annika.

Daisy sighed again. "Grandma makes nice apple turnovers."

His mother, baking pastries. Who'd think? But then, everyone dealt with difficulties in their own way. His mother's way was to disconnect, ignore things she didn't want to see.

Dissociate from life.

Dissociate from him.

Thankfully, she was back now, fully present. And he couldn't hold onto bitterness, or he'd lose whatever little family he had left. Which meant he'd have to stay in Texas.

"We have to give people a chance, right?" She probably didn't understand what he meant. But he just placed a kiss atop of her head, breathing in the sweet scent of her mango shampoo to calm his raw nerves.

All the roads led back to Texas, and his heart sank.

How could he say goodbye to Gwendolyn?

The answer was he couldn't. He'd tell her his secret and hope to start anew if she forgave him.

Gwendolyn resisted the urge to pace the spacious living room as time seemed to stand still and tension somehow held her in a body cast. The Christmas tree was still there, probably left until after the New Year. Lights twinkled just as they had during yesterday's lovely Christmas Day, as if not realizing the tragedy of today's events.

Jenna's fiancé's nephew had been kidnapped.

Her heart hammered in her chest. Yet she managed to prevent her voice from trembling by some miracle as she read the children a story. Reading a book to the little ones might not be her greatest idea, but it was the best she could come up with. She couldn't even think of any games when Vera, Jenna, and other members of the family she'd grown to love might be in danger. She drew a deep breath of pine needles and pies, the happy aromas so not fitting with the current mood.

Time stretched on with no news. The arrow on the grandfather clock seemed stuck in place as if Danica, with her penchant for glue, glued it to the clock's face.

Conner gave her an encouraging glance as he touched her hand. "Would you like me to continue the story?"

She shook her head, acting on autopilot.

Should she have joined Jenna and Vera? Her skills could be useful in such a situation. She'd offered, but the family had refused, asking her to stay with the children.

Gwendolyn had no difficulty comprehending why, though worry for the boy sliced her stomach in two. Jenna, as well as most of the Clark family, was assisting in the search. Somehow, they'd managed to keep the frightening news from the children.

Yet everyone, even Danica, was quiet as if sensing worry. The children exchanged glances with each other but didn't say a word. They sat on the rug and listened instead of darting around the house, most of the time in opposite directions.

The moment Gwendolyn's voice started cracking, she knew she needed to accept Conner's kind offer.

What was happening to Jenna and Vera now? Did they find the boy?

Gwendolyn shuddered. She knew too well how much damage violence in a family could do, and how quickly one's life could be turned upside down. This wonderful family didn't deserve such tragedy.

She could barely speak, so she passed the colorful children's book to Conner without saying a word. Her throat was too clogged up.

CHAPTER TEN

GWENDOLYN'S DREAM VISION of the family on a rug near a Christmas tree returned while he read the story. His hand found hers again as he continued reading, and she stilled, her heart thundering for a different reason now.

For one blissful moment, her dream was so close she could touch it like he touched her hand, could smell it like the pine needles and his intoxicating cologne.

Lord, please keep the Clark family safe in Your care, amen.

She put everything into that prayer.

Conner leaned toward her after he finished reading, his gaze more intense than usual, but no wonder in times like this.

"I need to tell you something," he whispered.

Liberty, the youngest daughter in the family, stormed inside the living room. Her signature green hair stuck up in different directions as if she either pulled on it or brushed her fingers through it too many times.

She gestured for Gwendolyn to follow. Worrying about the children, Gwendolyn glanced at Conner.

He nodded as he seemed to understand her without words. "It's okay. I'll read another story."

"Thanks." Her heart beating fast, she jumped to her feet, doing her best to gauge Liberty's expression.

Liberty snatched Gwendolyn into her bear hug once they reached the hall. "They rescued Andy. Everyone is fine. Well, Jenna was taken to the hospital, but Vera said it's a only a flesh wound."

Gwendolyn could breathe again.

During his half-sister's wedding, Conner watched from the back church pew, doing his best to remain hidden. Most of the small town seemed to have arrived for Jenna's wedding. But then, they were a prosperous family, weren't they? And a generous one, as well.

Two girls in pink dresses ran through the aisle with baskets, spreading petals, one of them Danica, of course.

"I wanna be a flower girl, too," his daughter whispered, snuggling closer to his side.

Both girls waved at her as they passed her, the scent of roses trailing them.

His rib cage constricted as he hugged his precious girl. "You will be. One day."

"When you get married, right?" Her eyes were so trusting, so innocent.

He coughed a little. Much as he'd enjoyed Gwendolyn's company, much as he admired her, he couldn't see himself getting married again. He still hadn't steeled himself to tell her why he was here, didn't want her to feel he'd only used her. Once she knew, most likely she'd be the one to push him away.

But Daisy didn't need to know that.

People smiled and greeted each other while they filled the pews as if they all were one big family. Well, some of them were indeed part of the large, rich Clark family.

The Clarks.

Unlike his, this family had plenty of children, who'd already welcomed his shy daughter into their circle in the park and during the Christmas celebration at the mansion. His gaze flickered to the children's pretty nanny—*Gwendolyn*—in one of the front seats. She'd sparked more of his interest than he wanted to admit, and their meetings—could they qualify as dates, when the children were always present?—had made his heart beat faster in a way it hadn't in years.

As if feeling his gaze, she glanced back, and her lips curved up as their gazes met and held. Blood rushed faster in his veins. He didn't need this sudden attraction, didn't want it. She should've been his ticket to get close to the family for his daughter's sake, and only that.

Then why couldn't he look away?

Because she'd become much more, so much more. Face it, he was falling in love.

The bridesmaids in emerald-green dresses with their husbands in tuxedos started their slow walk to the altar, and he switched his focus to the happy couples. For a moment, envy stabbed him. All of them seemed to have eyes only for each other, and he wondered how it would feel to experience profound love again.

But he'd loved once, and the pain of losing Annika was still sharp. He plastered a smile on his face for his daughter and hugged her.

"They are so pretty," she whispered.

"You're pretty, too." He squeezed her tighter. He did everything he could to boost her self-esteem, but it hadn't seemed to work too well.

"Wow!" She gaped at the bride as if not hearing him.

Jenna's long-sleeved dress was simpler than he'd expected, considering the family wealth, more in the sense of understated elegance than something designed to attract attention. No tiara or sparkling rhinestones. But with her smile shining so brightly, the bride didn't need any embellishments.

At a more attentive glance, her dress was embroidered with small stars, and the white belt featured a half-moon buckle, probably a nod to the groom's nephew, who according to Conner's daughter loved astronauts, stars, and planets.

As his half sister passed him, her gaze lingered on him longer than on the other guests, and something akin to understanding flashed in her striking blue eyes.

As if…

As if she understood who he was. Maybe she did run a background check on him. After all, she was an investigator. That was fine with him. His background was squeaky clean and crystal clear.

His intentions, however, weren't.

Guilt knifed him as his gaze switched to Gwendolyn again. Even if they didn't have a future together, she deserved to know the truth about him being related to the Clarks. And the fact was, despite all logic, he wanted to have a future with her.

Well, today or never. He owed it to her. He drew in a deep breath and held it.

How would she react? She might stop talking to him, and though he deserved it, he didn't want that to happen. He couldn't say goodbye to her yet.

Would he ever be able to?

After the ceremony, he and Daisy waited near the door until Gwendolyn stepped outside, and then he followed her. "May I speak to you, please? Alone?" Then he cupped a hand on Daisy's shoulder. "Sweetie Pie, is it okay if I talk to Miss Gwendolyn for a moment?"

"Okay, Daddy." She nodded with more confidence than he'd ever seen, and it steadied his trembling heart.

Liberty gave him an understanding nod and ushered the children forward, including Daisy.

Breathing frosty air, he took Gwendolyn aside before he could lose his courage. "I have to tell you something. The Clark family… the family you're working for… they don't know it yet, but they're my half siblings."

Her jaw slackened as she gasped. "What?"

The entire next day, Gwendolyn tried to wrap her mind around Conner's confession.

She'd already had trust issues after her mother had left her so easily and never allowed her to talk to Vanessa. In addition, her father had trained Gwendolyn to be suspicious and vigilant as part of the skills necessary to survive in the field they'd both chosen. Plus her ex-fiancé had cheated on her, and her so-called friend Gillian had betrayed her.

To question her trust in Conner after all that made her gut wrench.

Yet, long ago, she'd learned to smile even when her heart had been bleeding. So she'd plastered on a grin for the children's sake and gone on during the day like nothing had happened.

Conner promised her he'd tell the family soon, but could she believe him now?

Her heart flipped over in her chest.

Like Vera who'd married one of the Clark brothers earlier this month, all the other siblings in the Clark family seemed to have found true love and happiness. Gwendolyn was happy for them. She really was. But seeing their joyful love sharpened her loneliness.

Their family would continue being close-knit and there for each other while she would return to her empty apartment where not even a cat waited for her. Her father had taught her that pets needed stability, and their lifestyle was anything but.

Her heart shifted. Just like Daisy, Gwendolyn wanted to have a cat. Wanted to be needed, to stroke smooth fur, to elicit happy purrs, to feel that overwhelming tenderness when the cat settled on her lap to snuggle during the long winter nights. A pet wouldn't betray her like people had.

By the evening, tired of pretending everything was great, she looked forward to going to bed and studying the info Vera had sent her. Then disappearing into a dream. Hopefully, without a certain ex-cowboy in it.

Once she finished her work as a nanny-bodyguard for the day, she dragged her tired feet to her room and sank onto her bed.

Then her gut clenched. She'd never looked deep enough into her father's murder and wished she hadn't waited twenty-five years to do it. She read the file her friend had found on Ron, Odetta, and the sculptor until her vision was blurry.

Okay, maybe tears blurred her vision, but who wouldn't cry when their heart was broken?

Her phone rang, and her heartbeat increased at Conner's name on the screen. Her fingers lingered over the screen, but she couldn't talk to him. Not yet.

First, she needed to figure out her feelings for him.

Lord, can I trust Conner?

An incoming text beeped—*I miss you. And I'm sorry.*

Longing unraveled in her. She missed him and Daisy, too. More than she wanted to admit. But if he'd lied to her about one thing, couldn't he have lied about others? Or more likely, what else hadn't he told her? How could she believe she was anything more than a source of information to him?

Her chest hurt as she did her best to reread the file, but her thoughts kept returning to Conner. She changed into one of the sweatpants and T-shirts she usually slept in and slipped under the covers, a lump clogging her throat and tears burning her eyes.

She thought there was an attraction between them. More than

an attraction. But then, she'd been wrong before. Plenty of times.

For a long time, she stared at the ceiling, not sleepy despite this overwhelming tiredness.

Oh, how much she missed him! His smile, his support, his way of looking at her and seeming to see her soul and care about her.

Spending time with young children was so much better than with adults.

Children hadn't learned to lie yet.

CHAPTER ELEVEN

AFTER THE CHILDREN RETURNED to their parents the next evening, Gwendolyn put away enough toys to make a toy store proud, her heart heavy.

Liberty plopped down near her on the rug, her single green leaf-shaped earring dancing in her ear. "You missed the sleigh rides we did before Christmas, but we're doing them again. *And* you're going on the sleigh ride with Conner tonight."

"Excuse me?" Gwendolyn blinked. Surely, she'd misheard. But her heart started beating fast.

"You're going on a sleigh ride with Conner tonight. I'll finish up with the toys." Liberty smiled. "Go get ready."

Gwendolyn had never seen a woman so comfortable in her skin, plus size, green hair, and all. Maybe being adored by her husband and soon-to-be adopted son and being passionate about her veterinarian job had something to do with Liberty's happy glow.

Gwendolyn pretended she was too occupied with the important task of placing toys in boxes. "Um, I'd rather retire to my room earlier tonight. Or have a root canal."

Laughing, Liberty tossed a stuffed puppy at Gwendolyn's

head. "That wasn't a question. That was a reminder."

As Gwendolyn fumbled with the plush Dalmatian, she opened her mouth and promptly closed it. In the short time she'd known Liberty, Gwendolyn understood arguing with the youngest Clark daughter was futile.

Still, she tried. She wasn't ready to speak to Conner yet. "I... I have my reasons."

Liberty grimaced. "Yeah. He should've told us he's our half sibling from the get-go instead of sneaking around."

Gwendolyn gasped. "You know?"

"Yup. He told the family. Right after Jenna received the DNA test results to confirm it. I take it, he told you, too?"

"Yes. On Jenna's wedding day." Gwendolyn didn't want Liberty to think she'd kept that secret away from the family. "And... and you're okay with it?"

"At first, I wanted to punch Conner." Yes, that sounded like Liberty. "My brothers did, too. But then we decided to give him a chance. Well, the women decided, and the men agreed. Eventually. Knowing Jenna, she investigated Conner thoroughly, and we decided to trust him for now. Family is family, even though it's turning out we have far more family than we realized." Liberty rolled her eyes. "Besides, we all love Daisy. Mom's happy to have a new grandchild."

Gwendolyn's world shifted. "Wow. I mean... wow. I... I don't know whether I can be as forgiving as you all are."

"You have a kind nature you're trying to hide. Not everyone is going to take advantage of your kindness. I'll say a prayer for you. Anyway, I'm sure Conner and Daisy wouldn't want you to miss all that fun." Liberty got up as her adopted son ran to her, dimples denting his cheeks.

His hair stood up in an adorable cowlick. "We're gonna go for another sleigh ride!"

"Yes, we are." She gave Nehemiah a hug much gentler than

her usual ones, probably to avoid suffocating or crushing the boy.

Liberty's husband, now the accountant for Mending Hearts Ranch, greeted Gwendolyn with a handshake, then placed a kiss on his wife's slightly blushing cheek, his grin and dimples matching his boy's.

Gwendolyn suppressed a wave of envy. She wasn't an envious person to start with, and Liberty deserved her marital bliss. Liberty's outspoken no-nonsense hid a generous heart.

"Leave the rest of the toys. I'll get them later." Liberty glanced back as she walked toward the hall, her husband's arm wrapped around her shoulder. "Gwendolyn, please be ready in half an hour. We'll give you a car ride to where we have the horses and sleighs."

That was probably the polite equivalent of Liberty dragging Gwendolyn there. But then, what in other people might be considered rude and intrusive, in Liberty showed she cared.

Once again, wistfulness invaded Gwendolyn as she hurried to her room to get ready. She'd love to have Liberty as her friend. For a moment, resentment stung her. Conner had that precious gift of being related to this family and had hidden it from them for too long.

He'd said his concern was about his daughter, about the way they'd accept her. But wasn't there some of his own concern, too? Was he scared to get attached again after his wife's death?

If so, he'd never let himself get attached to her, either.

With those sad thoughts, Gwendolyn changed into her best slacks and a fun Christmas sweater Liberty had given her as a gift, in emerald green, of course. Gwendolyn wished she'd packed makeup or pretty clothes.

A slight unease developed in her stomach as she brushed her pitiful hair, and not only because she didn't know how to act with Conner.

She'd never liked being out in the open because it was much

more difficult to protect someone then, and even trips in the park made her nervous. She took a deep breath and dabbed her favorite perfume on her wrists, the scent gentle and nonintrusive. Really, her bodyguard duties were nominal now, and there was no reason to think the children might be in danger. Besides, evenings were her own, and she was off duty.

Her shoulders relaxed a little. For most of her career, she'd had to stay on high alert while on the job, and being able to enjoy herself should feel good.

Did she start healing in Cowboy Crossing?

Her heart warmed as if she belonged here more than to any of those other places she'd been in. But then a small lump formed in her throat. She swallowed the clog down but couldn't push away the fact that she'd have to leave soon.

A knock on the door preceded Liberty marching in without waiting for an answer. "Ready?"

Sure enough, Liberty wouldn't let her off the hook.

Gwendolyn nodded, though she wasn't ready for what was about to come.

Would she ever be?

Out of habit, she checked her surroundings as she opened the mansion's front door in a slit before moving forward when nothing looked suspicious. One could never be too careful. Her father had found it out the hard way.

She reviewed camera recordings often, checked the interior and exterior perimeter twice daily, and watched from the windows many times during the day. Still, after the threat had seemed to be over, she felt a sting of guilt for her high pay.

Tipping her face toward the setting sun, she took a deep breath of frosty air in a failed attempt to calm her jumping heart.

Then she followed the obnoxiously happy family and allowed herself to enjoy the magnificent panorama instead of scanning the environment for potential threats.

With the frosty trees and fences dusted in white powder and the ground thick with snow, the place looked like a winter wonderland. Tiny sparkles reflected in the snow like precious stones.

The myriad of Christmas lights still on after Christmas illuminated the wish hidden deep inside her soul. She wanted a different life from the one she'd led until now.

First, she needed to believe in herself, believe she had the strength to find what that life was.

On the short walk to the truck, Liberty's husband lifted their son onto his shoulders, eliciting a squeal.

Gwendolyn's treacherous heart skipped a beat as the motor roared to life and the truck took off, the air freshener giving off a whiff of green apples. One of the reasons a new life looked attractive was because she was falling for Conner and getting attached to his precious girl. Despite her inexperience in the romance department, she hoped she was observant enough to discern if the attraction was mutual. She'd thought it was.

Yet for them to have a chance at happiness together, she'd have to work through her trust issues, and he'd have to work through his abandonment ones. Not to mention figuring out how to resolve the geographical distance.

Her stomach clenched as she rested against the leather seat. Her having a dangerous profession wouldn't help.

Lord, what should I do?

Besides teaching her to pray, her father had told her he'd tried to learn something from every case he'd taken. He'd said that the Lord often showed us the things we needed to learn.

As she pulled out her phone from her pocket and studied photos on Odetta's social media, especially the ones where Odetta was with her husband, Gwendolyn wondered what she could learn here. Odetta's smile looked natural, not forced, as she gazed at her husband, and he looked at her with the same affection.

Gwendolyn scrolled down for more photos.

Vacations at the ocean. Entertainment parks. Picnics in their spacious yard. They looked like a happy family.

Lowering her phone, Gwendolyn peered out the window at the white wonderland. If Odetta could heal enough from physical and emotional abuse to fall in love and trust a man again, couldn't Gwendolyn do the same?

Conner omitting his blood ties to the Clarks didn't help, but maybe her trust issues weren't the only problem. She was so used to her loneliness that it was all she knew. She huddled into that loneliness as if it was a warm security blanket. The idea of risking betrayal again made her stomach clench tighter.

Her phone rang, and she squinted at the screen.

An unknown number again.

Tension built in her gut as she swiped the screen to answer and pressed it to her ear. "Hello?"

"Remember what you've done." The male voice spoke fast, and the line went dead.

A shiver traveled down her back though it was warm in the vehicle. What could this mean? What had she done? Or was this call for someone else?

She sent her friend a quick text with the new info. She felt the truck slowing down, and there was no time to call her.

When the truck stopped, Liberty glanced back. "I'll say a prayer for you. I hope it works out between you two. And if not, I'm sure Danica will find you a great guy."

"I'll help, too!" Nehemiah grinned.

"Thank you." Warmth spread inside Gwendolyn. Liberty seemed to treat everyone like family, even people like Gwendolyn who retreated into their shell like a turtle at the first sign of emotional danger. "And thank you for doing this."

Liberty winked at her. "Don't thank me. The sleigh ride was Danica's suggestion. And I see someone is here early."

"O–okay." Gwendolyn faced the window, and her heart picked up speed.

There he was, standing near the horses. He stroked the space between the black mare's eyes, then lifted his daughter so she could do the same. Small white flecks covered the beautiful horse's coat like snowflakes, and striped hooves stamped the snow as she shifted them.

The Appaloosa looked magnificent, but Gwendolyn's gaze quickly slid back to the man who made her heart beat faster.

He didn't see her yet. So, after she did her usual scan of the area, she took the opportunity to take him in.

Hmm. His whole demeanor changed when he was around horses.

He placed Daisy on the ground again and fed the mare an apple. Such wistfulness twisted his expression that Gwendolyn's insides twisted in response. Huh. She might not be the only one on the brink of life-changing decisions.

"He loves working with horses, doesn't he?" Liberty whispered.

"Yes." Gwendolyn nodded for emphasis.

From the way he'd talked about the ranch and the shine in his eyes as he spoke, she'd gathered how much he loved his previous job and lifestyle. Trading open spaces for stifling rooms and fragile art must've been difficult.

But he felt he needed to dedicate his life to managing his late wife's gallery. While she could respect that, her heart sank. She lifted her chin and exited the truck.

Daisy saw her first, yelped, and ran toward her. "Miss Gwendolyn! I missed you! We haven't seen you for ages!"

Gwendolyn caught the girl in her arms and hugged her while tenderness swept her whole. "I missed you, too." While "for ages" was only a day apart, she didn't correct Daisy.

A day without this little family did feel like "for ages" indeed.

The child's love was so pure, and Gwendolyn didn't remember the last time she'd received a gift like that, if ever.

If she could have a Christmas wish, even if it was too late for that, it would be to give this girl all the affection Daisy so obviously needed and Gwendolyn never had the chance to give her mother or sister.

A wish for a family for Conner and Daisy. Maybe even for herself?

"You're gonna go on the sleigh ride with me and Daddy, right?" Daisy tugged at Gwendolyn's sleeve, dragging her toward the horses and sleigh without waiting for an answer.

Daisy must've taken lessons from Danica and been a quick learner. Daisy's tiny nose scrunched in a funny way as she looked up and grinned. Gwendolyn's heart melted faster than snow in the spring sun.

As she walked along the fresh, crisp snow, she wondered if she could start fresh, too. Could there be a spring season with fragrant blooms of love in her life?

Her pulse spiked the moment she looked into Conner's mesmerizing eyes. There needed to be a second part to that wish.

She swallowed hard.

Lord, please help Conner accept what he lost. Give him and me a chance for the future. Amen.

Conner's heart leaped, making him want to rush to Gwendolyn the way his little girl had. But he forced himself to stay rooted in place, leaning into the mare for support, either moral or physical—or both.

The Appaloosa nickered, the sound somewhat comforting. Amazing how horses could sense the human's mood. More amazing how they could soothe it. How forgiving they could be.

While Conner had always been calm and kept his emotions in check around horses because they needed to know they could rely on him, this one forgave his distress.

A breeze played with the strands escaping Gwendolyn's knit hat, and the chill pinked her cheeks. And the joyful way his daughter greeted her made him realize he was falling for this woman.

The woman he could easily lose if he hadn't already.

Their goodbye had been tense after his admittance.

He lifted his daughter and placed her in the sleigh. "Here we go, Sweetie Pie."

"Thanks, Daddy."

Then he faced Gwendolyn, not sure how to act around her. She didn't respond to his call or text yesterday. "Um, hi."

"Hi." She ducked her head, soft curls slipping around her face as her fragile lashes kissed her cheeks.

"I wasn't sure you'd show up today." He frowned. That wouldn't win him the greeting-of-the-year award. He missed their easy camaraderie, missed it passionately.

"I… Well, you underestimated Liberty's and Danica's influence then," Gwendolyn told the snow.

Great.

His heart dipped into the same snow. So she'd come here because Liberty had made her. He had to admit *that* half sister was quite the woman, but that didn't mean he wanted her bullying someone he was coming to care about.

"You don't have to be here if you don't want to," he said in a low voice so his daughter wouldn't overhear. Daisy would be upset if Gwendolyn left.

The Clark family had been forgiving when he'd told them the secret. He'd been shocked. Thrilled to find out she had cousins, Daisy didn't mind at all that he hadn't told her earlier. But could Gwendolyn do the same? After many people had deceived her, her trust was threadbare, and his actions could've torn it completely.

His heart seemed to stop beating when he waited for her answer, and the only sound interrupting the silence was the horse's nickering.

He couldn't wait any longer. "I'm sorry I didn't tell you sooner. I really am. How about we start from scratch? Before my mistake. Get to know each other." He stuck out his hand. "Hello. I'm Conner. And this is my daughter, Daisy."

Gwendolyn looked up, and a bashful smile widened her lips. "I'm Gwendolyn. Great to meet you."

Hope unraveled inside him. "Great to meet you, too. Have a date with me tomorrow, please. Let me get to know you better. No secrets between us any longer. Daisy will be with us, if that's okay with you."

Her eyes lit up like lights on a Christmas tree. "You know, that's just the thing. I *want* to get to know you. I… want to see you. And Daisy, of course."

"Is that a yes to the date?"

"Yes."

His chest swelling, he couldn't help it. He lifted Gwendolyn up and twirled her around while his heartbeat became a staccato from having her in his arms.

Daisy squealed from her sleigh's seat in what he hoped was an approving delight.

Realizing what he'd done, he put Gwendolyn back on the snow. "Oops. I didn't overstep my boundaries, did I?"

Her lips curved up again. "You did, but I enjoyed it."

Attraction zipped through him. He took her delicate gloved fingers into his hand and helped her inside the sleigh before he could overstep those boundaries even further and kiss her. "Me, too. I'm enjoying every moment with you."

As they took off, he thought about what he'd just said. With Gwendolyn, he was learning to live again instead of surviving for his daughter's sake. He was coming to cherish every moment, like Annika had seemed to do once.

After all, the next moment was never guaranteed, and he knew it too well.

The chill deepened the pink in Gwendolyn's cheeks, making her look even more adorable, and her flamingo-hued knit hat that he guessed matched his daughter's on purpose, suited Gwendolyn.

Golden and peach hues swirled in the sky and tinted the pristinely white carpet spreading as far as the eye could see. It all added to the early evening's magic.

It was more than that, though.

Being in open spaces again, working with horses, just breathing in the freshness of frosty air exhilarated him. How special to share this time with two girls so dear to him! He let the reins rest loosely in his grip as he eyed the girls beside him—Daisy all aglow and Gwendolyn bright-eyed.

Warmth flowed from his heart, and then his chest constricted. He dammed up his joy before the flood of it could wash away his common sense. He didn't want to think he might lose Gwendolyn when her nanny contract was over. Or that he'd have to go back to the office, a place he'd had to put on like he'd had to put on a suit, for that matter.

He'd entered a dream—rode into it with jingle bells, really— but even practical and jaded guys could dream once in a while, right?

He hugged Gwendolyn and Daisy close as if they could escape from his dream and he needed them there to believe happiness was possible.

If he didn't know better, he'd think God was showing him what his life could be like. Conner's eyes dampened as the images of Tara and Annika flashed in front of his eyes.

Then, like in the past, God could give Conner the illusion of happiness before taking it all away. It didn't matter if that illusion lasted an evening or years.

"Daddy, Miss Gwendolyn, look, deer!" Daisy pointed to a small herd.

"Oh yes, I see." Gwendolyn smiled at his little girl.

Three does and a stag stilled, then looked up, and the next moment their white tails flashed as they hightailed it behind the trees. Only their tracks betrayed they'd ever been there.

A few pale evening stars appeared in the sky and twinkled but then hid behind the clouds as if reminding him everything in the world was temporary. The moonlight caressed the snow, painting it into bluish shadows more exquisite than anything he'd ever displayed in Annika's gallery.

He drew his wonderful girls closer and whispered into Gwendolyn's ear. "Have you ever thought happiness is only an illusion? Here today to disappear tomorrow?"

Something unreadable flashed in her moonlit amber eyes. "I don't know about that. But I do know some things most certainly are not illusions, like your love for your daughter. Your love for her is forever."

Yes, it was.

Just like the pain of losing Annika that he'd never wanted to repeat.

Chapter Twelve

"WHAT AM I GOING TO WEAR?" Gwendolyn stared at the measly wardrobe in her walk-in closet at the mansion.

She'd packed light for a job in the Show Me state. The clothes she'd taken had to qualify by three parameters: be comfortable, make her unnoticeable in a crowd, and not scare children. Based on how the children behaved sometimes, the third one should've been negotiable.

Swallowing a bitter taste, she dragged herself from the closet into her room. She hadn't counted on the possibility of a date when she'd agreed to this job.

She cringed as she sank onto a wooden chair near the oak desk. She'd been out of the dating circuit long enough to lose her dating skills, not that she'd had great dating skills to start with. Ever since... She rubbed her bare ring finger, her heart twisting as she twisted up her hands. It was better not to recall her ruined engagement.

Well, she had an evening off and two hours to prepare for this *date*—wow!—and no clue what to do. Why did she have this sudden desire to pretty up? Conner had seen her in all her undecorated glory and seemed to like her well enough.

But she wanted more than "like." She wanted admiration. She wanted love. She wanted passion.

She wanted too much.

After being raised by her father, she wasn't good around makeup or fashion. On the other hand, she could pull a rifle apart and put it back together.

In under fifteen minutes.

At the ripe age of nine.

Which might not be super useful when one needed to appeal to a man.

Lord, I need help. Please?

Liberty barged in, right after knocking and before Gwendolyn had a chance to respond. "I heard about your *date* tonight. And I hope you're not going looking like that."

If Gwendolyn didn't know how outspoken Liberty was, she might've gotten offended. "Like what?"

Liberty hustled her to the tall mirror on the wall. "For starters, you have flour on your shirt, I'd guess from making pancakes with the children in the morning. Then there's some substance on your shoulder I'd rather not identify."

"Apple purée from feeding the baby."

Liberty nodded, her single green leaf earring that matched her hair winking in her earlobe. "Right. That's what I thought this was, too. And on your stomach and on your knee…"

"I see." Gwendolyn cringed. "This must be from finger painting with the children after lunch. I strictly told them not to finger paint the wall and each other. I should've included myself in the list."

Liberty chuckled, the sound as strong and uninhibited as the woman herself. "Don't get me wrong. I'm all for children's art. But Conner might be a little concerned if you show up like this. Hmm, you even have maroon finger paint on your back between your shoulders! How did that get there?"

"Nehemiah must've jumped. Gotta love those kids."

A grin spread over Liberty's face. "We all do. Also, we need to do something about your hair."

Wincing, Gwendolyn couldn't help sneaking a glance at Liberty's bright hairdo. "I know it's a little dull and a little flimsy, but—"

Fingers through her emerald hair, Liberty propped her hip against the oak desk and ignored its squeaky complaint. "Don't worry. I'm not going to be the one helping you. My idea of dressing you up would be cutting your hair short, coloring it green"—Liberty winked when Gwendolyn winced again—"and putting you in jeans and cowboy boots. I'm going to ask my sister."

A whoosh of relief left Gwendolyn's lungs. "Thanks."

"Jenna lived in Paris for over two decades, and based on those fancy clothes of hers, she learned a thing or two about fashion."

Gwendolyn's eyes widened. Learned a thing or two? Tall, slim, and elegant, Jenna could've been a model. "Thank you, but I don't want to interrupt her honeymoon. And, even if she agrees to lend me her fabulous clothes, I won't be able to squeeze into them. I'm not as slender as she is." Gwendolyn grimaced. "Or tall, for that matter."

"Yeah, something must be wrong with her genes." Liberty cleared her throat. "As my sister-in-law Vera says, there should be a lot of a good person. I'm the proof. That means you are, too. Anyway, don't worry about the honeymoon. Jenna was gone so long she doesn't want to leave Mending Hearts for even a short trip. The newlyweds are hanging around here somewhere. As for clothes, Jenna knows how to sew."

Hope fluttered inside Gwendolyn. But she was too used to her expectations not coming through. "Maybe we should ask her first if she can help during her honeymoon?"

Liberty stared at her, then left the desk. It squeaked again, this time in gratitude. "Consider it done. Hmm, Vera's grandmother is good with coloring hair. She does it all the time when she's in too much of a hurry to go to the hairdresser."

Gwendolyn had seen her friend's grandmother. "She has *blue* hair!" She suddenly started to like her dull and flimsy hair.

Liberty beamed. "Yes, she's a one and only. Oh, and Vera's grandma has an old sewing machine, too. It still works. I can get fabric."

When Jenna joined them, Gwendolyn trudged after Liberty to the living room, marveling at the sisters' relationship, even after decades of them not seeing each other. They'd picked up as if they'd only been apart for a summer vacation.

How would it feel to have camaraderie and friendship like that with her sibling?

Gwendolyn's rib cage constricted. After they'd grown up apart thanks to their parents' agreement, she had tried to establish contact with Vanessa through their mother. But dear Mom always found excuses not to pass on the message until Gwendolyn gave up.

Once best friends, the sisters hadn't spoken to each other in too long. Maybe it was time to try to make contact again.

Then her rib cage squeezed even tighter, guilt reminding her about the older navy-blue sedan and the strange calls. She needed to look into her father's murder instead of having Vera do the whole job, and what was she doing?

Going on a date with a handsome guy *again*.

Déjà vu, anyone?

Gwendolyn sighed. "Maybe I shouldn't go."

Liberty stopped abruptly, and Gwendolyn bumped into her. "Oh no, you're going all right. Otherwise, I'll drag you to the restaurant. I'm not above calling Danica for reinforcement, either. Dara just might nudge you in the back with her nose, too."

Gwendolyn couldn't help chuckling.

Soon, Gwendolyn was in a chair getting highlights while the sisters paraded in and out of Jenna's childhood room with different outfits.

Liberty raised an eyebrow at the leopard-print jacket in Jenna's hands. "Isn't that going to look trashy?"

Gwendolyn winced again. She was doing a lot of wincing lately.

"No." Jenna shook her head. "I'm going to add decorations to make it look *stylish*. And it's going to be a short coat with a nice belt."

Gwendolyn released a breath she didn't realize she was holding, then looked in the mirror. "Um, what color are the highlights going to be?"

"Blonde." The older woman's hand stopped midair. "Unless you want to be more adventurous and color your hair black with orange highlights. You'll look like a tiger."

As if looking like a leopard wasn't bad enough!

"Blonde is good," Gwendolyn said quickly.

Jenna studied her while the highlights were drying out. "If I may suggest, it's not just about the clothes, makeup, and hair."

Liberty sliced her hand in the air. "Right. It's also about the boots, and I'm still suggesting cowboy ones."

Jenna's lips widened in a way men probably found enigmatic. "Yes, footwear is important. As well as accessories. But not nearly as much as inner confidence, the way a woman carries herself, her posture."

Well, some people like Jenna seemed to be born with a regal posture and stately confidence. Gwendolyn searched for her inner confidence, but she'd seemed to leave it behind during one of those far-too-many moves.

Jenna snapped her long fingers. "Let's teach you to walk. A book might be helpful."

"A book?" Gwendolyn nearly groaned. "I don't have time to

read right now." Though she did love reading. Books were her friends back when they'd moved constantly for her father's job and she hadn't had time to make human ones.

Jenna gestured to her head with its short black hairdo and those impossibly long bangs that fell on her electric-blue eyes, a striking combination. "I meant to put a book on your head while you walk."

Right. Gwendolyn was probably slouching too much.

Wishing Jenna didn't have to see those far-from-slim measurements, Gwendolyn tried not to squirm as the sisters measured her, then started working on the outfits. Huh, both women acted as if those were just numbers.

Maybe they were.

"Being stylish is ninety percent confidence. Knowing how to combine colors and patterns wouldn't hurt, either." Jenna cut the jacket, matching up the print as she pinned in excess fabric cut from its length to widen it. Then she added trim at the bottom and cuffs from a different fabric. "For example, if you combine animal prints and floral prints, the outfit is going to be too busy. Or if you combine green and red, you're going to look like a traffic light."

Liberty, who was sewing the pants, lifted her head. "Hmm. I have green hair, and I love my magenta jeans. You didn't say anything."

Jenna cleared her throat while her utter attention remained on the jacket. "Wellll… You have your own style."

Liberty grinned. "That I do."

"Let's talk about the gait." Jenna started sewing cut pieces together. "It's important to keep your back straight, shoulders back, stomach in, and flow smoothly. Look forward, not into the ground. In old times, women carried jugs with water on their heads. Their gaits were perfect, or they'd take an involuntary shower. These times, some women walk like they're trying to hammer nails into the floor with their feet."

Gwendolyn took mental notes.

"Huh." Liberty flicked hair away from her eyes. "That's the way I walk. I need to practice. We don't have large water jugs, but I made a three-cheese casserole this morning."

As she cut the thread, Jenna winked at Gwendolyn. "We might be left without dinner tonight."

"I heard that." Liberty laughed. "And by the way, I'm fine with combining red and green. I am who I am, and I'm fabulous. I prefer to stay true to myself, march to the beat of my own drum."

Gwendolyn stilled as the words solidified something inside her. For most of her life, she'd marched to the beat of her father's song, out of guilt and maybe out of convenience.

What was her own song? Had it even been written yet?

"I agree. Forget all I said and stay true to yourself. After all, everyone pays attention to the traffic light." Jenna nudged her sister in her shoulder.

"That's right." Liberty raised her chin and nudged Jenna back, but her sister barely remained standing.

Gwendolyn chuckled, but envy stung deeply. Even when Jenna and Liberty were bantering, their love for each other shone through.

Gwendolyn felt a strong urge to talk to Vanessa, not just sometime in the future but as soon as possible.

While Jenna styled Gwendolyn's hair, Gwendolyn's thoughts drifted away.

When she was growing up, her father's profession sounded so romantic. So noble. He'd put his life at risk to help other people. He was truly her hero.

Maybe it was the type of assignments she'd been getting, but she'd found out her job didn't just include guarding people's bodies, though there was that, true to the moniker. She'd guarded their secrets, too.

Most of the time, those were rather innocent. But sometimes, there were reasons they needed protection, reasons that didn't sit well with her conscience.

Welching on a gambling debt.

Taking advantage of a business partner.

Conducting unethical professional dealings.

And often those reasons weren't disclosed until after she'd signed a contract.

She'd learned the hard way to have an extensive talk with her future clients and do her research before taking on new assignments. Not only because she didn't want to twist her conscience, but also because, to protect them properly, she needed to know as much as possible about potential threats, just like a doctor needed to know about his patients' symptoms to treat them.

Even the details they weren't comfortable disclosing.

But unlike a doctor who could help people heal or at least treat their pain, she couldn't help her clients with their damaged consciences, friendships, or reputations.

Eventually, being a guardian of people's dirty secrets had worn her out. She'd applied for a job with a security company to protect buildings instead of people and stayed there until her contract expired. It felt like a betrayal of her father's legacy, but it gave her a necessary respite.

She'd only come back as a bodyguard because Vera asked for her help.

"Oh, I almost forgot. There was an envelope for you in the mail." Liberty left and returned with a white envelope.

No return address. Huh. Gwendolyn hesitated before opening it. But she'd forwarded her mail to this address for the time being, and she'd received a few Christmas cards.

This wasn't a classic business-sized envelope. Another Christmas card, arriving a little late?

She opened it, and her heart went cold. It was a photo of her father's favorite football team. What on earth?

Lord, is this a sign from You?
Or from my father?
And if not, what is this?

Chapter Thirteen

CONNER STARED at the woman who entered the restaurant door, and his jaw slackened. Surely, that couldn't be the shy woman he'd asked out.

Based on how male heads turned in her direction, he wasn't the only one mesmerized.

Gwendolyn wore a stylish leopard-print coat that suited her somehow, paired with a wide white belt and gloves and boots that softened the effect. Dressy slacks of his favorite caramel macchiato color hugged her apparently shapely legs and matched the silk scarf tied into an elaborate knot on her neck.

Soft makeup accentuated generous lashes and hazel eyes that looked bigger now, and sun-kissed highlights gave her new curls playfulness. Happily, though, makeup didn't cover up those freckles that added the touch of girlish innocence.

The bright shine in her eyes attracted him most of all. He couldn't look away.

He was used to being surrounded by priceless works of art, and she was one of them. He'd suspected it before, and now, he knew for sure.

His heart shifted at the reminder of the little time they had left together. Most likely, not enough for them both to open their hearts to love again.

"Miss Gwendolyn!" Daisy rushed to Gwendolyn and hugged her legs.

He froze. His daughter didn't take a shine to people easily, much less display her attention publicly. But she'd gotten attached to Gwendolyn already. When Conner and Daisy left Cowboy Crossing, they might both be leaving their hearts behind.

A frown accompanied his tightening jaw.

Not telling Gwendolyn from the start who he was also twisted up his conscience now. She'd given him a chance for a fresh start, but would she ever fully trust him again?

"Hello there, sweetie. Don't you look lovely tonight?" She hugged his daughter.

Daisy didn't say anything, just returned to her seat. Sometimes people took offense at his daughter's lack of response and considered her rude. But Gwendolyn didn't seem bothered.

As Gwendolyn sauntered toward him, those elegant over-the-knee white boots clicking against the tile, he managed to pick his jaw up from the floor. "You look... stunning."

She smiled. Even her smile looked different now, more mysterious and inviting all at once. "You look... surprised."

He should've stopped gawking sooner. He pulled out a chair for her, remembering his manners.

"Thank you, but I'd like to sit near the wall, please." She gestured to a different chair.

"Okay." He pulled that one out. Even though she wasn't a bodyguard on duty, the habits obviously stayed, and he winced at the reminder of her dangerous profession. His heart wouldn't survive losing the woman he loved a second time.

His stepsister's electric-blue eyes—just like Jenna's—filled with tears appeared in his mind, and guilt overwhelmed him again as when he'd been a teen. He'd lost too many people not to build a wall around his heart.

Yet he had a strange urge to run his fingers through Gwendolyn's teasing hair that must be soft to the touch. Go figure.

As he took off her coat, revealing an alabaster-white sweater with a long necklace of amber that matched her eyes perfectly, its three layers of beads gleaming, he leaned into her. She smelled differently, too, some new fleeting, delicate perfume that made him want to breathe her in and hold on for a while.

He couldn't explain why, the same way he couldn't—didn't want to—explain the flutter of his heart.

She slid off her white gloves, revealing a fresh pink polish that matched her lipstick. Then she smiled at Daisy. "I've got a present for you." She wriggled a fluffy toy kitten from her purse.

Daisy's eyes widened. For a moment, she stared. Then she hugged the kitten. "Wow. It's so cute! Thank you."

"You're welcome. And you're the cute one." Gwendolyn pressed playfully on Daisy's upturned nose.

His heart leaped into his throat. He'd needed so badly to see that sweet smile on his girl's face. He gave Gwendolyn a grateful glance. "You're good with children."

Something unreadable flashed in her eyes. "Thanks. But I have to be. It's my occupation for now."

Huh. Gwendolyn and his daughter had something in common. Neither one of them knew how to take a compliment.

Gwendolyn's gaze darted around the room as if she recorded every detail, stopping at the exit. Surely, she wasn't contemplating fleeing? She seemed a bit tense, just like in the park. Was she nervous? Or was it a habit of always being on high alert as a bodyguard?

Or… was there a different reason?

His heart sank to the tiled floor. She'd told him about the mysterious calls, messages, and that navy-blue sedan. He couldn't let something happen to her. Even if they went their separate ways, he needed to know she was okay. Somewhere in the world without him.

After the waitress took their drink orders, he read the menu to his daughter, who as always seemed undecided. On the contrary, he already knew what he wanted.

He wanted to know more about the woman in front of him.

No! He meant barbecue ribs, of course.

He reminded himself about their leaving soon before he could drown in those syrupy eyes. Or was it already too late for that?

The waitress brought their drinks. "Are you ready to order?"

The familiar deer-caught-in-the-headlights expression appeared in Daisy's eyes, and everything in him softened. During the few times he'd gone out on dates, he'd taken her with him, and his dates weren't thrilled.

They were even less thrilled when she made those dinners awkward by refusing to order food or asking to go home early. But his daughter was his priority, and he wanted that clear from the start. On all the previous dates, that was where it ended.

At the start.

Well, maybe he wasn't too enthusiastic about those dates, either. Finding a woman who'd compare to his Annika was…impossible. He glanced at the woman with him.

Maybe he never should've been looking for someone to compare to Annika. Maybe he should've been seeking someone uniquely special like Gwendolyn.

Shaking the thought away, he adjusted his daughter's braids. "It's okay if you need to take your time."

Based on the waitress's tapping her foot against the tile, she had a different opinion.

Her expression tender, Gwendolyn smiled at his girl. "How about I order a few appetizers and your dad does the same, and you try them and decide which ones you like. And maybe cocoa with marshmallows for you to drink. You liked the cocoa I made before, right?"

Daisy blinked a few times, then nodded. "Okay."

"Great." Gwendolyn beamed at the girl.

Dipping her head to her kitten toy, Daisy whispered something in its ear.

Gwendolyn was different from other women, and it warmed his soul. She realized his daughter wasn't *being* difficult. She just had a difficult life. So it wasn't only a beautiful frame that drew him to Gwendolyn. She seemed to have a beautiful heart, too.

Again, not a thought he should be having!

Since she'd worked with children for some time, maybe he could use her expertise. He loved Daisy with his whole heart, but he needed her to be able to integrate into society better. Besides, he'd remembered all too well how lonely he'd felt as a child. "Um, have you ever worked with challenging children?"

Her eyes narrowed a fraction. "Well, let's see. When I started nannying for the Clark family, Danica put glue on my chair. Then she added hot sauce to my already spicy chicken wings. Oh, and I had to chase her around the house, jumping over the toys scattered on the floor and doing my best not to collide with Dara."

"Oh, wow." He suddenly felt very grateful for Daisy's quiet nature. She could play with her dolls for hours and never got into any mischief. "And you stayed?"

Gwendolyn's lips tipped up as she sipped her tea, the tawny liquid reminding him of her eyes again. "I realized Danica just wanted to spend more time with her new mom and felt I was in the way. And Danica realized I wasn't going anywhere. I also have a habit to check chairs before I sit on them. I shared my spicy chicken wings with her. And thankfully, I can run rather fast and jump high, even if I don't look like it."

Huh.

His chest swelled further. So she wasn't just kind but tenacious, too. Great qualities for a mother. Whoa. "I'm sure they won't be able to find a nanny like you soon. Did you… Could you consider staying longer? I mean, at least until they find a replacement?" Though he had a feeling she couldn't be replaced.

Not in his heart.

"I do. For a week." She looked away.

His heart squeezed. Only a week. But with some people, even a few moments could be more important than a lifetime with others.

"I'm sure you'll be missed." And he didn't mean just by the family.

Her cocoa cup wobbled, and Daisy's lower lip stuck out. "Miss Gwendolyn, are you leaving soon?"

"Not soon, sweetheart." Gwendolyn smiled at his daughter, then looked up at him. "I'd die to be a part of a family like the Clarks."

Those words echoed in his ears long after she'd spoken them. And he'd lied to them. His stomach clenching, he briefly closed his eyes and rubbed the space pinching between them.

He refocused on Gwendolyn, wanting to know more about her. A plump bodyguard with a soft smile and adorable freckles, she intrigued him. And he told himself, the more he knew, the more opportunity he'd have to help her with the mysterious calls and messages, too. "I take it your family is not close-knit like theirs?"

Oh man. Of all the stupid things to ask someone who'd lost her father… Conner breathed in sharply the scents of barbecue and biscuits. What a faux pas!

Her eyes dimmed. Then she whispered, probably so Daisy wouldn't overhear. "I haven't spoken to my mother and sister in years. You know my father was shot. Grandpa died two years after that. That sums it up."

Compassion loosened the tightness in his stomach. He could relate to her all too well, though at least he still had his mother and his precious daughter. Gwendolyn seemed to be alone in the world.

He wanted to reach out to her, but he stopped himself. "I'm sorry. I was raised by a single parent, too. I never met my father." He cleared his throat. "Well, obviously. My stepfather turned out to be a cruel person." It was more than he'd told anyone in years, and he shouldn't have said that, considering Daisy was here.

"I'm sorry, too." Then Gwendolyn did something he didn't dare do.

She touched his hand. It was fleeting, and she pulled back because the waitress showed up with their orders. And still, he felt it. Oh, how he felt it.

Daisy observed the dishes with barbecue wings, cheese sticks, and stuffed mushrooms, and he tensed despite the enticing aroma.

But then she started happily munching, and his shoulders relaxed. The kindergarten teacher had called Daisy a spoiled kid because she was such a picky eater. But to him, she was a child who had difficulty navigating the world without her mother.

Gwendolyn whispered what he assumed was grace. He stilled. He'd grown up a believer, though his faith was more fledgling than strong. After Annika died and her parents refused to have anything to do with Daisy, that faith had withered altogether. He felt God had abandoned him like the people in his life did.

Now doubt needled. Annika would've wanted him to instill Christian values in their daughter.

"Daddy, eat." Daisy pushed the plate toward him. "Can we get more wings?" She thought a minute. "Pretty pretty please?"

He laughed, relieved. "We sure can."

As the evening progressed, so did the conversation.

Conner and Gwendolyn talked about their favorite music, movies, actors, books, friends, and shared the secrets of their childhoods they could say in front of Daisy. Gwendolyn told him how she'd dreamed about becoming part of the elite bodyguard company that traveled the world on important assignments, just like her father.

She used to pet-sit, too, and that part caused Daisy's acute interest. Gwendolyn told them stories about the animals' antics and showed a few funny cat photos. He'd never seen his daughter smile so much.

By the time their plates were cleared, he felt like he'd known Gwendolyn forever, and he didn't want to let her leave in a week. He didn't want to let her leave now, either.

But it was time. Reluctantly, he asked for the bill and bundled Daisy up in warm clothes.

As he opened the restaurant door, frosty air shivered over him, chilling him after the warmth inside. Gwendolyn lingered as her gaze swept over the parking lot before she stepped outside. Apprehension cooled him more than the fresh air.

His daughter needed stability. A globe-trotting bodyguard for a mother—if he could think that far—wouldn't give Daisy that, and he had to consider his daughter's interests before his own.

They walked outside, Gwendolyn's step brisker than he'd like, but then she looked at Daisy and slowed down. Stars twinkled around the gathering clouds, the crisp sky promising snow soon, and he wished the walk to Gwendolyn's truck was longer.

An older navy-blue sedan pulled out of the parking lot. One of its tinted windows was open just a slit, and a song from the eighties he couldn't name drifted to them. He tensed and stepped to shield Gwendolyn, either from the car or the memory.

She shook her head at him as if not accepting his protection and moved around him, her hand slipping into her purse. He had no doubt she was a quick draw, but his pulse quickened nonetheless.

Her gaze followed the car until it disappeared around the block. She paled so much her freckles stood out as starkly against her light skin as the bright stars contrasted the dark sky.

His teeth set on edge. "The same car?"

"Yes. More than that. That… that was my dad's favorite song," she whispered. Then she pulled her shoulders back, and her face took on a normal color.

He needed to do something about that. And he was going to see Gwendolyn as much as possible in the time they had left, even if it made it impossible not to fall all the way in love with her. She shouldn't be by herself.

He was contemplating how to ask her out again when Daisy tugged at Gwendolyn's sleeve. "Miss Gwendolyn, are we gonna see you tomorrow?" Daisy must have been taking those matchmaking lessons from her new friend seriously.

Conner wasn't complaining. He looked into Gwendolyn's eyes. "Are we? If you're free tomorrow, of course."

Her eyes widened. "Yes. No. I mean, I shouldn't...."

The Christmas lights decorating the restaurant eaves and wrapping around the trees reflected in her eyes, and once again, he couldn't decipher their expression.

Longing?

Caution?

Apprehension?

All of the above?

Probably all the feelings that whirled in him right now like a personal mini-blizzard. He ached for her to say yes because he couldn't wait to see her again.

"Well, if you can, would you like to see a movie sometime?" He glanced at his daughter, who looked up expectantly. "I mean, if you're both okay with fairy tales?"

"Yay, Daddy!" Daisy jumped up and down, the pompom on her hat bouncing in rhythm with her movements. Then she stuck her tongue out to catch a falling snowflake.

Hmm. He'd been right about the potential snowfall.

As Gwendolyn tipped her face to the sky, her eyelashes fluttered, delicate snowflakes covering them while more flakes danced around her lovely face. "Not only okay. I've started believing in them for the first time in my life."

He wished he could say the same.

Chapter Fourteen

THE NEXT DAY, Conner had mixed feelings as he brought Daisy for a playdate with Danica.

The Clark family mansion smelled of freshly baked cookies, and the children's laughter and voices filled it like sparkles filled some ornaments. Doubt wormed through him, and with it came his usual apprehension over whether Daisy would be okay there. A habit no amount of happy visits with her cousins seemed to break. And then in snuck joy strong enough to swell his chest as he thought of seeing Gwendolyn again.

Gwendolyn insisted he could trust Liberty with his daughter for the evening, and all he knew of his half-sister concurred with that.

But would either Liberty or Gwendolyn fully trust him again?

And he'd sensed hostility from that navy-blue sedan yesterday. He'd called Gwendolyn yesterday to wish her good night, and she'd told him she and Vera were investigating, as well as the police. He needed to talk to her more about it, in case he could help in any way. Thinking she might be in danger set his teeth on edge.

Liberty crouched before Daisy, who was staring at her feet.

Liberty's hair matched the most ridiculous Christmas sweater he'd ever seen, and she wore both proudly, even after Christmas. "It's high time you got to know your auntie Liberty better. We're going to play board games, and then Danica is going to bring her kitten."

As her head finally tilted up, Daisy's eyes lit up. Liberty had said the magic word. "A… a kitten?"

The woman's vigorous nod sent those emerald-hued curls flying around her face. "Would you like to stay with us while your daddy and Gwendolyn have coffee somewhere?"

Daisy scrunched her cute nose. "They can't have coffee here?"

Liberty's forehead wrinkled as if she didn't have an answer to that. So she just went for a nope.

Clearing his throat, Conner shifted his feet. "Sweetie Pie, you don't have to stay if you don't want to. Totally up to you." His daughter had always been clingy, but that was understandable under the circumstances, wasn't it?

Or maybe he was the one who'd been too clingy. He knew all too well how easy it was to lose someone he loved.

Never shy, Danica ran into the room, the small feet in magenta and forest-green socks—she must've taken fashion lessons from her auntie Liberty—tapping against the hardwood.

Danica snatched Daisy's hand while holding a squirming kitten with her other one. "Come on. We'll have fun. We always do."

"O–okay." Daisy finally nodded, her concentration now on the meowing pet.

"Good. We've got more Christmas cookies, too. And lots of games when you get tired of the kitten, though I doubt you'll get tired of that cutie." Liberty dared to wink at Daisy.

Then Liberty began herding the children to a cozy rug near that towering Christmas tree still generously decorated with those ornaments, some of which seemed homemade. Conner figured the holidays in this house lasted through New Year's Eve. It was never too early or too late for the Christmas spirit.

Everything in this house, from the many photos on the fireplace mantel to the plush toys littering the floor, screamed about love and care. Their father might not have been a great person, but the Clark family seemed to have chosen a legacy of love instead of resentment.

Something Conner should've done.

"I'll see you soon, Sweetie Pie." He hugged Daisy.

She hugged him back, filling his heart with tenderness. "Are you gonna be okay without me, Daddy?"

His eyes widened. Daisy worried about him? Usually, it was the other way around.

Liberty sauntered toward them and placed a hand on Daisy's shoulder. "Don't worry about your daddy. Gwendolyn will take care of him, right?"

Gwendolyn blinked as if she didn't expect it, then nodded and gave him a reassuring smile. "I… I will. And Daisy will be okay, too."

Danica grinned. "Yup. Daisy gonna be just fine. Come on. Games are not gonna play themselves. And here. You can pet my kitten." She handed Daisy the feline that Daisy hugged eagerly.

The kitten meowed but stopped squirming.

"What are you two still doing here?" Liberty gestured to the hall.

His pulse picked up at the chance to spend time with Gwendolyn alone, even if they were going to be at a public place. As much as he loved Daisy, some things couldn't be said in the presence of curious tiny ears.

As he helped Gwendolyn into her leopard-print coat, his fingers brushed against the smooth skin of her neck, and his pulse spiked even faster. She'd started affecting him too much.

Once she'd bundled up warm and cozy, he opened the front door for her, and the frosty air cooled his heated skin. Her gaze swept over the area outside before she stepped out. No surprise there.

"You look beautiful," he said as they walked to his rental truck.

She had this… soft glow about her he hadn't seen before. It was as if someone turned on the lights on a Christmas tree. It was beautiful already, but the lights further illuminated that beauty.

Or maybe, because he was getting to know her better, her inner beauty was shining through.

"Really? I mean, thank you." Her lips curved up slightly.

"Really." He opened the truck door for her. "I wish I could take you to a fancy restaurant to give you the romantic dinner you deserve."

Her gaze lingered on his face, heating his skin again despite the cold atmosphere. "I don't need a fancy restaurant. A simple meal is wonderful, especially when the company is great." Her cheeks pinked, and she climbed inside the vehicle.

He hummed a tune as he opened his door, settled into the driver's seat, and turned on the heat. Hmm. He didn't remember humming a tune since the time… since the time he'd left the ranch.

He started the engine.

Her gaze became pensive in the Christmas lights spilling into the windows. Was she thinking about her father? About the navy-blue sedan with tinted windows and snow-covered license plates? Or maybe about him not telling her the full truth?

"I could be a good listener." He glanced her way as he drove away from the mansion. "In fact, I'm a much better listener than a conversationalist."

He'd made an effort to go out a few times with the gallery patrons in those lonely years after losing Annika. But he wasn't one for small talk, and a lot of times, he'd found himself wishing he'd spent the time with his daughter instead. He missed working with horses, too.

Horses had never been ones for making small talk, either.

"I know it's silly to rehash the past. I mean, a quarter of a century has passed. But... I feel guilty I never managed to find the person responsible for Dad's death. That navy-blue car and other things keep reminding me of my mistake." Her shoulders slumped, and her voice lowered further with each word, the final one a painful whisper.

Empathy constricted his rib cage as they entered Cowboy Crossing. "You shouldn't feel guilty. But I understand the need for closure—more than you know. Maybe bouncing your ideas off someone would help. I volunteer."

"Thanks." Her voice grew stronger. "My friend is helping me, too. She's a former cop and a PI. But... How can we figure this out if even professionals failed to find the answer?"

"All we can do is try. That devastating feeling of helplessness gutted me after my wife died." Wow. He hadn't meant to share that. His shoulders inched upward, his whole body tensing as he turned onto the restaurant's street. "Why couldn't I prevent it? The same with my baby brother. With my stepsister. What was wrong with me? After Annika died, I stayed awake at night asking myself what I could've done differently. I... I started getting distracted. I felt lost."

"I'm so sorry." Her compassion loosened some of his tension. "What made you stop?"

His shoulders settling back where they belonged, he glanced at this wonderful woman beside him. "My daughter's scared eyes. I realized she was afraid something might happen to me, too. Sometimes we don't get answers. Sometimes we just need to move forward."

This... this connection between them...

Was he the only one who felt it? Or did it mean something to Gwendolyn, too?

He pulled up into a vacant spot and parked, then turned off the engine. He hurried around the truck and opened her door.

A car drove by and parked in another spot, and she tensed, following it with her gaze. Then her features relaxed as an elderly couple wobbled out of the vehicle, and Gwendolyn stepped out of his rental.

Inside, the restaurant smelled of barbecue ribs, french fries, and onion rings, the aromas hearty and homey. His stomach perked up at the prospect of being filled with the source of those scents. Holly displays still decorated tables, and soft carols drifted from speakers while the waitress took them to a vacant table.

He already knew Gwendolyn preferred to sit with her back to the wall, and he was right.

Yes, the Christmas season was about the birth of Christ, the most amazing gift from God, about grace and salvation. Annika had reminded him about it often. Still, all the years after Annika's death, he couldn't rejoice during this most wonderful time of the year, couldn't believe in God's miracles....

But this holiday season had become different. One of such miracles was right in front of his eyes. The miracle that would disappear in a week, however, and air whooshed from his lungs at the thought.

"Thank you." He took the menus from the waitress and handed one to Gwendolyn.

"Thanks. I'd like sweet tea with no sugar, please." Her gaze roamed the room as if she memorized every detail.

He asked for caramel macchiato, and the waitress left.

Gwendolyn's eyes turned pensive as she folded and unfolded the napkin. "I'm trying my best to find the answers in my father's murder."

He asked the most logical question, though she'd most likely asked herself that many times already. "Who could be interested in his death?"

She sighed as she studied the table as if she could find the answers on its holly-patterned tablecloth. "That's the thing. His profession was a dangerous one. Several times, he protected people from someone who had a grudge against them. I imagine, every time that 'someone' wasn't happy."

As she was looking down, her sun-kissed curls tumbled over her face, and her feathery soft lashes hid her beautiful eyes.

He barely resisted the urge to reach out and move aside the stray strands. He could imagine her skin to be smooth to the touch, and as his pulse spiked, concentrating on the conversation grew more difficult. "Okay. So they could develop a new grudge, this time against your father, shifting the blame onto him. Do you happen to have their names?"

She leaned back as the waitress brought their drinks, then took their orders, including his chicken wing takeout for Daisy.

Once the waitress left, Gwendolyn drew circles with her index finger on the tablecloth. The glass with her tea remained untouched so far. "I know a few cases, but I'm sure I don't know about just as many other cases." The circles she drew became abstract as her fingers trembled.

Compassion twisted his heart. This was difficult for her, and he ached to take her hands in his to show tangible support. He sipped his hot and flavorful drink to stop himself from reaching out to her. "That's a start."

Then she looked up. "Well, there's a guy named Ron Amspoker. He was an obsessive ex-husband who tried to shoot his ex-wife, a woman my father worked as a bodyguard for. She already took out a restraining order on Amspoker, but the man didn't get the message. When his plan failed, he shouted threats at my dad."

Conner brightened, sitting up straighter. "That's something already. Did the police check his alibi?"

She nibbled on her lower lip, and that drew his attention to her mouth, covered in shiny lip gloss. Looking at it caused all those unnecessary thoughts about kissing her. Argh. "Yeah. He had an alibi at the time."

Disappointment crumpled her lovely face, and this time he couldn't resist. He covered her hand with his, and pleasant tingles traveled along his skin from touching her hand.

Her eyes widening, she looked up at him, and her pink lips parted. But she didn't remove her hand, and a joyful jolt shot straight to his heart.

Did she still feel the same attraction toward him that he felt toward her? Did she think about a kiss? How could a man think rationally in a situation like this?

He did his best to gather his thoughts before they ran away like spooked horses. "Um, I heard sometimes alibis can't be relied on. Some people don't tell the truth when they vouch they were with the suspect when the crime was committed." He paused as he stroked her smooth, long fingers ever so slightly and was glad to hear her breathing quicken. "Granted, my knowledge is limited to TV crime dramas."

"Well..." She looked at their hands together on the table, then into his eyes, then at their hands again. "What were we talking about? Oh, right. Ron Amspoker had a strong alibi. He was in prison for aggravated assault causing bodily harm to his new girlfriend. I think the guards and cameras there can be trusted."

Huh. One couldn't argue with that. He didn't try.

The scents of barbecue and potatoes drifted to him as the waitress brought their order. Her cheeks pinking, Gwendolyn pulled her hand back, and he missed her warmth immediately.

As soon as the waitress left, Gwendolyn bowed her head and whispered grace.

After a hesitation, he said a half-hearted amen.

He hadn't regained his faith, but he started leaning in that direction. Amazing to think that, after everything that had happened to Gwendolyn, she remained a believer. She'd never preached to him, but simply seeing her example affected him.

He started on his barbecue ribs. But even yummy food couldn't distract him from the way the dim restaurant light played in her eyes, calling to him on a level that didn't seem possible. He had difficulty remembering what they had talked about.

Oh yes. Why, again, did he have the bright idea to talk about her father's murder on a date he'd wanted to be romantic and memorable for her? But he had to continue what he'd started. "What about other suspects?"

She sighed again, digging into her salad. "The second one had an even stronger alibi." She made sure to keep her voice low, though there weren't patrons right near them.

"Really?"

"He was dead at the time."

Chapter Fifteen

CONNER'S HAND with the rib stilled midair. "Huh."

"Anyway, according to Uncle John, my father's friend and colleague, the police didn't work too much on that version." Gwendolyn grimaced. "They thought my father wouldn't have gone to meet someone he couldn't trust in a deserted area in the middle of the night. I did find out that Amspoker asked one of the women who'd visited him in prison to meet with my father. She said she'd refused, and she had an alibi for the time of the murder. I asked Vera to verify that."

He hoped her facial expression wasn't an indication of how their date was going. "Okay, I see. It's a good thing being an investigator isn't my day job." The taste in his mouth turned bitter, and he did his best to chase it away with sweet caramel macchiato.

"No, that was a good question. Motive is important. Dad used to say that, with enough motive, people would find the opportunity. Or as the famous saying goes—where there's a will there's a way." Her mirthless chuckle fell flat as she savagely poked at her garden salad. "If you wonder who'd benefit from his death financially, that would be me."

Well, great. He frowned. He was losing his appetite, and she was massacring an innocent salad. Some date. This wasn't a fresh, romantic start he hoped for. "Maybe all this wasn't such a great idea."

"I later found out the police suspected me. But once they had proof I stayed in the restaurant where several people saw me while my father was killed, they let that version go too."

He pushed his half-empty plate aside, and she followed his gesture with a longing look. On a hunch, he opened the plastic container with the chicken wings he'd ordered for Daisy, glad he'd ordered extra.

"Please help yourself." He recalled the case with Danica. "They are barbecue. Not extra spicy."

She hesitated, then reached out for one with her fork. "Thanks." She cut it awkwardly.

"I don't know why, but ribs and chicken wings taste better when I eat them with my hands." He showed an example.

She brightened. "You know what? You're right." She started on the chicken wing with gusto, dipped it in the ranch sauce, and then even licked her fingers.

Blood rushed faster in his veins. Back to the case!

He took a deep breath of air filled with yummy scents.

What were they talking about?

Right.

"What about John? I'm sure your father would go to meet him, considering he was a friend and trusted partner. Did John benefit in any way?"

She wiped her hands on a napkin, lifted her tea glass, and studied him over the rim, her eyes sad. "Yes." She sipped her tea and set it back down. "His caseload became higher."

"Therefore, the profit margin, too." A pang sliced into him.

Man, he was bungling things tonight. He shouldn't have brought that up. By the looks of it, she needed to trust the guy, and it didn't seem like her circle of trust was big enough it could afford to shrink. Especially considering Conner had deceived her, too, by keeping his relationship to the Clarks secret so long.

Pain flashed in her eyes, and his guilt sliced even deeper this time. She tapped a sticky finger against her glass, smudging it. "You're right. But I'm sure the police checked his alibi. I'll talk to Vera about this angle. I was thinking about something else. That rebellious teen girl Dad was guarding in his last assignment… Brea seemed too compliant with what essentially was house arrest."

"You think she might've played a role? But isn't murder too drastic a method to get rid of him? Besides, one bodyguard could be replaced with another one." He pushed the wing container closer to her. He could easily order Daisy another one.

"She could've been desperate enough. Addiction is a strong motive. The girl's father, Dad's client, vouched for her, but he might've done it to protect his daughter. Then again, after Dad died, Mr. Cohen hired a new bodyguard for the girl, just like you said. So there goes that motive." She rubbed her face, smearing a bit of the barbecue sauce. "Either way, we can't ask Brea because she died from an overdose eight years after my father was shot." She paused. "But why would Dad go to meet with her in a deserted place?"

"She could've devised some plan to lure him in. Though I have no clue what that plan could've been." He had no clue how to think straight when Gwendolyn occupied his mind, either. "What about the girl's father, your dad's client?"

"I thought about it. That my father could've overheard something in the house that he shouldn't have." She rubbed her temples. "Vera is working that angle already. I don't know. I just don't know."

That speck of barbecue sauce in the corner of her mouth created unwanted thoughts. Was it his imagination, or did they crank up the heat in this place?

He snatched a napkin and handed it to her. "You have some

barbecue sauce on your face."

"Here?" She took the napkin and touched her cheek with it.

"Um, you missed it by an inch or so." Without a doubt, someone raised the temperature in the room. Staring at her mouth so much was not a good idea. Not a good idea at all.

"Here?" Her hand moved away from the speck.

Oh, for crying out loud!

If he looked at her mouth a moment longer, he'd never be able to stop thinking about kissing her.

He snatched another napkin and brushed it against her skin. Though innocent, the touch still sent a delightful wave through him. "Right… Right here."

A pinkish hue tinted her face. "Th–thank you."

He should've asked for ice water instead of caramel macchiato because the heat kept rising while Gwendolyn surely had no idea what turmoil she created inside him.

Their gazes met and held, and he felt like they were the only people in the world instead of a single couple in a restaurant becoming more crowded by the moment. His heartbeat went staccato. How would it feel to draw her close and brush his lips against hers, first slowly, then…

She looked away first and fiddled with the napkin again. "You must be wondering why I started looking into my father's death twenty-five years later."

He shifted back. That wasn't what he was wondering, but okay. He'd take any distraction. "The car that looks like your father's? The strange messages you're receiving?"

"Yes. Hearing the band he loved. Receiving a card with his favorite football team. I even got a phone call with a male voice calling me by the nickname my father gave me."

His eyes narrowed. It was worse than he'd thought. He didn't like it. He didn't like it one bit.

She sighed. "Some people think they see a ghost of a person. I see a ghost of a car, apparently. I'm not going crazy. These things *are* happening."

"I know. I've seen the car. I heard the music. Besides, I'd believe you even if I hadn't." He'd need to spend more time with her and be on the lookout for anything suspicious. Yet… he couldn't leave Daisy alone either, could he? But Gwendolyn shouldn't be alone with this happening.

"I'm amazed a wonderful woman like you is still single," he blurted out.

Real smooth, man.

He nearly slapped himself on the forehead. His dating skills weren't just rusty—they were corroded through. Even the horses would snicker or nicker or whicker at him if they heard him right now. He took a sip of his sweet drink to hide his faux pas.

But Gwendolyn gave a half shrug, obviously letting the remark slide. "Thank you for calling me wonderful. Dad didn't have a clue how to raise a daughter, so he raised me like a son. A son who'd take after him. He taught me martial arts, marksmanship, defensive driving, and alertness in all circumstances. Boys treated me like one of the guys. And then…" She paused, her eyes becoming misty as if she were remembering something that caused her pain.

He resisted the urge to grind his teeth and wished he could ask one of his half brothers how to talk to a woman. They should know. They all seemed happily married now.

After Annika's death, he'd never imagined he'd remarry, couldn't think he'd care for someone enough to risk the pain of possibly losing her.

But he cared about Gwendolyn already. He didn't know how to say it, so he simply reached out and touched the outline of her face with his fingertips, trying to show her how much she meant to him, how much he wanted to take away whatever made her suffer.

She gave a sharp intake of breath as her hazel eyes grew big and liquid like the amber tea in front of her.

He removed his hand, though he was eager to bring her closer. "You don't have to talk about it if it's difficult."

"The evening my father died… He wanted to spend it with me. Instead, I went on a date with a guy I just met." Her lips trembled, and her eyes dulled.

"So you blame yourself?" His heart sank. "Please don't. The only one at fault is the person who pulled the trigger."

"Well, I didn't date for a while after that. Years later, my neighbor seemed very much into me. We started dating, then got engaged. He had a great family, too. I heard jokes about mothers-in-law, but his mother treated me like the daughter she never had. He even had two adorable cats."

"The cats were important?" He raised an eyebrow.

Her lips twitched as she pushed the plate away. "Very. I felt I'd started healing. I'd found the people I belonged with. But it turned out to be the classic old story. Two weeks before the wedding, I discovered he was cheating on me with my friend—my maid of honor."

He felt like punching the guy. "It's his loss. Sorry that happened to you."

Okay, maybe not too sorry. She deserved better than a man who'd deceive her.

Great, that guilt just wouldn't stop needling him. Conner had deceived her, too.

"Thank you." She drained her tea as if suddenly very thirsty. "In the end, it might've been for the better. I realized I missed his mother and, well, the cats more than I missed him. Sometimes loneliness can make us do the wrong things. I ignored the signs when he canceled our dates at the last moment or stepped out to take calls. I craved having a family so much that I persuaded myself I was in love with the guy who could offer it to me. From then on, I decided never to be with someone to escape loneliness. I learned honesty in a relationship is essential."

He took in a deep breath of air filled with the scents of barbecue and freshly baked bread. "I'll never deceive you again."

She stared at him as if deciding whether to believe him. "I'm going to leave soon."

His heart sank. "I'd like to see you before then. As much as possible." For more reasons than one. "Daisy wants to see the ponies tomorrow. Join us, please."

Gwendolyn's lips curved up. "I do miss her. And… I'll miss you. Liberty is taking the children to the Children's Museum in the afternoon, so I'm free. I do have a meeting with my friend to discuss the investigation in the evening. But I can see you and Daisy tomorrow afternoon."

"Yes!" He grinned, his chest swelling.

Her phone beeped as if with an incoming text.

"Please feel free to check it. It might be important." Though he didn't want the evening to end, he gestured for the bill to the waitress.

Gwendolyn fished out her phone from her purse, and her eyes widened as she opened the text.

The air whooshed from his overfilled lungs, but he didn't ask her about what she'd read.

She volunteered that information. "I don't get it. It says, 'Your time is almost up. If you don't tell, I will.'"

Chapter Sixteen

CONNER KEPT HIS DAUGHTER close to him at the stable the next day, holding her hand tightly to make sure nothing happened to her.

Daisy looked around with big eyes, her mouth forming a perfect *O*. She looked extra cute in a pink helmet he'd bought her and tiny pink-embroidered cowboy boots. "Daddy, they are awesome. Can I pet them?"

He smiled. But, as much as he loved horses, his daughter's safety was his priority. "Not yet. Horses are prey animals, so they get spooked easily. Then they can buck or bite. Let them get used to us and our scent." At the sleigh ride, he'd waited for some time before approaching the snowflake Appaloosa.

"Oh. Okay, Daddy."

He finally got the chance to wear his Wranglers and cowboy boots, as well as a cowboy hat, and he felt so much more comfortable in them than in the suits he wore to work now.

Gwendolyn wasn't here yet, and his heart dipped. Was she late? Or did she change her mind?

He took the chance to get familiar with the place. It was his kind of place, after all. The stable was well kept and large with many stalls and a system to heat water in the winter to have a constant source of fresh water. Horses who in their turn seemed to study him and who looked healthy and content.

He breathed in the familiar scents of hay and leather again that calmed his frayed nerves, transferring him to his childhood when he'd still believed in the best in people. Longing disturbed him and yet, somehow, soothed him.

Argh. He didn't need to rehash everything he'd missed by walking away from the foreman job he'd worked so hard to get.

His appreciative gaze roamed over the magnificent horses who whinnied at him and Daisy. Thankfully, the animals didn't exhibit any signs of unfriendliness like flaring nostrils or pulled-back ears.

One of the horses attracted his attention, probably because he saw Snowflake in every snowflake Appaloosa he'd encountered as if he could return the one he'd had to let go. His father could've helped keep her instead of letting her be sold, eventually to the people who'd mistreated her, but he'd chosen not to.

Conner swallowed hard. He needed to let resentment go. If not for himself, then for his daughter's sake.

"I like this one." Daisy pointed at the snowflake Appaloosa who whinnied softly.

"Me, too," he admitted. "But let's start with ponies, okay?"

His girl nodded, her head bobbing in a funny way in that cute pink helmet. She trusted him, and his heart skipped a beat as he hoped she never lost that trust.

He moved in the direction of the Appaloosa as if drawn by a magnet. The horse brought her head up, legs poised as if ready to take off at a gallop. Her tail raised.

Uh-oh. He was scaring her.

He stopped and waited, making sure his posture and facial expression exhibited calm confidence without being threatening. He took a few long breaths to have that calmness he wanted to portray inside him, too. Horses could sense humans' moods, could read facial expressions, and didn't like being around nervous people. Especially when those people were strangers.

Establishing trust was paramount.

After a few minutes, the tail moved down, and the horse's legs were all firmly on the ground. The head lowered. Good. Her posture was getting more relaxed.

He stifled his nostalgia. Placement mats evenly covered the cement floor. The bedding looked clean, so the place was mucked regularly. Mangers raised from the ground to keep the hay from getting soiled waited for feeding time. But the most important part—the horses looked healthy and muscular. They clearly spent most of the year on the pasture and were taken out daily and exercised in winter.

They looked… happy.

He'd like to work here.

He pushed the thought away. He had a different life and different obligations now.

"Let me take you to the ponies." Gwendolyn's voice was soft, and yet it startled him.

He whirled around, his heart beating fast. So much for calmness.

Daisy grinned and waved at Gwendolyn, omitting the exuberant greeting she usually gave the nanny, probably due to the lesson not to be loud around horses. Gwendolyn smiled and waved back at the girl.

"Thanks." He gave one more glance at the snowflake Appaloosa as if he needed to commit the image to memory. Then he and Daisy followed Gwendolyn.

She led him to a separate smaller building sheltering Shetland ponies and Norwegian Fjords. The latter probably had been bought for when the children grew up. Fjords were smaller than other breeds but larger than ponies. Like the other stable, this well taken care of place impressed him.

"The family bought them for when children want larger horses." Gwendolyn seemed to read his mind. "Also because the Clarks are running a program of summer and winter camps for foster teens now."

He closed his eyes, then opened them. He should've told them from the beginning who he was. He should have! What a miracle they accepted him and he'd received an open invitation to visit any time, though the guys didn't seem too happy.

Daisy looked around, wide-eyed. "Wow! And I can choose any one?"

"I've brought the children here before, so I'm somewhat familiar with the place and animals. I'd suggest..." Gwendolyn pointed at a pony to the left. "He has a more mild character, I was told."

Perfect. He placed a protective hand on Daisy's shoulder. "Ponies are often playful but can be naughty, as well." A few of them neighed as if to confirm it, but then he winced from a sting of guilt for stereotyping ponies. "How about you groom him first? It's good for the pony and would be a great way to bond."

Gwendolyn's gaze became pensive as if she thought about something else. "Establishing a bond is important. Even essential."

He studied her. "But then it's difficult when one has to break that bond."

She looked away, and he winced. Just like him, she'd had to break the bond with the people who mattered to her, and he didn't want to remind her. And he didn't want to lose her, but their bond would have to be broken in less than a week.

His hand moved toward her, but before he could say anything, Daisy tugged on his coat sleeve. "Daddy, where's the bucket with brushes?"

"Brushes? Oh yes, right." He glanced over the stable.

"I'll get it." Gwendolyn left.

While she was away, he and Daisy approached the pony.

"Horses have blind spots right in front of them and behind them. So never, never approach them from behind. Remember they were prey animals, so move forward slowly to show you're no threat. Imagine you're a pony. You want to feel safe."

"I'm no threat, Daddy." Daisy grinned up at him. "I'm a friend."

He let the pony adjust to the girl first, watching the body language carefully. The pony's tail was down, and his posture peaceful.

"Here we go." Gwendolyn returned with a bucket filled with grooming essentials.

The pony greeted her like an old acquaintance, and it soothed something inside Conner. People said animals could often sense the human's character, and he agreed.

Pleased they had many grooming tools, he picked up the rubber currycomb first. "This one is to remove shedding hair, dried sweat, and mud. Do it like this." He moved the rubber comb in circles.

"Okay, Daddy." Daisy gently rubbed the pony in circular motions as she took the currycomb. "Like that?"

"Yes."

Gwendolyn picked up the rubber mitt. "I'll work with this one."

"It's best to use it on the legs and head," he said. "Those parts are more sensitive."

"I know." Her lips curved up. "I'll be gentle. My grandpa used to work on a ranch, so he took me with him from time to time. I found it easier to relate to horses than to people." True to her word, she gently removed debris first from the pony's head, then legs.

So they had even more in common than he'd realized. A woman after his own heart.

"Daddy, I'm done!" Daisy placed the currycomb aside. "Now what?"

"We'll use the dandy brush." He took a brush with long bristles from the bucket. "See how the rubber brush brought up dirt to the surface? We need to remove it. Remember to follow the direction in which the hair grows. I'll do this part, okay?" As Gwendolyn and Daisy nodded, he removed dirt in quick movements.

Daisy grinned, and Gwendolyn smiled at him. He enjoyed this mundane task more than he'd enjoyed elegant exhibition openings with champagne he'd never liked.

"Now this, right?" Daisy picked a body brush with much softer bristles.

He nodded, relishing every moment. "You're learning fast. Yes, we'll polish the coat." He demonstrated how with long careful movements. "But you know how you get ticklish under your armpits? A horse can get ticklish on the belly near their flanks."

Daisy giggled as if he tickled her already. "Really? Huh. They get ticklish, too."

The pony moved his head up and down as if nodding.

"He said yes! He said yes!" Daisy screamed.

Several ponies neighed nervously.

Gwendolyn pressed a finger close to her lips. "Shhh. They are afraid of loud noises. Anything they don't recognize can create an urge to flee."

"Oh." Daisy blinked. "I don't want them to run away. I'll be careful. Let me shine the pony."

Conner didn't think *shine* was the right term, but no reason to correct his daughter. He exchanged glances with Gwendolyn, and she smiled as if she thought the same thing.

He knew then this would be one of the best days he'd had in years.

Once Daisy was done, he reached for the clean cloth. "Okay, time for—"

"Extra shine?" Daisy said excitedly, then in a much lower

tone, "Oops."

He chuckled. "That, too. But we'll also dampen a cloth to wash around the eyes, ears, and nose." He started on the nose and let Daisy do the rest. The pony seemed quiet and timid, and Conner wished he and Daisy had more time to get to know him better. But then, it took years to get to know a horse well, often a lifetime.

"What about his forehead and chin?" Daisy asked once she finished, and Gwendolyn hurried to rinse the cloth.

"Good question. We'll use the face brush for that. See how it has soft bristles? Don't forget about his jaw and throat-latch areas, too." He did it for the most part and let Daisy finish the job while Gwendolyn cleaned the brushes.

"We're not going to bathe him, are we?" Gwendolyn stroked the star on the pony's forehead.

"Hmm, no. It's too cold for that right now."

"Daddy, we gotta do something." Daisy picked up the sponge.

"Yes, we *gotta*. Run it under the warm water, and we'll clean his face, neck, and where the saddle and girth had been."

Then came the mane and tail. They used the detangler first, making sure not to pull any hair out, and then the girls had fun braiding the mane.

"Daddy, how old was the oldest horse who ever lived?" Daisy asked while braiding, a happy grin on both Daisy's and the pony's faces.

"Sixty-two. You're doing a great job, Sweetie Pie." Maybe being around horses could have the same healing effect on his daughter as it had on him and Gwendolyn. Daisy seemed happy here, and that made him happy, too. At least, for now.

He recalled the work on the gallery he had to do online in the evening. Duty called—sometimes literally. So this peaceful respite wouldn't last long. On the other hand, his mother had sounded upbeat as he'd checked on her every day, and he was grateful.

"Why are those horses"—Daisy pointed at the Fjords—"not

like the ones we saw before?" Apparently, her curious mind never rested.

"They are different breeds." Gwendolyn slowed down on braiding so Daisy could keep up. "There are around four hundred breeds of horses, actually."

"I'm impressed you know that," he whispered to Gwendolyn.

"All these horses are tame, and mustangs are wild, right?" Daisy grinned at the work of her hands.

"Mustangs are domestic horses that escaped," he said. "The only wild horse is the Przhevalsky horse that originated in Mongolia. By the way, braided horses were once a status symbol, but it also helped keep the reins from tangling up."

Gwendolyn smiled as she finished braiding. "I'm impressed you know all this, too."

He shrugged as if it were no big deal. "I'm a man of the horse."

Whoa. A low breath slid from his lungs. How true that was!

"The pony looks beautiful. You've done an awesome job." Gwendolyn quietly high-fived Daisy.

Daisy beamed.

"You're so great with her," he said as he cleaned the grooming tools.

She gave the same nonchalant shrug he'd done. "Turns out, I'm a children's person."

If you're a children's person, then why do you work as a bodyguard?

He didn't ask it, only nodded. "That you are." He used the hoof pick to clean the hooves, then had Daisy wash her hands and put on her gloves.

Then Gwendolyn tensed. Her eyes narrowed, and she looked at the entrance as if she heard something. He listened intently and heard steps in the crunching snow and voices outside.

Liberty and Danica walked inside, and a few ponies neighed in greeting.

"Who is ready for riding lessons?" Without waiting for an answer, Liberty marched to the ponies, and her gaze roamed over them as if giving a quick assessment.

"I am!" Daisy jumped up and down. Then her hand flew to her mouth. "Oops."

"It's okay." Liberty glanced back and winked at her. "But first, your pony will need riding gear." She pointed toward the saddles, bridles, reins, halters, and so on.

"Right." He wished he'd bought Daisy a saddle that would fit her exactly. Maybe one day… He brushed aside the thought.

Ponies were okay with him, but with time, Daisy would want to mount a horse, and he was afraid for her to fall. He'd always be afraid for her to fall. She was his entire world.

He inspected the gear, glad to find it clean and in great condition.

Once the pony they'd groomed was ready and outside, Liberty took the rope. "I'll take care of Daisy and Danica. You two can just—"

"Take a walk!" Danica announced, her grin a bit too innocent not to look suspicious.

He eyed Daisy as he placed his hand on the reins, torn between his desire to spend time with Gwendolyn and his worry for his daughter. "Will you be okay?"

"Daddy, please! I'm not a baby." Daisy scrunched her nose in her funny way.

He lifted her up and placed her in the saddle. "To me, you'll always be my baby."

"Daddy!"

"Okay, Sweetie Pie. Be careful." While he was drawn to Gwendolyn, it took an effort to let the reins go with his child.

"We will be." Liberty gave him a reassuring look.

"Don't worry. We'll stay close." Gwendolyn studied him.

"Now, why don't we go visit the Appaloosa you liked so much? I'm sure she could use some grooming and bonding, too."

So she'd noticed.

They returned to the other stable, and this time, he brought the bucket with the cleaning tools. The Appaloosa didn't show any signs of distress as he approached her but studied him with curious eyes. He stood in close proximity, then moved his hand toward her. The mare didn't move, so he stroked the smooth coat between her eyes, his lungs filling with hope.

He didn't say a word, but he'd learned that, with horses, one often didn't need to.

"She welcomes you," Gwendolyn whispered.

Who'd think a simple task could soothe a soul so much?

As he started with the rubber currycomb again, he brought up the topic that didn't soothe him at all. "Any more scary calls or ghost-car sightings?"

She picked up another tool. "Not yet. Let's… let's talk about something else for now."

"Okay, but… Can I join you in the meeting with Vera to discuss the investigation tonight? Maybe my fresh eye could be useful."

She moved the brush in careful motions over the mare's coat, then nodded. "Okay. I… I reached out to my sister. She's coming here soon. We've been apart for over three decades. You reuniting with your family helped me realize how much I missed mine."

"I'm glad." And he was. He wanted the best for Gwendolyn.

They worked in companionable silence, and he was taken back to many years ago. Then he blurted out, "One of my dreams was to become a trainer for mistreated horses. To try to heal their broken spirits." Maybe in that process, he could heal his, too.

She leaned toward him, the gentle scent of her perfume mixing with the scent of hay. "It's not my right to say, but you should go live your dream. You love horses and have a talent with them."

Longing stirred him with a stronger force than he'd expected. "I… I can't. My mother might need my help. And I have a responsibility to run the art gallery. It meant a lot to Annika. And it's Daisy's legacy."

Gwendolyn placed the brush aside and touched his hand, sending waves of excitement through him. "You know what would mean even more to her and to your daughter than you running the gallery? For you to be happy. To do what you love."

Her words took root, but he shook his head, then picked up a rubber mitten and worked on the Appaloosa's legs. "It's not about me. I've already had managers mess up several exhibitions. I can't risk it again."

She looked him in the eyes, without blinking. "I understand you studied a lot to manage the gallery—you've given years of your life to make sure it's the best it can be. And I understand you had bad experience with the people you hired to run the gallery before. But there are good managers out there, too. Why don't you find one?"

When she looked at him like that, as if she cared like few people had done before her, rational thought became difficult. "The assistant manager I have now is better than the others were. But the gallery is my responsibility. I can't be selfish and walk away from my obligations."

Like his biological father had walked from his responsibility. Like his mother had emotionally checked out when her husband had mistreated his daughter. Not to mention his stepfather who instead of caring for his child had abused her. Like they'd let his baby brother die.

Gwendolyn shook her head so vigorously, her sun-kissed curls went flying. "It's not selfish. God gives us a talent for a reason. The way you talked to me about horses… You have a light in your eyes that you don't have when you talk about the gallery. And when you talk *to* horses, even when you don't say anything, you come alive. Training horses is your talent. That's what you were born to do."

"I can bring Daisy with me to the gallery often enough. I'm still afraid to bring her to the stable where she might get hurt."

She nodded as if he'd said something she'd suspected. "That's exactly it. You're holding on tightly to your daughter because of what happened to your wife, your stepsister, your baby brother. Too many losses for one person. But you have to let Daisy breathe, live, and learn to do things on her own. You can't be by her side twenty-four-seven."

"I'm doing my best to be a good father," he whispered as he managed to tear his gaze from her face and suppressed the urge to check on his daughter. He could hear Daisy giggle from here.

Why couldn't Gwendolyn understand something so simple?

"You are a great father. But you'll be an even better father when she sees you happy." Gwendolyn hesitated, then continued while she worked with one of the brushes. "Once, Liberty returned from spending all night in the stable with a horse who'd had colic, totally exhausted and bruised. I asked her how she could do it. I mean, colic, deworming, checking for ticks and other parasites in summer, pulling a young calf when the cow had difficulty birthing…"

"What did she say?" he asked when Gwendolyn paused, then returned to their task. Maybe he needed this bonding process more than the Appaloosa did.

"She said she loved her job so much that even unpleasant tasks didn't bother her. She. Just. Loved. It. The same way when I did the job assignments I didn't like, everything irritated me. So… What kind of father would Daisy rather see?"

The horse neighed as if seconding the question.

"I can't fail another person like I failed Annika, Tara, my brother, Snowflake." Pain sliced through him.

"You didn't fail them."

He winced at her conviction. She didn't understand.

He was done grooming, and he couldn't be near the horses in a state of distress, so he asked Gwendolyn to go outside. Besides, he needed to see that Daisy was okay. He took a few deep breaths to ensure he was calm while he stayed close to the horse.

He'd make sure to find out her name. And he wanted badly to get to know her better, as well as other horses. For many years, he'd found relationships with horses much more rewarding than with people. He gave the mare a long look, hoping it wasn't goodbye yet.

Then he and Gwendolyn cleaned the tools and their hands and stepped out.

With Liberty leading the pony on a rope and Daisy sitting comfortably in her saddle, Conner and Gwendolyn walked on the crisp snow, and he told her things he'd only told the horses before. About Tara's disappearance.

Then about Annika's accident.

"If only I didn't insist on us going out that evening, Annika would still be alive. If I was stronger at the time, I could've protected Tara." He closed his eyes, then opened them. "You see a ghost car. I don't see the ghost of Tara, but I feel her presence. Isn't it crazy? The more years pass, the less I want to believe she's gone."

"It's not crazy at all."

"Throughout the years, I saw a few cars following me. I mean, nothing ever happened, so I stopped worrying about it. Then the day of the accident…" He didn't want to relive the memories, but he needed to tell someone. After all, he didn't have horses to talk to any longer.

Gwendolyn touched his hand as her steps slowed on the crunching snow, which probably wasn't easy for her because she seemed to be on the higher alert in open spaces. "Take your time. Do you think someone could've caused the accident?"

"No, that's not it. A cat dashed in front of us, and Annika swerved off the road to avoid hitting the cat. She lost control of the vehicle and hit a tree instead. I... I lost consciousness. I only remember the scent of burning rubber, the pain, the sound of my own scream. I came to in the ambulance." He paused, trying to figure out how to explain the rest.

"See? You couldn't have saved her. You should stop blaming yourself. And, for what it's worth, I'd probably swerve to avoid hitting a cat, too." Soft and soothing, her voice poured over him like a healing balm to his wound. "It wasn't your fault."

He looked at his daughter in the distance, indeed the best legacy he could have from Annika.

"Later, the police told me they received a call from someone named Calista Smith. The person driving by saw the accident. Neither my wife nor I were thrown out of the car. Calista Smith somehow pulled us out before the car exploded. Annika died before she made it to the hospital. I survived with broken bones." His heart was crushed like his bones had been.

"That was heroic on her part. And I'm so sorry it happened to you." Compassion laced Gwendolyn's words.

He breathed in the frosty air. "I tried to find her. I wanted to thank her. I mean, I don't even know how a woman could pull me out of the vehicle." He winced, hoping he didn't sound sexist.

"Must be a very strong woman. Probably a surge of adrenaline helped."

"Well, I couldn't find her. A person with that name didn't exist." He'd been grieving too much to question it at the time, but he'd started searching for an explanation later. The explanation he'd come up with sounded crazy to him.

"Maybe someone didn't want the praise." Gwendolyn paused, then stepped closer. "I'm grateful to God that He spared you. That Daisy has you to raise her. That you exist."

He couldn't help it. He stroked Gwendolyn's fingers, causing her eyes to widen. "Have I told you lately how amazing you are?"

Her lips twitched up a little. "I'm not amazing. I'm just a woman who wants you to be happy. Even…" She swallowed hard. "Even if I'm not there to witness it."

He placed a kiss on her cheek, breathing her enticing scent. "Ditto."

Though he'd much rather have her witness it. He wanted to find a way for them to be together. To take that risk.

Her eyes turned liquid again, and neither one of them said a word.

Then she whispered, "As for the legacy… The best legacy we can give to the people who came before us and would come after us is the legacy of love and happiness."

CHAPTER SEVENTEEN

IN THE EVENING, Conner did his best to ignore the unease in his stomach as he had to leave his daughter with an unusual babysitter. He followed Gwendolyn and Vera Clark to one of the mansion offices. "Um, are you sure Daisy will be okay with your husband?"

Vera laughed. "You don't have any reason to worry."

He wasn't a hovering parent now. He *had* reason to worry. Up till now, he'd only left Daisy with Gwendolyn or Liberty. Maverick, one of the Clarks' golden boys, was famous for being a reckless race car champion before his retirement. That image didn't go great with babysitting skills—right?

While Conner understood that discussing a murder case wasn't for curious little ears, he glanced back, ready to scoop up Daisy if she needed him.

The picture in the living room stopped him, and his jaw slackened. Was this the guy who'd worn dashing tuxedos to parties or slick racing uniforms to the track?

Maverick sat at a small round desk, rocking the baby in one arm. Nearby, Danica and Daisy were hard at work, adding large fabric triangles to a headband, which probably meant cat ears. And glitter. Lots of glitter.

A kitten curled up on the fourth chair, peacefully asleep.

Daisy was so concentrated on the task, the tip of her tongue stuck out just like the kitten's. Unlike his daughter, whose white socks and cowboy boots matched, Danica wore one azure blue sock and one matching the orange cat ears she was making. Her shoes were pink and orange, respectively, as if she'd gotten dressed without looking. Conner had braided Daisy's hair that morning, but Danica wore her chestnut hair in messy waves.

"Uncle Maverick, this ear doesn't want to stay glued." Danica scowled at the offending piece.

"Let me help you." Maverick adjusted the piece to the headband, then placed it on the girl's head. "All done. Looks beautiful."

Daisy placed hers on her head and smiled shyly.

"Yours looks great, too." Maverick rocked the baby again, then reached for the markers. "Now, who's up for having whiskers painted?"

"Me! Me!" both girls squealed.

Vera stopped and followed his gaze. She wore her long blonde hair in a braid and had the happy glow of a woman content with her life. "Just in case you wondered, Danica didn't get dressed in a hurry. She likes that style. She must be taking on my sister-in-law's love for bright colors."

She didn't need to say which sister-in-law.

Daisy grinned at him, then waved, and he waved back before she returned to her task.

He caught Gwendolyn's gaze, understanding and reassurance in her eyes. "I told you. Daisy will be fine with Maverick and Danica."

Okay then.

Conner entered the room as joyful sadness shivered over him. He wanted Daisy to do well among her peers, had worried when she hadn't. But a tiny pang said she didn't need him quite so desperately any longer.

"Daisy still loves you and needs you," Gwendolyn whispered as if reading his mind. "She always will."

But maybe it's time for you to live your own life....

Gwendolyn didn't say it, but he could guess it.

He notched his chin up a bit.

A window hugged by creamy curtains allowed warm light into a room sparse in furniture but rich in electronics. A whiteboard occupied one of the caramel-hued walls while local maps covered another. Twin oak bookshelves contained tomes on forensics. Three oak chairs matched the desk in simplistic sturdiness. Small bronze equine statues serving as bookends and an antique bronze lamp with a matte shade offered the only decoration.

Vera moved to the oak desk with a computer, printer, and stack of folders. "My husband turned out great with children. He even agreed to a fingernail painting session after he puts the baby down for a nap, so don't be surprised later. That said, I declined Danica's request for my lipstick this morning because even Maverick's patience might have its limits." Vera gestured for them to sit down.

Conner pulled out a desk chair for Gwendolyn, and when she sank onto it as if feeling weak, his gut tightened.

Gwendolyn shook her head. "I hate to break it to you, but the lipstick might've been for the kitten. Don't worry, though, I explained things to the girls."

Despite her easygoing tone, tension pulled her features. Discussing her father's murder again must be gut-wrenching, and as his hand moved toward her nearly on its own accord, he had to shove his hands into his pockets to stop from reaching out.

Her face went intentionally blank. "Thank you for doing this for me, Vera. Especially now that you retired from investigations."

Vera propped her hip against the simple desk. "I guess we always want what we don't have. Or maybe Jenna's passion for investigation is contagious. Either way, I was excited to work on this case. I missed helping people find truth and justice." Then her eyes dimmed. "I mean… Sorry. I know this is painful for you."

"Don't be sorry." Gwendolyn, the kind soul that she was, managed a wobbly smile. "You're helping me."

"Well, helping myself, too. Jenna and I want to start a detective agency. This case could be the beginning for us."

Gwendolyn's lips twitched up a little more. "I'm glad your sister-in-law returned home and found happiness with the ranch foreman."

A gleam appeared in Vera's eyes as she tipped her imaginary hat. "What can I say? We love cowboys here."

He sure hoped that statement applied to Gwendolyn. Not that… that he was a cowboy any longer. He drew in a deep breath to lift the sudden weight from his chest.

Then Gwendolyn sobered as she patted the folders. "Now, I've used a lot of your time already. Let's get to the case. It's going to be difficult to find the culprit twenty-five years later. Besides, unlike now, there was no camera footage, no passersby with cell phone cameras to record something useful."

Vera spread her hands. "I know! Those were prehistoric times. Anyway, that's when human connections become more important than ever. I pulled some strings, and those strings pulled more strings. And then my grandmother did the same. Well, she mostly pulled at her current boyfriend, who is the chief of police here, and he did the rest."

"That sounds like a lot of pulling." He couldn't help himself.

"No kidding." Vera opened the top folder and removed several photos. "My sister-in-law, Heather, searched the web. It's great to have an IT person in the family. She was glad to be useful. Her husband barely allows her to do anything since she's pregnant with the twins. Hmm, I hope she covered her tracks well."

He preferred not to ask why Heather needed to cover her

online tracks, and neither did Gwendolyn.

"If it gets too much, let me know." Vera handed Gwendolyn the folder. "I got ahold of some police files and traveled to the crime scene, too."

Gwendolyn paled and bit into her lower lip as she looked at the photos, her freckles becoming more pronounced.

He squeezed her forearm, wishing he could spare her the pain. "If it's too much…"

The hollowness in her eyes as she looked up emptied something inside him. "I need to do this."

Her gaze assessing, Vera folded her arms across her chest. "Maybe it's best if I just tell you the results."

"I need to do this." Gwendolyn's voice grew stronger.

He squeezed Gwendolyn's arm again and backed off. He could respect that determination.

"Okay then." Vera wrote "The Crime Scene" on the board and started pinning up photos with magnets. "Black-and-white ones are from the file. Colored ones are current. Amazingly, that property's still abandoned. No one was interested in it, except as you can see, the homeless and people using it as a place to buy drugs."

Her eyes narrowing, Gwendolyn sat straighter, and a blankness overcame her as if she did her best to disassociate herself.

The last thing Conner wanted was for Gwendolyn to see how her father bled out on the asphalt. Apparently, he wasn't alone in that. Vera seemed to leave out the more gruesome photos.

"The time of death was between eight p.m. and ten p.m." Vera wrote on the board as she spoke. "A homeless woman stumbled on him and reported it to the police. He was shot from close range. Suspiciously close."

"Which means he knew his shooter." Gwendolyn spoke without emotion.

"Trusted him or her, too. Now, an interesting part. The

weapon was a Glock. Forensics identified the bullet they extracted from his body as having been fired from a weapon registered to him."

Gwendolyn gasped. "How did I miss this important part? The police must've told me." She covered her face with her hands. "Was I… was I so out of it I didn't remember?"

He moved his chair closer, his heart breaking for her. She might've suppressed the memories. "Gwendolyn, it's not your fault." He tried to hug her. But she stayed stiff in his embrace, so he let her go.

When Gwendolyn looked up, her eyes were blank. "So he was killed from his own gun. Could he… could he have killed himself?"

Vera shook her head. "The gun was found in his hands, but no gunpowder residue was on his skin. The police checked the woman who'd found him, and there was no residue on her skin, either. And I imagine it would be difficult for her to get close enough to him to pull out *his* gun if she wanted to shoot and rob him. He was a person who was used to being on high alert, too."

Gwendolyn nodded as if still processing the information. "Okay, so let's move on to the real suspects then."

"Right." Vera wrote "SUSPECTS" on the board in large letters. "I might be grasping at straws here."

"I understand," Gwendolyn whispered.

First, Vera pinned the photo of a young blonde girl smiling into the camera. "Here we have your father's client's daughter, Brea Cohen. I doubt she'd shoot your father because she'd only get a new bodyguard. But the desire to get a fix could be stronger than logic. Sadly, the girl is dead."

She paused, and they all mourned the loss of a young life.

"That's why I wanted to talk to her father and your dad's client, Mr. Cohen." Then Vera pinned the photo of a man with white hair and a matching unkempt beard. His devastated pale eyes seemed to look beyond the horizon.

Gwendolyn hugged her arms around her middle. "That's the photo of the sculptor from the flyer. He can be a suspect, too—if Dad overheard or saw something in the house, something the man wouldn't want known. Mr. Cohen is also opening an exhibition soon, after decades of silence. I mean, I'm glad if it's a sign of healing from the tragic loss of his daughter."

"But why now?" Conner rubbed his forehead.

Vera scrawled a question mark near the photo. "Yes, why now? He and his daughter were each other's alibi for that night, which doesn't inspire confidence. The female employee who was supposed to watch Brea's room at night confirmed the girl's alibi, too. But something is more interesting. Mr. Cohen is currently nowhere to be found. His housekeeper said he left for a Christmas vacation. The first one since she started working for him seven years ago. He told her he was going to visit his cousin in Delaware. The cousin hadn't heard from him for a year."

Whoa. Conner's jaw tightened. "I don't like it."

Vera pursed her lips. "Me, either. I'll keep searching." Then she pinned the photo of a clean-shaven man with green eyes. "Ron Amspoker."

Women might find the guy attractive.

Conner eyed Vera. "I understand he has an alibi, but he could've hired, bribed, threatened, or cajoled someone to do his dirty work."

"I'm following up on his communications from prison at the time as much as I can. Which brings me to Odetta." Vera added a photo of a woman with short chocolate-hued hair and a bright smile. "Odetta's alibi was confirmed. However, the restaurant where she worked wasn't that far from the abandoned warehouse where your father was shot."

"So still a suspect." Gwendolyn grimaced. "And now, Odetta has way more to lose than she did then. Could she... could she become dangerous?"

A shiver ran down his spine. She had a point. If Gwendolyn stood between Odetta and her newfound happiness, Odetta could decide to take desperate measures.

Frowning, Vera straightened the photo. "We need to make sure you're never alone. And I might find someone to shadow Odetta, to be on the safe side."

Gwendolyn's phone rang, and he tensed. Could this be that mysterious caller again? He shifted closer, wanting to yank the phone and tell that person what he thought about those threats.

But, as Gwendolyn fished her phone out of her pocket, she said, "It's Uncle John."

"Take it, please," Vera and Conner said in unison.

Gwendolyn put the call on speakerphone.

"Hello, Gwendolyn." A loud baritone boomed from the speakers. "Just wanted to make sure you're okay. The invitation to come over and spend time with me and my children and grandchildren is still standing."

"I'll be fine. Thank you, though."

"Just be careful." Hurried words followed a pause. "Also, I–I remembered something. Shortly before his death, your father mentioned a woman who called him. She had an alcoholic name."

Gwendolyn blinked. "Excuse me?"

"Well, like Tequila. No, not that."

"Brandy?"

"Yes! That one." A deep exhale traveled down the line. "I don't know about all of your father's cases. It might not be much help, but—"

"I appreciate it."

"I'll let you go. I'll call if I think of anything else." He disconnected.

For a few seconds, Gwendolyn stared at her phone as if trying to remember if she'd seen the name Brandy anywhere in the files.

Then her gaze moved from Vera to Conner. "Does this help us any?"

"It might." Vera wrote the name on the board with a marker.

Head tipped down, arms tight around herself, eyes closed, Gwendolyn obviously strained her memory.

"Maybe it was someone from years before the murder happened." He wanted to reach to her, help her, but, as much as he ached to see her at peace, he was helpless to make it happen.

Then Gwendolyn lifted her head and snapped her fingers. "Oh, I know. Three years before he died, a case nearly wrecked my father. His client swindled his business partner out of their business. Dad didn't know about it before signing up. Well, that business partner was so devastated he tried to shoot dad's client. Dad had to open fire to protect the client, fatally injuring the guy. Dad felt guilty, even offered assistance to the family, but they refused."

Conner's frown deepened as he leaned forward. "Let me guess. The wife's name was Brandy."

"No, daughter's. She was in bad shape after losing her father. She would've been eighteen at the time of Dad's death." Gwendolyn sighed.

He nodded. "Time to find her then."

"I'll do my best." Vera placed her marker on the desk. "I'll need the last name and any details you have, please."

"I'll email them to you." Gwendolyn's lower lip trembled.

"Um…" Vera glanced out the window, clearly uncomfortable. "There's also that guy you were supposed to have dinner with that evening. I'm having difficulty finding him. I might have a suspicious mind, given my line of work, but I don't believe it's a coincidence."

Sitting up straighter, Gwendolyn gasped. "You think he might've been an accomplice?"

Vera nodded. "That's a possibility."

A shudder went through Gwendolyn.

Hurting to see her like this, Conner reached for her hands. "It's going to be all right. I… I'll pray for you."

Her lips slid open, forming a little *O*. "What? You said you haven't prayed since your wife's death."

"I…" He drew a deep breath of her gentle perfume, looked into her kind tormented eyes. "I'm going to try for you."

Vera cleared her throat. "Maybe that's enough for today."

"No." Gwendolyn pulled her hands back, her mouth setting and her chin lifting. "Let's continue."

"Okay then." Vera pinned another photo under Suspects. With a receding hairline leaving him close to bald and a paunch, this guy still seemed to age better than the sculptor. Though his face was wrinkled, his blue eyes were bright. "Uncle John. Sorry, but he did have a motive, and your father trusted him enough to meet up at a questionable site, I'm sure."

"Yes. I know," Gwendolyn said through gritted teeth.

Vera turned around, looking guilty for casting doubt on someone her friend trusted. "The police checked his alibi. His late wife said he was with her all night."

Gwendolyn swallowed hard. "O–okay. Now, what do we know about that navy-blue sedan I keep seeing?" Was she trying to change the topic? "All the things that remind me of Dad? I know it's difficult to find a car without knowing the license—"

Vera held up a hand. "Difficult but not impossible. Heather and I are working on it."

He was impressed and said so.

"Please." Vera waved off his praise. "This is my job, and I'm starting to like it again. Now, I need to check on my husband, the baby, and the children. And Danica's kitten. She mentioned wanting to paint its nails, too."

Despite the grim mood, Conner couldn't help chuckling. He was glad he and Daisy could become part of this family, though his situation was still a bit precarious. The Clark men didn't fully accept him yet.

Later, as he and Daisy stepped out of the mansion, her mittened hand in his, her cat ears underneath her hood, the door opened and closed behind him, and he turned around.

Vera stood on the porch. "You're falling in love with my friend, aren't you?"

Women in this family didn't waste time.

He liked it. "More than half the way there already." Then he lowered his voice. "But we both have issues from the past we haven't resolved yet. Besides, I live in Texas. It's a long way from here to Texas."

Hands on her hips, Vera pinned him with a stare. "It's an even longer way from Russia to the US. But if my great-grandparents thought your way, I wouldn't exist."

Chapter Eighteen

AFTER HER LONG DAY running after children—marathon runners should consider babysitting as part of their training program—Gwendolyn appreciated the peace and quiet of Conner's room in the Cowboy Crossing Bed & Breakfast.

She smiled as he appeared in the room, more handsome than ever, masculine even in a fun snowman Christmas sweater.

Yesterday's image of him in a brown cowboy hat, Wrangler jeans, and cowboy boots appeared uninvited, and her heartbeat increased.

Be still, my heart.

Maybe opposites attracted in friendships and not just in love. Like Daisy's friendship with Danica, who was her polar opposite, so was Gwendolyn's friendship with Vera and—please!—Liberty. Vera's toughness and Liberty's outspokenness complemented Gwendolyn's soft shyness. Gwendolyn had rarely reached out to people, so when the women of the family reached out to her, it was a relief.

God didn't mean for her to be alone, after all.

But then… Wasn't she going to be alone again once she left Cowboy Crossing?

Daisy clapped as Conner placed a popcorn bowl on the coffee table, and its buttery aroma spread in the small but cozy room. "Thanks, Daddy."

It had taken them a few days to get together for that movie he'd suggested during their first actual date. Yes, they were dating!

"Happy to do it, Sweetie Pie." He planted a kiss atop his daughter's head, then handed the remote control to Gwendolyn. "Daisy, we're going to let our guest tonight choose a movie, okay?"

"Yes, Daddy." Daisy climbed onto the sofa and snuggled up to Gwendolyn.

The wave of tenderness invoked by the girl's trust was difficult to ignore. Gwendolyn surprised herself by choosing a children's Christmas movie she thought Daisy might like.

It had been a while since she'd seen a Christmas movie. She'd done her best to book work for the holidays each year. Working was better than spending them alone or even with friends. This holiday season had changed her.

Transformed her into a different person.

But was she brave enough to reach for her dreams now?

As they started watching the movie and Conner's arm wrapped around her shoulders, her pulse quickened, and longing unraveled inside her.

A longing for a family and okay!—a cat to share her Christmases like in the movie. Hmm, Daisy adored cats. What if…

Gwendolyn did a mental headshake. No, best not to think about it. And as much as Gwendolyn loved felines, a cat might remind Conner about the accident when he'd lost his wife.

Hmm… His words about a stranger pulling him out of a car about to explode niggled at her, but she wasn't sure why.

Daisy munched on popcorn and laughed at the child's antics in the movie, and more tenderness claimed Gwendolyn's heart.

She whispered to Conner, getting an intoxicating whiff of his cologne. "You asked at the sleigh ride whether happiness was only an illusion. For me, happiness is what I feel right here. Right now."

She didn't add "with you," but she didn't need to. It was clear enough, wasn't it? Her breath caught. Did she say too much?

He brushed his lips against her cheek. "I feel the same way."

As his hot breath caressed her ear, it was a good thing Daisy was snuggled up against her, or Gwendolyn might do something crazy like kiss him.

Daisy handed her the popcorn. "Eat some, please, Miss Gwendolyn."

The smile on that adorable face tugged at her as she munched on buttery popcorn too. That smile reminded her of other adorable grins that greeted her every day.

Hmm, her contract with this family turned out to be a blessing. Working with children was exhausting but rewarding. They were so much fun and still so pure, so trusting, so untouched by the dirt of the world that she'd blossomed among that purity like never before.

By the end of the movie, Daisy's eyes closed, her breathing evened out, and she seemed to drift off to sleep. She whispered something, and Gwendolyn leaned toward the girl to catch the words.

"I like you, Miss Gwendolyn. Come home with us."

Everything inside Gwendolyn stayed still as she looked up at Conner. Thankfully, the girl didn't expect an answer as her eyes stayed closed and her breathing evened out further.

Because Gwendolyn could only give her one answer.

It wasn't possible. Was it?

She looked into Conner's brown eyes and realized he didn't hear what his daughter had just said. But did he feel the same way?

A different movie started, about horses and a struggling family, and she could relate to how they healed each other. She felt he could relate to it, too. As his fingers laced through hers, a pleasant wave washed over her, and she placed her head on his shoulder. There was that connection again. She could relate to him better than to anyone else.

As if God had created this man just for her.

As if Daisy could be her daughter.

The connection felt wonderful. Maybe it was good to look out from her shell of loneliness and feel the sunshine of a bond on her skin.

"It was about the horse for me, too," she said quietly.

Not a horse. The.

"It often is." His gaze warmed.

She dared to venture out a little more. "She was a chestnut mare. Maybe the color attracted me to her first." She gestured to her hair. "She was a thoroughbred, a former racehorse. After retirement, she was passed from one hand to another before she ended up with Grandpa."

Moving from one place to the other was another thing she could relate to. No wonder she took one look into those eyes and felt a kindred spirit. That didn't change even when the mare had kicked and bucked.

"Let me guess," Conner filled in her pause. "She was labeled difficult. I dealt with horses like that. People were upset with them when in reality horses were scared of a new environment. Besides, some people don't know how to communicate with horses, and they blame animals for that. What did your grandpa do?"

"Nothing." She waited for his reaction. For years after her father's death, she felt like that horse with a broken spirit.

He nodded, his understanding blanketing her. "That's what I'd do, too."

So he knew what she meant. Doing nothing signified giving the horse time to adjust to an unfamiliar environment and a new herd. Allowing her to accept the new human as part of the herd before asking her to do things.

Of course, Gwendolyn had groomed the horse, fed her, mucked her stall, made sure she was healthy, had a veterinarian visit her, and so on. But for some time, she'd let the horse be.

She'd learned another valuable lesson from Grandpa and horses those days. "We should learn to be still. Only in those times, can we listen to God. And in a lesser degree, listen to ourselves."

Conner didn't say anything, but his gaze became pensive. "I haven't listened to God in too long. Much less to myself. I feared what I might hear."

"There's no time like now."

Huh.

When did the movie end?

"True. There's no time like now." His gaze moved to her lips, and his breathing quickened. Then he looked into her eyes again and brushed her curls aside, causing a quick breath intake. "I'm going to put Daisy in bed. Don't leave, okay?"

"Okay." That pleasant wave spread in her again.

She wanted to follow him as he carried the little girl into her room. But her phone vibrated with an incoming call—thankfully, she'd turned off the sound—and she stayed on the couch.

She checked the screen, and Vera's name transferred her to reality. She swiped to answer and pressed the phone to her ear. "Hello, Vera."

"Is this a bad time?"

She glanced at the hall. Even if Conner returned while she talked, he'd understand. "No."

"Okay. No suspicious activity with Odetta so far. I talked to Ron, and naturally, he denied ever wanting to harm your father. He said he's been trying to change his past around. Then he started giving me compliments. Imagine that. I stopped that fast. He lives in Kansas now. His parole officer and employer both confirmed he hasn't left the town for months. I don't think he's the person driving the navy-blue sedan. Besides, he wouldn't know those details about your father's favorite things."

Good point. Gwendolyn shivered. "Do you think the sculptor, Mr. Cohen, might be it?"

"It's a possibility. I'm checking all the rental companies for anyone who rented a car with that description. Despite it being older, I have a feeling it's a rental—probably from a low-rate rental company."

Gwendolyn heard footsteps, and her heartbeat increased. "Thank you for everything."

"You're welcome. I'm still looking for Brandy. I'll keep you posted." Vera disconnected.

That was what a true friend did. Vera was there in the time Gwendolyn needed her. As a newlywed with a doting husband and a baby—even if the baby wasn't hers, Vera adored the child—she had every right to dedicate her time to them. Not to a friend she hadn't seen in a while. But she'd come through for Gwendolyn.

Friends like that were gifts from God. Gwendolyn's heart squeezed. She didn't want to move away. She'd miss them all. Sometime during this holiday season, she'd left her shell and allowed people in. What was she going to do now?

Conner entered the room, smiling. "Daisy is asleep. But she woke long enough to ask whether we're going to see you tomorrow."

Gwendolyn couldn't help but return his smile. "Yes. I mean, I hope so."

Despite him not being truthful with her from the beginning, she started to see that a man like that was a gift from God, too.

But did she dare to accept it?

Her pulse spiked as he claimed the cushion near her, and his proximity and spicy cologne wreaked havoc on her senses. This was the first time they'd been alone without a little chaperone, restaurant patrons, or at least horses present.

Her head spun from the thought. She knew they wouldn't go further than kissing, but even the thought of a kiss made her dizzy. Their gazes met and held, apprehension swirling between them. Losing herself in his mesmerizing eyes, she didn't want to be found.

He traced the outline of her jaw with his fingertips. "All I can think of right now is kissing you."

Her eyes widened, and her heart started thundering. She did her best to hold on to a rational thought. "Wait. Before I get carried away…"

He smiled again, and that smile could melt the Antarctic. "Before *we* get carried away."

He was so close that, if she angled her face a little, she could claim his lips with hers. Somehow, she managed to relay Vera's conversation.

"I don't want anything to happen to you. Gwendolyn, I… You…" His eyes darkened. "You mean a lot to me."

She felt as if she were floating on clouds already. "Yes. I mean… I–I feel the same way about you." A pleasant wave of anticipation rippled through her.

When he brushed his lips against hers, tentatively, slowly, euphoria conquered every cell in her body.
Then a child's yell filtered through her mental fog. "Daddy, I wanna glass of milk!"

Chapter Nineteen

ONCE DAISY was safely in bed again—after drinking two glasses of milk, then about an hour later a few sips of orange juice, then later getting her plush cat—and Gwendolyn was gone far too soon for his liking, Conner called his mother.

She was a night owl, after all, and he didn't want to skip a day without talking to her.

Warmth spread through him as he sat on the couch, still exhilarated by his kiss with Gwendolyn. Even though it had been interrupted, he'd remember it forever. It and the priceless look in Gwendolyn's eyes. He probably still had a goofy smile.

He listened to the long beeps, and by the time his mother picked it up, his gut had tightened. Well, it was his fault for calling so late. She must be asleep already.

"I need to tell you something." With her voice trembling, she offered no greeting.

The tightening became painful. Did she have a setback?

No, no, no.

Lord, please!

The pause stretched until he had to glance at the screen to verify she was still on the line.

"""

"Are you… are you okay?" The longer the pause stretched, the tauter his nerves stretched, too. Now, they were ready to snap.

"I am fine. It is… It's difficult for me to say. First of all, I know I wasn't a great mother, and I'm sorry. Thank you… thank you for forgiving me."

Light with relief, he let his body flop back against the couch cushions. She wasn't sick again.

Thank You, Lord.

Huh. Two prayers in a row? He didn't have time to dwell on it. "I realize you had a difficult life raising me alone. And you're my mother."

A long sigh reverberated through the line. "I don't deserve you. You and Daisy are the best things that ever happened to me. I love you."

He barely refrained from whistling. His mother adored her granddaughter all right, but this was a big difference from the "I wish he were never born" that he wished he'd never overheard.

"I… I don't know what to say." "I love you, too" would be the fitting answer, but his relationship with his mother was more an obligation than love. Maybe it was time to change that.

After seeing how much Gwendolyn missed her parents, he did start feeling warmth toward his mother that could grow into love. He hoped it would.

"That's not all I wanted to say." Another sigh, an even longer one, whistled through the line.

He tensed again. "What happened?"

"I was desperately afraid to lose you. I married not just for myself but also to give you a father."

What?

Unexpected heat roiled him like lava as he saw Tara's tears again, the bruises and scars on her legs, felt the pain from the belt buckle. He smelled stale cigarettes from the man's breath as his stepfather made Conner watch his stepsister crying because it was "all Conner's fault." He'd failed as a big brother. Failed miserably.

To think Conner would want that kind of father?

"An abusive one!" Despite his anger, he managed to keep his voice down so he didn't disturb his daughter.

"He never abused *you*," she snapped, her tone defensive. "Well, except at the end, but I did leave then."

Somehow, he resisted the urge to grind his teeth. He slumped deeper against the back of the couch and crossed an ankle over his knee, the wonderful evening's euphoria gone.

Was she clueless, or did she close her eyes to what she didn't want to see?

"He played favorites for a long time, which only made it worse for me. At first, I strove to gain his approval, man up, be strong like him. But I wouldn't mistreat my stepsister to please him, and it angered him." Just like the cries of the sickly baby had.

No wonder his stepfather was against the "unnecessary surgery." He'd been irritated since the moment the baby was born, upset he'd have "another mouth to feed."

Conner should've found the funds to save the baby. He should have! His little brother was his responsibility, too. His eyes burned with tears of loss, but he couldn't cry.

Men didn't cry, after all.

Silence ensued, and he checked the phone screen again.

She was there. Just quiet.

Like she always was.

Probably disassociating from cruel reality like she'd done before. Disappearing into work and later into TV sitcoms was the way she'd survived. Canned onscreen laughter replaced the real kind in their house.

"I made many mistakes." She started sobbing. "More than you realize. Your biological father… never refused to help you."

"What?" He gasped, slamming both feet to the floor and nearly dropping the phone.

"He didn't know about you. I never told him. Days before I found out, he broke up with me. He said he made a horrible mistake. That he couldn't leave his wife." She sobbed full force now. "I'm so sorry. Once I knew, I never said anything. I was afraid he'd take you away from me—like he did with his youngest daughter. He could hire the best lawyers, claim I was neglectful or something. I couldn't let that happen. I couldn't lose you."

He had difficulty breathing. All these years he'd resented his father, and the man never knew Conner existed. It didn't justify an affair, but there was no abandonment. All his life, he'd considered himself unwanted, a burden for both of his parents.

He felt as if he'd just fallen from a horse and hit his head.

There was even ringing in his ears.

"So when I asked you to talk to him about helping us when my brother needed surgery, when my stepsister needed a safe place…" A lump clogged his throat, preventing him from continuing.

"I lied to you. I was afraid you'd never forgive me. I hoped things would get better on their own." Sobs stopped, then resumed.

"You… How…" He struggled to think, much less say a word.

When secrets stayed hidden, they could kill. His baby brother didn't get better. Neither did his stepsister's life. The horse he'd adored was sold.

How different all their lives could be if his mother had told him sooner. Resentment brewed again, but he couldn't let it poison him.

His mother could've kept this secret forever, and he would've never met the Clarks, never been able to give Daisy great cousins, aunts, and uncles, never would've fallen in love with Gwendolyn.

Whoa.

What had he just thought?

As the image of Gwendolyn with her kind hazel eyes, sun-kissed curls, and adorable freckles appeared in front of him, he realized it was true. His chest swelled. He loved her.

He didn't mean to, didn't want to, but he did. And he had no way back from it. It was possible to love again, even for a jaded man like him.

"Please forgive me." The whisper was so quiet he barely heard it.

"I… I am trying to." He wanted to fill his life with love, not hatred. He was worth it. Daisy was worth it. Gwendolyn was worth it. He needed to be a better man for them.

"Oh, and one more thing."

He held in a groan. One painful secret revealed should be enough for the evening. "What… what is it?"

"I don't want to keep you tied to me. I heard the way you talk about Gwendolyn. If… if you're serious about her and she feels the same for you, you should be together. If Gwendolyn agrees to come here, great. If not, go where your heart leads you." His mother paused. "Just make sure she's a better mom to Daisy than I ever was to you. Though that won't be difficult, will it?"

CHAPTER TWENTY

THE NEXT DAY, Gwendolyn, Vera, Conner, and Daisy had tea at the mansion. Later, they were going to visit the owner of the navy-blue sedan Vera had found. Of course, once Daisy joined the children and Liberty who were supposed to return from the pony rides anytime.

Apprehension tightened Gwendolyn's gut, and Conner covered her hand with his as if in silent support. She gave him a grateful glance, thankful she didn't have to go through this alone. His touch warmed her better than the cup of honey-sweetened hot tea she'd just finished.

Voices sounded outside, and Gwendolyn tensed.

"Let's check what the commotion is about." Vera rose, and the rest followed.

They walked into the hall, and Daisy ran to Danica as if she didn't see her friend "for ages." Well, there was another reason for the enthusiastic greeting, too.

"Oh, a kitty!" Daisy squealed.

Gwendolyn greeted everyone and helped the children out of their coats. It was a bit problematic with Danica and Nehemiah as they were holding a fluffy white cat that seemed too large for one child to lift. Gwendolyn's heart flip-flopped in her chest. The pet looked so much like Cuddles, the Persian cat she'd had as a child, the one her mother took when she'd left with Vanessa.

"Are we having a new member in the family?" Gwendolyn looked from the children to Liberty.

As a veterinarian, Liberty had most likely already checked the animal for any diseases, or, well, inhabitants in its fur. Danica was famous for bringing in stray pets from the street, and this entire side of town that had adopted more cats and dogs than they'd ever dreamed could attest to that.

Liberty chuckled as she stroked the cat, and the pet purred. "The cat is healthy but without tags. Doesn't look like she lived on the streets. Probably the owner dropped her off from a car. I'll check the missing animals' ads anyway."

"Daddy, can *we* keep the kitty?" Daisy lifted her pleading eyes with those dreamy lashes at her father.

Yep, Gwendolyn knew this was coming. The cat stirred as if she needed to examine her new home.

So Danica and Nehemiah placed her on the floor, and while Gwendolyn helped the girl out of her coat, Danica looked at her with a wry smile. Gwendolyn knew what was coming next, too.

"This kitten needs a home." Danica gave a nod with such conviction her hat slipped off. "Let's see what human she's gonna choose."

Conner chuckled. "Kitten?"

That didn't faze Danica as she marched into the hall, the cat trotting after her. "A *grown-up* kitten."

Gwendolyn laughed. "One can't argue with that."

"We have pet food for Danica's kitty as well as occasions like this. I'll go find it." Liberty strode to the kitchen.

The cat looked around, sniffed the air, sneezed once. Then she trudged toward Gwendolyn, sat near her legs, and started washing her fur.

"She chose you!" Danica and Daisy screamed in unison.

Uh-oh. Gwendolyn blinked. "This is a coincidence."

The feline stretched and then rubbed against Gwendolyn's leg.

"Nope." Danica shook her head, sending her chestnut curls flying. "Miss Gwendolyn, she chose *you*."

Even if one couldn't rewrite the past, Gwendolyn could still have a cat again. She couldn't help smiling. "I–I guess I could keep her in my room until we find the rightful owner."

"Well, well, well." Liberty put a pet food bowl in front of the cat's nose, then placed her arms on Nehemiah's shoulders, the boy wearing adorable dimples. "Gwendolyn, I have a feeling the cat owns you now."

Daisy's eyes were a little sad, and her pink lips pressed together in a way that resembled the cat's downturned mouth.

Gwendolyn knew how the girl felt, so she flicked one of Daisy's braids to draw a smile. "You can spend as much time with the cat as you want. You can even name her."

The girl blinked, a smile opening her lips. "Really?"

"Really."

But what would happen when Gwendolyn returned to her place? Gwendolyn remembered all too well the pain when Cuddles had been taken away from her. She didn't want to do that to Daisy. The feline meowed her demand, and she realized Liberty was right.

"I'll name her Marshmallow." Daisy grinned.

Conner lifted Marshmallow and stroked her, and the feline had the audacity to purr, the traitor. Then he squatted on the floor and let his daughter carefully stroke Marshmallow, too.

That was the moment Gwendolyn realized how much she liked Conner—well, way more than liked.

She'd learned early in life that appearances could be deceitful, but her grandpa had taught her that a person's character could be decided based on how they treated children and animals.

Conner clearly loved his daughter. Gwendolyn had been

mesmerized when she'd seen him with the horses. And she was smitten after seeing him with this cat who'd needed a home as much as her heart did.

There were people around, and Gwendolyn needed to move. But she stayed rooted to the hardwood floor and stared.

She loved so many things about Conner. His slightly unkempt beard that showed he wasn't into appearances. His full-bodied contagious laugh that made her laugh, too. His eyes that crinkled when he smiled at her, especially if she was the reason for that smile. She even admired the scars on his arms that he'd received while trying to defend his stepsister, though she wished she could spare him the pain.

And she loved how he believed in her even when she doubted herself. That she'd find her father's murderer or her path in life.

She didn't agree with him trading the profession he loved for one he didn't care for, but she loved that he could sacrifice so much in memory of someone dear to him.

His gallery had exhibited not only famous artists but also new and upcoming ones, too, and sponsored free art classes for children. She loved how giving he was.

She loved how he could talk about horses for hours and knew them better than some people knew their friends. She loved his compassion toward his mother, even after she'd told him yesterday what she'd done.

But, probably most of all, Gwendolyn loved how he made her feel alive again. With him, she'd dared to sing, though she couldn't carry a tune. She'd eaten barbecue wings with her bare hands. She'd become confident about her looks and stood tall instead of hunching. She'd stopped watching life through the window and started experiencing it, including the most amazing kiss of her lifetime, even if an interrupted one.

"Well, what are we going to do?" He studied Gwendolyn as he stroked Marshmallow again. "We can't divide the cat."

Marshmallow lifted her head and mewed in outrage. Gwendolyn winced as the statement reminded her of her mother's words when she'd left Gwendolyn with a broken heart.

Conner leaned to his daughter. "Okay, how about we get you a kitten when we get back to Houston?" He glanced at Danica who wore a yellow sweater and salad-green pants, resembling a sunflower. "Or I'm sure your friend here will get us a stray by then."

Danica grinned. "I'm gonna do my best," she said with an air of importance.

"Yay! Thank you, Daddy!" Daisy squealed. "That way, you won't feel lonely when I'm not with you."

"Wait. We're gonna get him Miss Gwendolyn," Danica whispered, but everyone heard.

Heat rose up Gwendolyn's neck.

Then it sank in as Conner lifted his daughter, his eyes wide. "So you wanted to stay with me not because you didn't like to be with other children but because you didn't want me to be lonely?"

She nodded. "You didn't like me to leave. I want you to be happy. Not sad."

What a kind soul. Gwendolyn's heart went out to her, but Conner's words stuck in her memory—*When we're back in Houston.*

It wasn't only about the cat. One couldn't divide a heart, either.

"So you found who the navy-blue sedan with tinted windows and a bow decoration belonged to." Her heart in her throat, Gwendolyn looked at Vera from the back passenger seat of Vera's car.

Conner took her hand in his, making her grateful he was with her in this. She'd walked through life on her own for so long—

stumbling, falling, getting hurt, and wobbling back up—that it meant a lot to have someone to rely on.

Vera turned onto a snowy street where most of the houses still had their Christmas decorations. "Yup. Curious people in Cowboy Crossing helped. The first such car belongs to an eighty-year-old lady, who returned yesterday from visiting her family in another state. The car was safely tucked in the garage and doesn't have the decorations you mentioned. The second one was a rental from Springfield that had me concerned. Mr. Cohen, that famous sculptor who was your father's last client, rented it. He rented a house in Cowboy Crossing, too, instead of staying at the B&B, which didn't surprise me."

"Do you think he sent me the threats, too?" Gwendolyn asked.

"I don't have proof because most of them were from burner phones. The card he sent you had no fingerprints. But one time, he slipped and sent you an email from a laptop. My sister-in-law tracked down the IP address."

Gwendolyn stared ahead as they approached a quaint mint-green wood-framed building generously covered by snow. It reminded Gwendolyn of one of the ornaments on the Clarks' Christmas tree.

What color would she like her own house to be? Would Conner and Daisy have the same tastes?

Right. While they were going to leave soon, Gwendolyn planned their life together. Her lungs constricted.

She did her best to switch back into professional mood, though having her hand in his made her brain foggy. "Do you… do you think this confirms he had something to do with my father's murder?"

Conner squeezed her fingers as if to show her he was here—with her. She forced a wobbly smile. Without him, she might not have enough courage to go through with this.

Vera parked at the curb and turned off the engine. "I have a strange feeling about this. Why would he threaten you if he shot your dad? Why the masquerade with the car? All the reminders about your father? Also, I have to tell you our visit might be in vain. We're not the police. He doesn't have to talk to us. He doesn't even have to open the door to us."

"Understood." And Gwendolyn did.

But she'd carried the mountain of the mystery of her father's death for too long, and she needed answers to unearth herself from it.

Lord, please give me some answers.

They surveyed the street before getting out and racing to the door, the air fresh and frosty after the warm car. Conner positioned himself as if he wanted to shield her, and it struck her as funny because she was usually the one shielding others.

Was it time to change? Could she allow someone to shield her from the storms of life instead of weathering them on her own?

Vera rang the bell while Gwendolyn's heart beat fast, and only Conner's arm on her shoulder strengthened her. She placed her hand in her purse, calmed somewhat by the smoothness of her weapon. She knew her friend was packing, too.

Unanimously, they positioned themselves on the two sides of the white door, in case bullets greeted them instead of words.

Apparently, they were right to do so.

The door opened, and Gwendolyn flinched at the gun barrel pointing from its crack.

Mr. Cohen looked worse than in his photos. His wrinkled shirt and pants hung off his gaunt frame as if several sizes too big for him while his tousled hair probably hadn't seen a comb in a while.

Even worse, his pale eyes were wild. "How dare you to show up here?"

Vera didn't flinch. "I'm Vera Clark, and I'm a former police officer. I currently hold a PI license, and Gwendolyn here is my client." Vera lifted her hands in a placating gesture, then showed him her ID. "People know where we are, and the police will be patrolling this street. I strongly suggest you put the weapon away and join us for a talk. No one needs to get hurt."

Vera must have nerves of steel, because Gwendolyn was trembling at the desolate look in Mr. Cohen's eyes. A desperate man couldn't be trusted. She and Vera might have great reactions, but no one could outrun a bullet.

Conner stepped forward as if trying to shield her again. Maybe it was a mistake to allow him to come with her. She didn't want *him* to get a bullet.

"Please," Gwendolyn added, ready to drop on the ground and roll if the man didn't listen to reason.

"Who are you?" The guy gestured to Conner.

"I'm Gwendolyn's boyfriend," he said calmly.

Whaaaat? *Boyfriend*? Her jaw slackened, but she put it back in place.

"I was going to ask you today," he mouthed to her.

A shadow passed over the man's face, but the gun lowered. "Why should I talk to you?"

Time to choose her words carefully. "My father held you in high regard. Talk to me at least to honor his memory." Gwendolyn met his gaze head-on. "Besides, I believe we both need some answers."

"I'm sure you're armed. But then, I don't have anything to lose." Mr. Cohen waved them inside. "Place your weapons on the coffee table and take off your coats and boots."

The growl of a motor announced a car's arrival. True to Vera's words, a police cruiser parked on the opposite side of the street, making Gwendolyn grateful for Vera's connections.

Vera placed her hand on her hip, close to her holster, as she stepped inside first. "Or we can wait for the police to question you. We already have proof the threats were sent to Miss Gwendolyn from your laptop."

He chuckled as he closed the door. "You wouldn't go to the police with that. It's not in your best interests."

Gwendolyn eyed him, her brows puckering. "Why would you say that?"

His shoulders slumped. "Because you wouldn't want anyone to know you killed your father."

CHAPTER TWENTY-ONE

GWENDOLYN BLINKED and then blinked again. "What?"

No doubt, she'd misheard.

The man shuffled to the window, his worn slippers whispering against the hardwood floor. He peeped through the blinds, probably checking whether the police cruiser was still there. "Well, either we can start shooting each other and give the police something extra to do, or we can start talking."

Vera narrowed her eyes. To her credit, the guy's shocking statement didn't faze her. "Your gun goes onto the coffee table, too. The same time as ours."

She and Gwendolyn exchanged looks, and Gwendolyn gave her a barely perceptible nod. Mr. Cohen appeared gaunt and weak while she and Vera were trained in hand-to-hand combat. They all placed weapons on the table, and Conner helped her and Vera take off their coats. They did draw the line at the boots, though.

Mr. Cohen gestured to the cheerful floral-patterned sofa mocking the grim mood. It wasn't a social visit, but Gwendolyn might as well sit because her legs didn't seem to want to hold her up. Conner claimed the spot near her, a protective arm on her shoulder giving her much-needed strength.

The sculptor lowered himself into an armchair matching the sofa. "I only wanted justice for a man who became a friend to me." His voice was as hollow as the gun barrel he'd been pointing before. "I tried to call to your conscience, Gwendolyn. It doesn't look like you have one."

As a shiver racked her body, she tried to speak. But no word left her dry mouth.

Conner tightened his arm on her shoulders, bringing her closer, and whispered in her ear. "I believe you. We'll figure this out."

His trust warmed her.

"What made you suspect Miss Gwendolyn?" Vera's voice was even as she spoke. "Some recent discovery?"

"I… I finally had the courage to go through my daughter's things in the attic. I discovered her journal. That night…" He stopped and rubbed a shaky hand over his face.

"Take your time." Surprising softness accompanied Vera's words.

"That night, Brea escaped from the house after I went to sleep. The woman who was supposed to be watching her fell asleep, too. It was all my fault. I should've hired a substitute bodyguard when your father wanted a few days off. I should have…" He closed his eyes and kneaded his forehead, his shoulders slumping forward.

Despite Mr. Cohen's hostility, Gwendolyn ached. She could relate to grief and self-blame more than she'd ever wanted to. "No need to blame yourself. You did what you could."

"Brea went to buy drugs. She parked away from the place and went on foot to the abandoned warehouse. Yes, this was crazy on her part."

But addicts cared about their fix more than they cared about their lives. It sounded logical so far—unlike his shocking accusation. Her thoughts in havoc, Gwendolyn leaned forward and nodded to encourage him.

"Her dealer was running late, so she had to wait. She saw your father's car pull up to the parking lot. She thought he'd tracked her down and hid inside the building. Then another car arrived." Mr. Cohen's gaze lifted, his glare slamming into Gwendolyn. "She saw you stand close to your father. My daughter was relieved he wasn't there because of her, though she didn't understand why he'd meet you there. Then a shot fired, and he crumpled to the ground. You rushed into the car and took off."

Any compassion seeped out of her.

His words—his daughter's words, if Gwendolyn were to believe him—didn't make sense.

At all.

"This can't be true." Conner brought Gwendolyn closer still.

Moving his glare to Conner, Mr. Cohen set his jaw. "It is."

Vera lifted her hand in a peaceful gesture. "It was dark. How could your daughter recognize Gwendolyn, especially from a distance?"

Wow. Good thing Vera had an analytical mind—good thing she'd visited the scene recently, too. Gwendolyn recalled the files she'd read and calculated the distance from where her father was found to the abandoned building. It was significant.

That glare wavered, and the furrows on his forehead deepened. Was that doubt in his eyes? If so, it disappeared as his chin jutted out. "The headlights were on."

"Even if the lights were on, distinguishing facial features enough to say for sure…would be difficult," Conner said.

"Stop trying to defend your girlfriend!" The sculptor started rising from his seat, one finger shaking at Conner. "Gwendolyn visited our house several times. She wore the same color pants, jacket, and boots that day." His accusing finger jerked to Gwendolyn. "My daughter had a good visual memory. The person who shot your father had the same height, the same build, the same clothes and footwear, even the same hair and face as you. How do you explain that?"

She couldn't.

At least, not yet.

Vera crossed her arms over her chest. "What if he was only wounded? Brea didn't check on him?"

"She was too scared." Mr. Cohen slouched forward, shaking his head at the ground. "You're trying to take me away from the point, but you won't be able to."

"Why didn't your daughter go to the police?" Vera mimicked the man's slumped shoulders and vocal tone.

"According to what Brea wrote, she didn't think anyone would believe a drug addict. Besides, she didn't trust the police. But from the journal, that decision plagued her for years. She realized she'd made a grave mistake by not speaking up."

Vera had once told her investigations would be so much easier if people didn't lie or withhold information. How right her friend was!

"We'll need a copy of the journal." Gwendolyn drew her eyebrows together. "We'll also need other samples of your daughter's writing."

He shrugged. "Fine. I've got nothing to hide." He didn't add "unlike you," but he didn't need to.

Gwendolyn's gut twisted. All this time she'd been looking in the wrong places.

"Why didn't you take the journal to the police when you discovered it?" Vera asked.

Gwendolyn wanted to know that, too. Could the journal be fake?

"I didn't think it was enough proof." His gaze moved to Gwendolyn. "I wanted you to confess."

"I had nothing to do with my father's murder," Gwendolyn said the words quietly but clearly. "You withheld useful information and went on a rampage of vengeful self-righteousness."

His face crumpled. "I wasn't thinking straight. I miss my daughter so much. Despite my art's success, life without her is meaningless."

"I'm very sorry," Gwendolyn whispered. "I really am."

His gaze sharpened. "I'm asking again. How do you explain my daughter's words?"

Gwendolyn gathered a few ideas, but it was too early to share them with the guy. Especially since—with all her heart—she hoped she was wrong.

"We'll find the explanation." Conner's voice was firm.

Vera rose to her feet. "I suggest you give your evidence to the police."

Closing his eyes, Mr. Cohen hesitated, then opened them and looked Gwendolyn in the eye. "I will, but I'll honor your father's memory and give you a chance. I give you twenty-four hours to turn yourself in. Don't try to do what you did with your father. If I'm found dead, the evidence goes straight to the police."

Gwendolyn staggered to her feet, thankful Conner's hand held her up. She was right. He would help her when she fell down or fell apart.

Repeating her innocence was no use. She exchanged glances with Vera and Conner, determination set deep in her friend's and—wow!—boyfriend's eyes.

They understood each other without words. They had twenty-four hours to find the killer and get the proof. Otherwise, Gwendolyn might be arrested for a crime she didn't commit.

Rest was overrated, especially when one's life could come to a screeching halt.

Reeling from the accusation, Gwendolyn followed them into the mansion. Even the children's loud greetings, meeting them in the hall, did little to cheer her up. Conner helped her shrug out of her coat while Vera's husband did the same for her.

Feeling weak with fatigue, Gwendolyn forced a smile. She hugged each of the children, careful since this time Danica and Daisy held up the large cat.

Conner hugged and kissed his daughter, then talked to her about something that barely registered in Gwendolyn's mind.

Gwendolyn petted Marshmallow, the cat's smooth fur calming something inside her.

The animal meowed unhappily as if sensing her mood. Liberty took one look at Gwendolyn and herded the children to the kitchen. "How about everybody wash their hands, get some cocoa, and then help bake cookies?"

The children gave an enthusiastic yelp, but the cat meowed again as if not excited by the prospect of cookies.

Conner placed another kiss on his daughter's head. "Sweetie Pie, are you okay to stay with Miss Liberty, Danica, and the others while I talk to Miss Gwendolyn some more?"

"Yes, Daddy. I like it here."

Conner's face twisted up, half-wounded and half-grateful.

When Vera led them to the same office they'd used earlier, he pulled out a chair for Gwendolyn. "Are you okay?"

"What do you think?" Her voice sounded sharper than she'd intended, and she cringed but had no strength to say anything else.

"Yes. Sorry." He brushed the back of his hand against her cheek. "God will make this right. The Clarks started a prayer chain for you."

"Yup. He asked us." Vera nodded as she stepped close to the board.

So he'd gone to the family and asked them to pray for her, though his half brothers were still somewhat hostile.

"Thank you," Gwendolyn whispered before sinking onto the chair while her legs felt like cooked noodles. Then she rocked back and forth while studying the photocopy of Brea's journal he'd given them.

"I'll have Heather run this through some computer program to verify the writing is authentic." Vera's voice was soft as if she didn't want to inflict any more hurt.

"Thanks." Gwendolyn found the passage Mr. Cohen had told them about. "He said the truth."

It was all in the journal, and Gwendolyn blinked fast before the pages could blur.

"There should be some explanation to this. There should be." Conner moved behind her chair and placed his hands on her shoulders.

She touched his left hand with her right one, needing the bond with him more than ever.

Then she peered at the journal as if she expected the words to disappear, but they were still there. Was this what a horse felt when she was led in a direction she didn't want to go but wasn't given a choice?

"Are you up for a discussion?" Vera's eyes were concerned, too.

Gwendolyn gathered her strength, reaching to Conner to borrow his.

But first, she needed to reach to the Lord. Even with Conner's help, she couldn't get through this without Him.

Lord, please help us.

"Let's sum up what we know." Vera started writing on the board fast as if their time was almost up, which it was. "Brea's father vouched she was with him at the time of the murder. He lied to protect her. So no alibi for either one of them. I guess Cohen paid the female employee to confirm his daughter's alibi. Opportunity: Brea was at the crime scene at the time of the murder.

Motive: Brea wanted to be rid of the person standing between her and drugs."

Gwendolyn did her best to think straight. "Let's say my dad returned to his job because I canceled our dinner, saw Brea escaping, and followed her."

"Right." More confidence filled Conner's voice. "At the scene, he asked Brea to go back. Instead, she pulled his gun and shot him. Then she came up with the idea to pin it on you. And that's one of the angles the defense might use if… well, you know."

Gwendolyn flinched. "Yes, I know. Then why didn't she go to the police with her fake statement?"

"Her father answered that. She realized her credibility might be questioned."

Made sense. "Fair enough. Now let's imagine she wrote the truth. Which means someone of my height and build impersonated me."

They went through the suspects again before Conner patted her shoulder and pushed from his seat. "You need something to eat—we all do. I'll be back."

While he stepped out to make sandwiches, Gwendolyn scooted closer to her friend and took a deep breath. Time to face it. "I have an idea."

They discussed that version until he returned carrying a tray of turkey and cheese sandwiches from the kitchen.

Gwendolyn didn't feel hungry but ate at Conner's insistence, though she couldn't taste anything.

After sipping her tea, Vera pinned a new photo to the board. "That's Brandy."

Gwendolyn perked up a little. "You found her? That's awesome."

"She has the same height and build as you. With a wig and the right clothes and boots, she might pass as you at night, though it would be a stretch.”

“How much did you gauge from your talk with her?” Conner asked.

Vera grimaced as she wolfed down her sandwich and wiped mustard from her lips. “Not much, sorry. Brandy admitted blaming your father for her dad’s death. But she was at her friend’s wedding at the time. I’ve sent a request to check her background and her alibi.”

“What about Uncle John’s and the sculptor’s backgrounds?” Gwendolyn waved toward their pictures.

“Pretty clean. And so were their hands when the police checked them for gunpowder residue. Though, admittedly, some time passed, giving them opportunity to wash them.”

Gwendolyn’s phone pinged with an incoming text, and she reached for it.

“It’s my sister.” She opened the text. “Vanessa just arrived in Cowboy Crossing. She wants to see me first thing in the morning.”

Vera shot her a concerned look. “We have very little time left. Not enough, frankly.”

“Yes.” Gwendolyn’s heart squeezed. “And I have little in the sense of family. I have to go and see her tomorrow.”

“Then get some sleep.” Conner hugged her, helping the broken spot inside her.

Lord, please help us.

“Will you stay up?” Gwendolyn studied her friend, torn between gratitude and guilt.

Vera nodded. “I need to try to put this puzzle together. I’d like to keep you alive and around. I’m selfish that way.”

“If I can help in any way, please count on me.” Conner’s gaze was sober as he walked Gwendolyn from the room.

She knew he meant it, too. This was a guy who’d do everything for her.

At her bedroom door, she wrapped her arms around his neck,

staring into his eyes. Would she dare to tell him about her feelings?

She started, "You're the best thing that ever happened to me. Well, you and Daisy. I want to tell you—"

Her phone beeped with an incoming message. Tensing, she wanted to ignore it.

"Check it. It might be important." He snugged his arms around her waist, his voice understanding.

She reached into her pocket, then stared at the screen as blood seemed to drain away from her head.

You'll pay. Or Daisy will.

Gwendolyn suppressed a shudder as she did her best to keep her smile intact. She had no clue what the sender had hinted at. She needed to think.

"I… I have to go." Even as she said the words, she missed Conner already. And she couldn't work up cheerfulness to say goodbye to his daughter.

His eyes dimmed, but he nodded. "I understand. Please try to get some rest."

His head dipped as if he wanted to kiss her, but she couldn't let it happen, not with the idea that was forming.

So she shifted, and he kissed her cheek instead. She didn't want to risk changing her mind, so she slipped inside her room and fell rather than sat on her bed.

You'll pay. Or Daisy will.

This was an alarming threat, and she doubted it was coming from the sculptor this time.

The memory of the recent kidnapping where Jenna and Vera risked their lives to save the boy made Gwendolyn's insides go cold. The boy had been kidnaped because of Jenna. What if…

What if whoever sent her mysterious messages tried to do the same, kidnap the one who was the most vulnerable?

Daisy.

Gwendolyn's heart shattered, and this time she couldn't stop tears from spilling. Conner and Daisy were going to leave soon anyway, so why prolong the inevitable?

The soft melody of her ringtone made her wince, and all the cells in her body went on high alert. Was this going to be another threat?

Later, she hung up after a brief conversation with the human resources director of the elite international bodyguard firm. He'd apologized for the late call in her time zone and offered her a job. She'd had her résumé on file with them for a long time, but vacancies rarely came up. She'd mentioned in her résumé she'd be fine with international travel, and they had assignments coming up in Europe.

In other times, she'd be jumping up and down like Danica or Daisy. But Gwendolyn only felt emptiness now. As soon as she resolved the mystery of her father's murder, she'd leave Cowboy Crossing. She'd never put Daisy in danger.

Lord, please keep Conner and Daisy safe in Your care.

Her fingers gathered the smooth bedspread into a fist while more tears spilled. Gwendolyn knew what she had to do to keep Daisy safe. Gwendolyn would have to stay away from the little girl and her father.

Even if it broke her heart.

After all, their happiness and safety mattered much more.

Chapter Twenty-Two

"WHAT?" HIS JAW SLACKENING, Conner glanced toward the room where Daisy was still sleeping. Then he lowered his voice as he stared at Gwendolyn in the B&B hall early the next morning. "What did you say?"

What she said simply couldn't be right.

Misery settled in her eyes as she slumped against the wall. "It's best for us to stop seeing each other."

"Why? I thought—"

She lifted her hand in a universal stop sign. "Why prolong the inevitable? You're going to return to Texas soon."

"I… I was going to come up with something. Anything. I can't say goodbye to you." He thumbed the ring in his pocket, the one Daisy had made, as a sense of overwhelming loss settled over him. He'd thought—hoped!—Gwendolyn felt the way he did.

No, he wasn't going to give up this easily.

He took her hands in his, grateful when she didn't remove them. Speaking with the turmoil in him was difficult, but he had to try. "Is this about the geographic distance? We can figure out something. If it's about that ridiculous accusation, I'll hire the best lawyers out there. We're in this together. I'll stay here as long as necessary."

"I appreciate it all. I–I"—her voice broke—"I really do."

Maybe if he told her he loved her, she wouldn't walk away. Or if she told him the reason, he could make this right. "Then *why*? I know you've been hurt before. But I'm not like your ex-fiancé. I'll never cheat on you. I won't keep a secret from you again."

So much longing gleamed in her eyes. "I know."

How could he change her mind? He *had* to change her mind! "I care about you, very much, and I felt… I felt you cared about me, too."

She closed her eyes and opened them. "I do, but—"

"I love you."

Her eyes widened. She jerked her hands away—not the reaction he'd hoped for. "Please don't make it more difficult. It's better this way."

Agony sliced his heart. "Better for who?"

"Everyone. I… I received a job offer. A great one. It's an elite international bodyguard company. There will be a generous salary, great bonuses, and the opportunity to travel the world. They have an opening because one employee got shot."

He winced as his gut tightened. "Sounds dangerous. What if next time they have a vacancy, it's because…" He didn't want to finish the sentence.

He didn't need to.

"Yes. I know." She hung her head.

He hugged her, hoping this wouldn't be the last time he'd have the opportunity. "If that job is your dream, if that's what you want, then I'm glad for you. But don't walk away from what we have."

He didn't know how to work it out with the world between them, but he'd have to figure it out. Maybe his new family would help? Looking at their happiness, he was starting to learn that family came not only with obligations but also with blessings.

"I've got to go. Or I'll be running late for the meeting with my sister. Please kiss Daisy for me." Her lips twisted up as she eased out of his embrace.

"She'll miss you. And I miss you already." His heart shattered—his daughter would be devastated.

Tears shimmered in Gwendolyn's eyes. "I'll miss you both. More than you can imagine." Then she stiffened as if she'd said too much. "I need to accept this for what it is. It was just two lonely souls attracted to each other. Besides, I was a source of information for you."

He wiped her tears with his thumb and kissed her salty cheeks. "You're part of my soul now. It's not a simple attraction, at least not for me. You're the woman I love with everything I've got." He wanted to add, "And the one I want to marry and have be a mother for my daughter." But it didn't seem like a good time to say it.

But he did treat her like his source of information in the beginning, didn't he?

Maybe he deserved what he got now.

His heart broken for a second time.

Gwendolyn could hardly believe she was sharing over-sweetened tea in a small rental house with the sister she hadn't seen in two decades. The scene felt as surreal as her goodbye to Conner, as if she watched someone else out the window walk away from the best thing that ever happened to her.

And still, here she was.

She needed to concentrate on the present because, if she thought about Conner and Daisy, she'd fall apart.

Vanessa smiled as she placed a pastry plate on the dining table. "I am glad we can be a family again. It's about time, right?"

"Right." Gwendolyn studied her sister over the rim of her

porcelain cup, looking for the person who'd once been her best friend.

Vanessa changed—a lot.

She'd colored her long straight hair strawberry blonde, a color that suited her well. She was no longer plump, and her muscles were well toned. Makeup hid her freckles, and her nose—now delicate, straight, and narrow—betrayed a nose job. Was it an impression from the blush makeup, or were Vanessa's cheekbones higher now?

A hollowness carved out Gwendolyn's heart, taking the place of any joy at their long-overdue reunion. If she'd met Vanessa on the street, Gwendolyn would've walked right by without recognizing her sister. She should've found her a long time ago.

Vanessa's jewelry and clothes seemed expensive, but not flashy. Overall, she exuded enviable confidence. Her designer crimson-hued pantsuit matched her lipstick but contrasted the rustic interior of the house with its simple wooden furniture and black-and-white farm photos the color of drizzling mist.

It was raining inside Gwendolyn's soul, too, but her sister wasn't the one to blame.

Where was that cheerful girl with chubby cheeks and pigtails? The one with laughter in her hazel eyes as they'd chased each other around the large house? The one who'd shared the last cookie with Gwendolyn or taken her for a bicycle ride?

"I should've reached out to you sooner," Gwendolyn whispered.

"Same here." Vanessa stared at her hot tea as the mint aroma spread in the room. "How is your tea?"

"Great." Gwendolyn glanced at her cup, where her fingers hugged the smooth, warm porcelain. Only half left. She didn't reach out for the pastries, and Vanessa didn't move them toward her. "So… how have you been?" Gwendolyn cringed at the stillness between them.

Small talk didn't work great right now. And neither of them seemed to want to talk about their parents, as if the connection between them was as fragile as a thin thread and could tear apart if they hung such heavy stuff on it.

Vanessa ran manicured nails through her beautifully styled hair, her tea remaining untouched. "I got married twice. Both times to a doctor. The first died, the second, I divorced. Each marriage left me with some money. Before you say anything, I earned every penny of it, especially the first time. No children. No pets. But I'm famous for giving the best parties around. What about you?"

"Single. Never married. No children, either." Argh. Did Gwendolyn sound as depressing to her sister as she did to herself?

But she'd been so close to happiness over the holidays—to having everything she'd ever wanted—and the wounded expression in Conner's eyes still tore at her. No, it was too painful to think about.

She searched for the call of blood inside herself, so strong and demanding in her childhood, and found nothing except regret about missed opportunities. Maybe it was for the best. "Though I do have a pet now. Marshmallow. A large and fluffy cat."

"I see. Would you like more tea?" Vanessa smiled softly.

"No thank you. It's weird. My mind is getting... foggier, I guess. What... what do you do for a living?" Her words came out quiet, her speech slurred.

Vanessa lifted her tea, then replaced it with a slight rattle. "Looking for a new husband. Those settlements don't last forever."

"At least, you're honest." Gwendolyn swayed in her seat from left to right. "Ohhh. It's like... it's like the room moved in front of me. And my heart feels funny." She pressed a hand to her chest.

Vanessa's hazel eyes narrowed slightly. "Really? I guess it's a lot to take in after not seeing each other for so long. Drink some more tea. It will help."

Gwendolyn picked up her cup but dropped it back to the

saucer. She stared at the person who pretty much represented the entire family she had left in the world. "Have you… have you ever thought about the way our father died?" There. She said it. She placed the heaviest of the heavy stuff on the fragile thread.

"Such a tragedy." Vanessa sighed. "You said on the phone you started investigating his death. Why now? And… have you discovered much?"

When Gwendolyn didn't reply, Vanessa added, "It concerns me, too. I have a right to know."

Gwendolyn shared the condensed version of what she'd learned from the sculptor. Then she slumped against the back of the chair. "I… I don't feel well."

Something flashed in Vanessa's eyes. Satisfaction or worry? "What happened? Are you weak?"

"Yes. And dizzy." Gwendolyn got up, then sank right back on the chair. "That's strange."

Vanessa removed Gwendolyn's cup with its dregs of tea from the table. Her own cup was still full.

"Why don't you lie down for a while?" No mistaking the gleam in her sister's eyes as she leaned forward.

"Yes. Probably a good idea." Gwendolyn rubbed her temples. "I'll need your help to get to bed, I think. I… I just miss Dad so much. Do you… do you miss him, too?"

Vanessa's mouth twisted as she sat on a chair closer to Gwendolyn. "Why would I? He left us."

"What? No! He made an agreement with our mother. He wanted to talk to you, but Mom didn't allow any contact."

"That's a lie! Not what my mother said."

Gwendolyn sucked in a shallow breath, then a gasp slid from her mouth. "Our father wasn't perfect, but I can assure you—he was a good, honorable man."

"Yeah, keep telling that to yourself," Vanessa muttered. "Maybe he was a good father to you, but he didn't care about me."

"Our mother didn't want him to see you. She probably told you things about him that weren't true."

"He didn't even pay child support! He couldn't be bothered!" Fury twisted Vanessa's face.

"No. Not true. He sent funds every month. He sent you expensive gifts, too." Gwendolyn's voice became weaker and weaker, and her arms hung by the sides of the chair.

Vanessa leaped from her chair and paced. "That's a lie. He didn't! I never received any gifts from him. And he didn't leave me anything! I deserved the inheritance as much as you did. I thought he felt guilty neglecting me. He promised to change the will and didn't."

Gwendolyn's mouth went dry. "How… how did you know about the will? There was no contact between you two. Or… was there? No. Dad wouldn't have kept it a secret from me."

Vanessa paused in the middle of the room. "I asked him to."

"I do need to lie down." Gwendolyn rose, then sank onto the chair again, faster than the previous time. "I… I'm going to pass out. I'm getting worried. Maybe you should call an ambulance."

"Maybe I should." Vanessa shrugged as she left for the kitchen. She came back with a paper towel and a cleaning solution and started wiping down surfaces.

The table's sharp edges cut into Gwendolyn's grasping fingers. "There's a reason I feel this way, isn't there? Did you put… something in my cup?" Her speech became more slurred. Her hand groped for her purse.

"Looking for your gun?" A smile twitched Vanessa's wine-hued lips. "Don't bother. Besides, you're not in good enough condition to shoot anyway."

"Did you poison me? But why? We're sisters."

Vanessa wiped down the door handles. "You left me no choice. You should've let things be. No need to look into a twenty-five-year-old murder."

Betrayal hurting her heart, Gwendolyn let her gaze follow her sister. "Was it… was it you who impersonated me when meeting with our father?"

Another careless shrug. "You figured it out. Thankfully for me, a bit too late."

"You shot our father, and you poisoned me." Gwendolyn shook her head as if she still couldn't believe it. "The cute guy I met at the grocery store—the one who asked me out and never showed up—he's connected to you somehow, right?"

"Oh, just a guy who was in love with me. I asked him for a favor. I needed you out of the way for the evening Dad had off. I didn't think you'd stay in the restaurant waiting for the boy for hours, giving you an alibi. " Vanessa shrugged. "It doesn't matter anymore. I might as well tell you. I killed Dad because he deserved it. You don't know what life with our darling mother looked like. She only cared about maintaining a lavish lifestyle. She passed me from one nanny to the next until she sent me off to boarding school. Neither the girls nor the teachers there were kind to a plump freckled kid with braces."

"You could've come to live with us," Gwendolyn whispered.

Vanessa glanced around the room as if satisfied she'd left no fingerprints, then scowled. "Mom said Dad didn't want to raise another brat any more than my stepdads did. I needed the inheritance. It was my way to freedom and the life I deserved."

"But you shot Dad before he had a chance to change the will." A fact, not a question.

"Well, he should've changed it sooner! I had to marry an old rich guy I despised because Mother was divorced again and spent her settlement faster than I could sneeze."

Gwendolyn blinked at Vanessa's sense of entitlement and lack of remorse. "You thought you'd get away with Dad's murder…."

"I already did, didn't I? I'm going to get away with this one, too." An eerie calmness whispered through Vanessa's voice. "It's a pity you had to put your unshapely Meyers nose where it didn't belong. Maybe we could have had a sisterly relationship, after all."

"What have you done? I trusted you with my life!" Gwendolyn's heart shattered for the second time in a short time. "Our father trusted you with his!"

Vanessa sneered. "I imagine, if you live through this, you'll never trust anyone again. But you won't live, so it won't be an issue."

That was it.

Trust. That was the reason she'd walked away from her happiness, besides wanting to protect Daisy from danger. She could've explained to Conner what was happening. Instead, she'd chosen to run because she hadn't learned to trust.

A tiny morsel of doubt for Conner lingered after he'd withheld information about being the Clarks' half sibling.

She'd prayed to God regularly, but she hadn't relied on Him believing He'd let bad things happen to her.

Since two of her friends had betrayed her, so she had difficulty trusting friends. And since her fiancé cheated on her, she wasn't sure she could trust her heart and her judgment.

Before she could trust God and people, she needed to trust herself.

Her sister's deceit should've crushed what little trust Gwendolyn had left. Instead, it multiplied it. She shouldn't judge God by people's actions but trust Him with her whole heart, not part of it.

She shouldn't judge the rest of the world by a few individuals because there were way more good, kind people like the Clark family and Conner and his daughter.

And she needed to trust herself and the man God had chosen for her.

Conner's image appeared in front of her eyes, and her heart longed for him. Then she saw herself walking down the aisle toward him, wearing an elegant white gown after Daisy and Danica spread rose petals. They would be such adorable flower girls, and Danica already had a lot of experience. Gwendolyn saw Conner dressed in a tuxedo, standing at the altar, smiling at her. Saw so much love in his mesmerizing eyes.

Conner was the man she loved.

Maybe this wasn't the best time to realize it because, right now, her most urgent need was to simply survive.

Lord, please help me. And please forgive me for not fully trusting You before.

"The name you rented this place with… it's fake, isn't it?" Her voice dipped to a whisper. "And your blonde hair is a wig? You've had plastic surgery, too, right?"

Vanessa shrugged as she put on gloves and a coat and picked up her purse and carry-on. "One has to take precautions. Oh, don't try to look for a phone." She waved Gwendolyn's phone at her. She'd grabbed it from where Gwendolyn had set it down earlier. "I've got yours, so no one will see our communications, and you won't find another phone in the place. I doubt you'll make it to the road in your condition. There's a reason I rented a house on the outskirts. No neighbors. No one is going to find you for a while."

"I told someone I was meeting you here," Gwendolyn whispered as her eyes fluttered closed and she opened them again.

Vanessa's forehead wrinkled, and she paused with her hand on the dining room door. "I didn't think you'd be close enough to anyone for that. Well, no problem. I'll be long gone by the time anyone comes looking for you. I have an alibi prepared, just in case."

"Help me, please," Gwendolyn gasped, as she collapsed to the floor.

Soft fingers groped for her wrist. "Hmm. Still a pulse, but not for much longer. Goodbye, dear sister."

Chapter Twenty-Three

HIS HEART BEATING FAST, Conner drove up to the place on the outskirts of Cowboy Crossing. He'd called Vera and extracted the address from her with great difficulty. He couldn't understand why she was so reluctant to give it to him or why she clipped her words with such a sharp tone.

Gwendolyn was meeting her sister this morning. The reunion after so many years should be a joyous event. But something about it had him twitched. It was taking too long. He'd hoped she'd be back at the Clarks by now, but she wasn't.

He frowned as he sped up and passed a car. He was grateful Liberty agreed to babysit Daisy, and Danica was thrilled for company. Still, the familiar guilt for leaving his daughter, even for minutes, stabbed him. Yet Daisy wanted him to bring Gwendolyn back and kept asking about her.

Then premonition tightened his chest.

He couldn't let Gwendolyn go.

He had to make one more attempt. He fingered the ring in his pocket. Daisy had made it from wire and a plastic bead instead of gold and diamonds, but he'd gladly buy Gwendolyn a diamond ring later. He just wanted a chance with her.

Was he selfish for wanting a future with Gwendolyn? Could a globe-trotting bodyguard, in danger of being shot anytime, become the mother Daisy needed?

Lord, please guide me.

He needed to see Gwendolyn, to make sure she was all right, and he floored the gas pedal. The rental jerked forward as the motor growled unhappily.

Her words should've confirmed everyone he'd loved abandoned him. But now he knew the truth. His father had never abandoned him. He hadn't known about Conner. His mother, while she'd emotionally checked out a lot, was fully present now and had even shown kindness he didn't expect.

The Clark family was there for him, though he'd deceived them by omission.

God had never abandoned him, though Conner had believed that when Annika died. Instead, Conner abandoned God all these years.

And maybe, just maybe, Gwendolyn would stay, too. She had feelings for him. He couldn't be wrong about that. And he didn't hear any enthusiasm when she'd talked about her new job.

The wail of the siren made him flinch. What... what was going on?

He pulled to the side of the road as an ambulance passed him, lights flashing. The unease in his stomach increased while he pulled back to the road and floored the gas pedal again.

According to the GPS, he was nearing the address. Right around the curve in the road. Which meant...

Cold traveled down his spine. Was the ambulance for Gwendolyn?

Oh no! She was in danger, and he'd let her go meet her sister alone. What was he thinking?

Lord, please help Gwendolyn!

It was a coincidence. It had to be.

But, as he turned the corner, his heart slipped to the brake he pressed on as he drove closer. Already, a bunch of cars had parked on the curb beside the ambulance. Several police cars. Even the car he recognized as Vera's. The police officers stood near yellow crime-scene tape marking off the area.

He dashed out of the rental as soon as he brought it to the stop, his heart thundering.

It shouldn't…

It couldn't…

Then things fell into place. How could he be so blind? It would be easy for a sister to impersonate Gwendolyn at the time of the murder, to put the blame on her in case Vanessa was discovered.

Such a foolish mistake on his part could cost Gwendolyn's life.

Or…

Had it already? He had to get inside!

But, even before the police officers stopped him, Vera did. "You can't go inside. You need to let the police do their job."

He stared through her. He wouldn't stoop to pushing her aside, so he needed to make her understand. "I have to see Gwendolyn." He spoke past the lump in his throat. "I *need* to see her. Please!"

Vera cringed. Her blonde hair, usually braided, was tangled now, and circles around her eyes showed a sleepless night. "I understand. I do. But the police are not going to let you go in anyway."

Two police officers led a handcuffed strawberry blonde out of the house, her head hung low as they placed her in the patrol car.

He followed her with his gaze, trying to make sense out of the situation. "Is this… is this Gwendolyn's sister?"

Vera nodded, then brightened as Liberty and Jenna jumped out of Liberty's truck and rushed to her. Neither one of them had even buttoned their coats.

Liberty hugged him immediately. "Don't worry about your daughter. My brother is with Daisy. The girls are painting his fingernails right now. Everyone in the family is praying for Gwendolyn. Is she okay?"

Vera turned to her sisters-in-law. "The paramedics are with her now. Chances are, she'll be okay."

Conner was able to breathe again. Gwendolyn was alive. There was still hope.

He said the most ardent prayer in his life.

Vera steeled her gaze. "I'll keep you all posted. And Liberty, I have a few ideas I'll text you. Now, why don't you take Conner home?"

He shook his head, planted his feet. "I'm not going to leave."

Liberty placed her hands on her hips. "If Vera says we need to go and she'll keep us posted, then she means it. Now, don't make me carry you."

He knew his half-sister meant it. Reluctantly, his soul hungry for a glimpse of Gwendolyn, for reassurance she'd survived, he turned away.

Nostalgia pierced Gwendolyn's heart while Vera drove her from the police station to the mansion.

Vanessa was under arrest, and the medical personnel had checked Gwendolyn and given her a clean bill of health. After all, she hadn't swallowed the poisoned tea, except for the first tiny sip. Instead, she'd poured it into a hidden sponge. The concealed pocket in her voluminous black infinity scarf made the perfect place to tuck it. Now the sponge and the scarf were with the police as evidence.

When Vera's research uncovered that Vanessa's first husband had died from an allegedly accidental overdose of his heart medication, she'd gone prepared. The sickly sweet tea warned her that she'd been right—extra sugar to cover the bitter drug.

It was over, but she didn't feel any accomplishment.

All she had to do now was to pack her bags and leave Cowboy Crossing. The children should be safe now, and the mystery was solved.

"Thank you for investigating Vanessa, getting help from the police, and setting up the wire. I couldn't have done it without your help." She sent a grateful glance her friend's way.

Vera made a turn to the familiar street. "Now that I have the freedom to choose my cases, I like doing my job. Well, except for the part where you sounded like you were dying. You're a good actress. You scared even me for a minute there."

Gwendolyn recalled the moment she'd pretended to faint.

Then the moment when her sister had leaned to her—not to help her, but to make sure she didn't have a pulse—Gwendolyn had jerked Vanessa's leg, toppling her sibling to the floor.

Cuffing Vanessa's hands behind her back, while her dear sister was sputtering and screaming, only took a matter of seconds.

Thankfully, Vera had signalled the police to storm inside then, and they'd arrested Vanessa. Then it had taken a while for the paramedics to check Gwendolyn, then for her to give the police officer her statement.

"Nah. I'm far from a good actress. But I was motivated to stay alive. I was afraid at first that Vanessa would hug me and detect the wire. Thankfully, my sister isn't the hugging type."

"Unlike my sister-in-law." Vera slowed around the curve in the road. "I still can't get used to her bear hugs." She cleared her throat. "Okay, I'm sort of a messenger here. The family doesn't want you to leave. Besides, you know the children won't forgive us if we let you go. Though, of course, we realize the nanny job might not be something you're looking for. And you do have your dream job on the table."

Gwendolyn chuckled without mirth. "I had doubts about the job I'm looking for—had them for a while. Conner said my father would be proud of me no matter what I did. My dad would want me to spend my life doing something that makes my heart sing."

"You have no idea how much I agree with that. Okay, it's a very far reach, but the grapevine says there's an opening for a kindergarten teacher. Part-time, though."

Gwendolyn took a deep breath. And then a soft melody played in her head. Maybe her heart was singing already. "Thank you. You and your family are amazing. I mean, I'm not even related to you—"

Vera lifted her hand. "Please. I have little in the sense of family, too, and they took me in like one of their own. I was told once it's not about the family you have but about the family God gives you on your journey. I've found that to be true. I understand if you leave. You do have a great job offer, and you deserve your dream job. But know you'll always have a place to come back to."

"This means so much to me." Feelings overwhelmed Gwendolyn as they drove up to the mansion.

For some inexplicable reason, she'd expected Conner and Daisy to meet her there, but they hadn't. Maybe they had left for Houston already. Her stomach tightened.

She'd pushed him away, and there was no way back, no matter how much she wanted there to be.

As she and Vera walked to the front door, Gwendolyn's heart grew heavy.

Vera opened the door, and Gwendolyn stepped inside an unusually quiet house. She held in a sigh. Vera had exaggerated the family's affection for Gwendolyn. People didn't even come to say goodbye to her, and the children hadn't missed her at all.

Her heart dropped to the hardwood floor, brightly polished, as always. But then, what had she expected? Even her own sister had tried to kill her. The Clark family didn't owe her anything.

It was time to go then. She was going to turn down the offer for the job she'd once dreamed about and apply for a kindergarten teacher's position in Springfield. Or just take her time to consider what she wanted to do next.

She'd miss all of them. But apparently, she wasn't going to be missed.

Her eyes prickled, and she blinked fast. She should've been used to goodbyes. Even if no one besides Vera had bothered to say goodbye.

"Let's go to the backyard while we're still dressed warm." Vera gestured toward the door.

Sniffling, Gwendolyn followed her.

As she stepped into the backyard, her jaw slackened.

"Surprise!" everyone screamed.

The adults held up a Welcome Home sign while the children… This couldn't be right. Gwendolyn blinked fast again, doing her best to clear her blurry vision.

Four children held up a poster board each, Daisy grinning most of all.

WILL

YOU

MARRY

ME?

A snow*woman* in the middle of the yard had the same sign in bright pink letters matching her hat.

Conner walked to Gwendolyn, carrying Marshmallow. "I just want you to know I love you—"

"Daddy, you're supposed to say '*We* love you.'" Daisy's grin widened.

"Right. Daisy and I love you. With all our hearts. *We* want you to be part of our family. I want to spend the rest of my life with you."

Struggling to believe what was happening, Gwendolyn could

only gape.

Was this all for real?

"I understand if you want to become part of the elite international bodyguard firm. If you want to travel the world. I won't stand in the way of your dream job," he continued, his eyes inquiring.

She finally found her voice. "It's not my dream job any longer." She whispered in a low voice as she leaned to him, inhaling the scent of happiness and intoxicating cologne. "There's often a danger of being shot at. I don't particularly like being shot at." Well, once she was stabbed with a knife. She didn't particularly like that, either. "I do like spending time with children," she said much louder.

"Yay!" the children screamed, and Danica high-fived Daisy.

Gwendolyn looked into his eyes where she found love, trust, and acceptance. "As for traveling the world, this small town is more than enough for me. You, my darlings, are my world. What else could I wish for?" She kissed a beaming Daisy.

Danica elbowed Daisy. "You can say it now."

"Oh yes." Daisy perked up. "How about a little brother or sister for me?"

Heat crept up Gwendolyn's cheeks.

Conner cleared his throat. "I'd love that, but we're getting ahead of ourselves. We need to get married first."

"Okay, but then you're gonna work hard on the little brother or sister." Clearly, Daisy wouldn't let that part go anytime soon.

A simple handmade ring gleamed on the cat's collar, and Gwendolyn's heart nearly stopped when he removed it, then passed Marshmallow to Liberty.

He dropped on one knee. "Gwendolyn, will you marry me? Will you make me the happiest man alive? I understand if you need to think about it—"

"I don't," she interrupted him.

Chapter Twenty-Four

"I DIDN'T TRULY LIVE before I met you. I was afraid to experience things, feel too much, get too close to people. I got hurt so much before that I stayed outside, watching life through a window. You and the children taught me to laugh again, sing, walk tall, and breathe with my entire lungs." She took a deep breath of frosty air as if to confirm it. "I love you with my whole heart. I can't wait to marry you."

"I love you so much." He kissed her, filling her heart with more joy than she'd thought she could handle.

Everyone shouted congratulations as he slipped the ring on her finger, and Marshmallow meowed loudly.

Through the happy fog, Gwendolyn heard Daisy say, "And now we don't have to share Marshmallow. We can all live together."

Danica's cousin—well, Daisy's cousin, too—said with an air of importance. "I'm gonna have a little brother and a sister soon. I can share them until you get your own, Daisy."

Gwendolyn couldn't help laughing. Joy shared multiplied, and sorrow shared diminished. She couldn't wait to share it all with this big, boisterous family.

A week later.

Gwendolyn stole a glance around the restaurant dining table where she and Conner had their first date. Her heart—and okay, her stomach—was full. The scents of barbecue and french fries hung in the air, just like then.

Her wedding ceremony was exactly like in her vision, only better. Jenna had helped sew the wedding gown from Gwendolyn's dream. Vera, Jenna, Heather, and Liberty became her bridesmaids, looking scrumptious in long-sleeved caramel-hued dresses. Danica and Daisy were the flower girls, of course, and they'd spread petals with the same generosity Gwendolyn had once poured sprinkles on cookies.

Landon and Nehemiah carried the pillow with the ring together.

The children said Marshmallow was a contender to be a ring bearer, too, but thankfully, the boys were too eager to do it. Jenna's friend who had a bridal studio did the photos and a video recording, and somehow, the cat turned out in many pictures, thankfully, with a smile.

The winter wedding meant everyone had to wear their coats outside. But Gwendolyn couldn't wait to be married to Conner— no way was she waiting until spring. Besides, spring bloomed in her heart already.

White ribbons and bouquets, homey food, and friendly smiles bedecked the restaurant for their reception. More than a wedding celebration, it felt like a homecoming. Amazing the family could make reservations and preparations in such a short time, but nothing about this family—her family?—should surprise her any longer.

Her Christmas wishes came true as if God gave them all to her at once, even what she hadn't asked for.

While she still missed her father terribly and was heartbroken over the revelation about her sister, Gwendolyn had her closure. And she could stop blaming herself for leaving him alone that evening. Her sister would've found another opportunity.

Gwendolyn's chest constricted, but then Conner covered her hand with his. The tightness loosened as pleasant tingles traveled from his touch all the way to her heart. Overwhelming love expanding her rib cage, she smiled up at him, so handsome in his tuxedo.

Love…

This must be one of the most amazing Christmas gifts ever.

God's love.

Love of all these people. She didn't come to Cowboy Crossing to find the love of her life, and yet she did.

Utensils clanked against porcelain dishes, and children's laughter interrupted adults' chatter. She had a family that accepted her in their midst with open arms, no questions asked.

Conner was a rightful member of this family, though he'd gone about it wrong at first. But they'd forgiven him and accepted him and his little girl as if they'd known them from day one. Gratitude warmed Gwendolyn's heart.

A family for Christmas…

"Miss Gwendolyn, I love you." Daisy lifted her large brown eyes at Gwendolyn from the chair nearby.

Gwendolyn melted like honey in her tea. "I love you, too."

A daughter…

It was fine that Daisy didn't call her "Mommy" yet or might never call her that. In Gwendolyn's mind and her heart, Daisy was her daughter, and that was it.

Her pulse picked up when Conner laced his fingers through hers. "Have I told you today how much I love you?"

She grinned. "Only twenty times. So I'm expecting twenty more."

A home…

The Clarks had invited them to stay at the mansion as long as they wanted to and had offered them part of the land. Conner, Gwendolyn, and Daisy were going to build a house, a paddock, and a stable, with input from Daisy, of course, who seemed mostly interested in the opportunity to have a pony.

Conner received a job at Mending Hearts Ranch and gladly took it for now, but she remembered his dream and would support him in it. To have a place for horses with broken spirits.

Her gaze stopped at his mother, who saluted her with a glass of apple cider and a generous smile.

Her heart warming, Gwendolyn did the same in return, then beamed at Conner. "I'm so glad your mother accepted me." His mother had already congratulated them and seemed to be happy for them.

He chuckled as he placed a kiss on her cheek, making heat rise inside her. "Are you kidding me? She loves you already. You're impossible not to love. She might stay in Cowboy Crossing for a while. Vera's grandmother said she could introduce her to a few bachelors and maybe take her scuba diving later on."

Gwendolyn's gaze flicked to the blue-haired lady in a matching pantsuit, whose toasts at the reception had made everyone laugh. "Oh boy."

"You can say that again. My mother was reluctant at first, but I told her it's never too late for love. But then she might not need much help."

Gwendolyn smiled at Uncle John paying compliments to Conner's mother and passing her biscuits. "Praying she'll find her happiness. And Uncle John."

"I'll pray for that, too." Conner's eyes were luminous, and she couldn't tear her gaze away.

All the voices faded away. Her mind still had difficulty grasping that her dream came true when she least expected it. She gave thanks to the Lord.

"So true. It's never too late to discover the meaning of love." She wondered if all people understood that concept, in a broader sense. With Vera's help, she'd tracked down her mother and sent a wedding invitation. Her mother had never replied, and Gwendolyn wasn't sure whether the pain she felt was disappointment or guilty relief.

Conner's eyes shadowed, then brightened as he placed a kiss atop Daisy's head. "Well, Daisy and I have a large brand-new family who does know the meaning of love, right, Sweetie Pie?"

"Right, Daddy." Daisy giggled. "And I have a brand-new mommy!"

Joyous tears threatened to spill, so Gwendolyn hugged Daisy tightly and hid them, the sweet scent of mango shampoo filling her lungs. "I love you so much."

"Love you, too." Daisy smiled up at her when Gwendolyn let her go.

This was what bliss looked like.

Liberty rushed to her, more exuberant than ever, and that was saying something. "I didn't think I'd ever have to wear a bridesmaid dress again, but here we go. Stand up now." Liberty paired the caramel-hued silk dress with cowboy boots and a white cowboy hat, probably as a compromise. When Gwendolyn obeyed, Liberty squished her in a hug. "Welcome to the family."

Gwendolyn wasn't sure, but she suspected her new sister lifted her off the tiled floor. Was her wedding dress too tight, or was it difficult to breathe? "Th–thank you."

Liberty let her go.

"My turn." Jenna's embrace, though more elegant and less suffocating, held the same warmth. "Welcome to the family. I couldn't be happier to have a new sister."

Meanwhile, Liberty snatched Conner in her signature bear hug, and Gwendolyn hoped the sound she heard wasn't his bones cracking.

She didn't even have a chance to thank Jenna as Vera hugged her, too, then more people gave her and Conner hugs and congratulations. They didn't just say it—they meant it, too.

Later, as she passed around the room giving out little wedding favors her new sisters had helped her make, she stopped by the gift table. A blue envelope attracted her attention because it was addressed only to her. All the other gifts were addressed to both her and Conner.

On a whim, she opened the envelope and the double-wedding-ring embossed card it contained. Her eyes widened at the large stack of cash inside. But even more, the inscription caused her to inhale sharply.

Take care of him and love him deeply.

The words were typed, and there was no signature—just a small drawing of a… cat?

She replaced the envelope. Conner had told her all about Tara's disappearance. Tara was identified based on a necklace and her father's confirmation. But the man hadn't wanted the police to look for his daughter. What if…

Then there was the case of Conner thinking someone followed him.… Could the drawing signify his stepsister's middle name?

Deep in thought, Gwendolyn waved to Vera who passed the baby to her husband and hurried to her.

Without a word, Gwendolyn showed her friend the envelope, and they stepped aside from the crowd. "I think this is from Conner's missing stepsister." A pang of conscience twinged her over not discussing it with him first. She'd tell him in a few minutes. She remembered all too well what keeping secrets could do to erode trust. "I need to discuss this with him first, but—if he agrees to it—do you think you can find her?"

Vera narrowed her eyes a fraction. "Often, if people don't want to be found, they have a good reason for it. That said, I'll do everything I can to help. I'm sure Jenna will be glad to help, too, and Heather will be thrilled to have another opportunity to use her online research skills."

Gwendolyn smiled at her friend, grateful Vera would always be there for her. "Thank you so much."

"In fact…" Her friend paused as if she considered an idea.

"Yes?" Gwendolyn raised an eyebrow, stilling as she was about to head back to Conner.

"We already have interesting cases at our new detective agency, including a case for one of the Clarks' cousins. His ex-wife died from an overdose in a rehab center, and he wants to make sure it was an accident."

Gwendolyn's lips pursed as she recalled Brea who died from an overdose, as well. Was this a coincidence?

Vera continued. "I know you have different career goals now, but you're welcome to join us any time. You can choose your hours. The girls will be thrilled to have you."

She hugged her friend in earnest. "I'll think about it."

Then she returned to Conner, who kissed her again, sending a jolt of pleasure through her. She'd already found everything she needed. But how would it feel to be part of the sisterhood? The answer was simple. It would feel wonderful.

"I can't wait to spend the rest of my life with you." His warm breath caressed her ear.

"Ditto."

She could trust these people's words and her own heart now. *Thank You, Lord.*

Epilogue

HER GUT TIGHTENED, and she tensed. She glanced around the street near the coffee shop she'd just exited, doing her best to determine what caused that unease.

Years of living on the streets in her teens had taught Tara—who'd used her middle name for years—to always be on guard, even if she was safe now. She suppressed a shudder at the memories as she made careful steps forward and watched reflections in the shop windows.

Those times of hunger and humiliation were thankfully gone. As she caught her reflection, a slight jolt of satisfaction zinged through her over turning her life around, the feeling as warm and sweet as the coffee she'd just enjoyed.

No sign of torn clothes sizes too big, thin dirty hair, sunken cheeks, or desperate eyes in the reflection. Her light cream-colored coat was stylish, just like her matching boots, and her shiny blonde hair covered her shoulders in waves, slightly messy thanks to the fresh breeze. She loved the Show Me state in spring, the symbol of renewal—of nature and her life.

It might be a crazy idea to move here from Texas, but she wanted to stay close to her stepbrother, even if she couldn't reveal

"

she was still alive to Conner yet. He was the only family she had left, as her father couldn't be considered family. The move wasn't a hardship. She'd moved a lot from one state to the other before, though she realized one could never escape memories.

Thankfully she could work online for the most part. No need to hunt for a job.

She shouldn't be too smug. Her life had been turned upside down once, and it could happen again.

Why the recent unease, though? Maybe her subconscious had picked up on something her consciousness hadn't. But what?

Uh-oh. The bulky bearded man across the road was watching her. She saw him reflected in the glass and felt rather than noticed the sharp gaze drilling a hole in her back.

A shiver ran down her spine, and she resisted the urge to run her hands over her forearms. One would think that, after years of living in a cardboard box, she'd be more resistant to the cold, internal or external.

Her fingers slid into her purse to find the reassuring cool smoothness of her gun. Then she flinched. The weapon wasn't there. Of all days to forget it at home after she'd taken it out to clean it.

Unforgivable mistake.

She grimaced as she made a few steps, then stopped, and studied the man's reflection in a different shop window. This was one of the days when everything seemed to go wrong. She'd burned her breakfast, missed an important phone call, left her car at the dealership, and now this.

On the other hand, if she'd told her miserable fifteen-year-old self about her day, that girl would laugh at her and say, "I wish I had your problems."

Time to move.

A premonition twisted her heart.

As she walked, the man moved in the same direction, and her

heartbeat increased. She slipped inside a clothing boutique and browsed dresses without much interest. She shifted aside as a woman with perfume so strong Tara nearly sneezed snatched a nearby dress.

When she left the store, the guy was still there. The beard covered most of his face, and his brown hat was drawn low. When he threw away an empty pack of cigarettes, bile rose inside her, and she did her best to push it down as goose bumps erupted over her skin. The name on the pack was a coincidence.

It had to be.

Breathe.

But, as she inhaled the fresh spring air, she could still smell the cigarette smoke. Could feel the sharp pain from the belt buckle, hear her father's mocking laugh. Then an image of another bearded man invaded her memory, and this time it included his large, strong hands pressed to her neck, strangling her.

Every breath came at a cost.

Even as she started running, she knew she was fine now. She'd come a long way from that scared, helpless teenager.

But the command "flee" was ingrained too deep in her mind. Her concentration was on the man, so when she noticed a pothole, it was too late. Her ankle twisted, pain shooting through her leg. As dirty water sprayed her cream-colored coat, she barely avoided landing in a puddle. Her training had prevented her from falling, allowing her to regroup in time, but it was a small consolation for her hurting ankle.

Horror filled her as the feeling of no escape overpowered her again.

She wouldn't be able to run with her sore ankle. The man marched to her across the street.

No way out.

No!

A cab! None was coming.

Her body shuddered. She stopped thinking rationally, and instincts took over. Her gaze slid to a car right near her, an older model that wouldn't be so difficult to steal.

What was she thinking? This was crazy. Totally crazy. She knew how to boost a car from the days she'd learned way more than she'd ever wanted to. But she was never, ever going to take a car for a ride again. She led a life with dignity now and taught other women to do the same.

The man was closer, and just as before, taking another breath became difficult. She opened her mouth to scream, but no word came out as if there was too much pressure on her windpipe again, not allowing air out—or in.

You're helpless! There's nothing you can do.

There was. The car alarm might shriek, scaring the guy away, and that was all she needed.

The alarm didn't shriek as she opened the door. She felt in a daze. What was she doing?

Stupid! So stupid.

Okay, she'd return the car in a few minutes. Then training took over, and the motor woke up, growling happily.

The man knocked on her window, making her flinch. The man didn't threaten her, didn't harm her yet, but she remembered large hands on her throat, pressure on her windpipe again. She had to get out of here.

Now!

So she did.

She'd circle around the street and return the vehicle to its place. No one would be the wiser. Her heartbeat calmed down somewhat from the staccato as she drove away. She'd be back as soon as she could be sure the man was gone.

Then a child's voice from the back seat reached her. "Who are you? Where are we going? Are we there yet?"

Her heart about stopped beating before resuming its staccato.

What in the world?

She glanced in the rearview mirror before returning her attention to the road. How hadn't she noticed a child in the back seat? Why hadn't she checked in the first place? "What are you doing here?"

"Waiting for my daddy."

Her hands flew up in the air in frustration before clenching on the steering wheel.

Really, what kind of an irresponsible father leaves a child in the car?

THE END

THANK YOU FOR READING

Thank you for reading *Show Me a Family for Christmas*. If you write even several words on Amazon, BookBub, and/or Goodreads, it'll mean a lot to me. You can make a difference! I'm grateful to every person who reads my books, and every review matters to me.

What do you think about the series about single father cowboys and curvy heroines? This series has been so much fun to write! If you'd like to read Tara and Roberto's story, that's Book 7, *Show Me a Mistaken Identity*.

I do love hearing from readers, and if you email me at alexaverde7@gmail.com, or visit me on Goodreads, Facebook, BookBub, or Twitter, you'll make my heart sing. And if you'd like to know about my upcoming releases, please follow me on Amazon. Of course, I'd be thrilled if you looked at my other books, and I pray and hope they'll bring you joy and encouragement.

For giveaways, news, free ebooks, and recipes, please sign up for my newsletter. Subscribers have access to exclusive subscriber-only contests, subscriber free ebooks, and book news. Emails won't arrive more than weekly; your email address will never be passed on to anyone else, and you can unsubscribe at any time. Also, you'll get the download link for a FREE sweet Christian romance ebook, *Season of Mercy*, as soon as you confirm your email address as a thank you gift.

Thank you very much for sharing your time with me and my books, and I hope we'll meet again. God bless you.

With love,
Alexa Verde

ABOUT ALEXA VERDE

ALEXA VERDE writes sweet, wholesome books about faith, love, and murder. She has had 200 short stories, articles, and poems published in the five languages that she speaks. She has bachelor's degrees in English and Spanish, a master's in Russian, and enjoys writing about characters with diverse cultures. She's worn the hats of reporter, teacher, translator, model (even one day counts!), caretaker, and secretary, but thinks that the writer's hat suits her the best.

After traveling the world and living in both hemispheres, she calls a small town in south Texas home. The latter is an inspiration for the fictional setting of her series *Rios Azules Christmas* and *Secrets of Rios Azules*.

Please visit Alexa's website for more of her books and to sign up for her email newsletter: www.alexaverde.com

You can also find Alexa on social media:
Facebook : alexaverdeauthor
Twitter : alexaverde3
Goodreads : 8180452.Alexa_Verde
Bookbub : authors/alexa-verde
Amazon : amazon.com/author/alexaverde

BOOKS BY ALEXA VERDE

Christian Contemporary Romance
COWBOY CROSSING
Show Me A Marriage of Convenience (Book 1) (Kade and Heather
Show Me A Second Chance (Book 2) (Mac and Kimberly)
Show Me The Boss (Book 3) (Liberty and Kansas)
Show Me Best Friends (Book 4) (Maverick and Vera)
Show Me my Brother's Best Friend (Book 5) (Jenna and Riley)
Show Me a Family for Christmas (Book 6) (Conner and Gwendolyn)
Show Me a Mistaken Identity (Book 7) (Cat and Roberto)
Show Me a Fake Fiancé (Book 8) (Nelly and Constanzo)
Show Me a Stand-In Husband (Book 9) (Aurora and Carter)

RIOS AZULES CHRISTMAS SERIES
In Love by Christmas Box Set (Season of Miracles, Season of Joy, Season of Hope)
Season of Miracles (*Book 1*) (Arturo and Lana)
Season of Joy (*Book 2*) (Dylan and Joy)
Season of Hope (*Book 3*) (Brandon and Kelly)

Christmas Love & Joy Box Set (Season of Love, Season of Miracles, Season of Joy)

RIOS AZULES ROMANCES: THE MACALISTERS SERIES
Season of Romance (*Book 1*) (Andrey and Melinda)
Season of Love (*Book 2*) (Petr and Lacy-Jane)
Season of Amor (*Book 3*) (Ray and Sylvia)

ACKNOWLEDGMENTS

Special thanks go to:

First of all, thank You to God for putting up with me and for all the blessings!

A million thanks to you, my readers, for reading my books, for sending me encouragement, and for supporting me.

My gratitude goes to Renate for giving me valuable information about German traditions and beta-reading the book, as well as to Sarah S. for helping me with the parts of the novel about horses. You're wonderful!

Many thanks to my friend, Autumn Macarthur. I don't know how I'd survive without you. You're the best part of me.

Heartfelt thanks to author Jessie Gussman for coming up with the idea for this series and for helping me so much on the way. Jessie, you make me laugh, you make me smile, and you make the world a better place.

Many thanks to my street team, Alexa's Amazing Readers, and to my beta readers, whom I love to pieces. Kim, Trudy, Debbie, Paula, Karen, Tandy, Susan, Mary Jane, Glenda, Julie, Jean, Deanna, Sarah, and Andrea, you're all amazing (I'm sorry if I forgot to name someone!). Thank you, Renate, Teresa C., June S., and Heleen, for helping me to name the cats. Thank you, Renate, Patty F., Carol W., and Lynn S., for naming the hero.

I thank you my wonderful editor, Deirdre, for coming through for me every time.